Twice upon a Time

Twice upon a Time

R. D. AMUNDSON

iUniverse, Inc.
Bloomington

Twice upon a Time

iUniverse books may be ordered through booksellers or by contacting:

iUniverse
1663 Liberty Drive
Bloomington, IN 47403
www.iuniverse.com
1-800-Authors (1-800-288-4677)

ISBN: 978-1-4759-4916-2 (sc)
ISBN: 978-1-4759-4918-6 (hc)
ISBN: 978-1-4759-4917-9 (ebk)

Library of Congress Control Number: 2012916762

Printed in the United States of America

iUniverse rev. date:09/19/2012

Chapter One

"**M**om! Mom!" I hollered as I burst into the kitchen, leaving muddy tracks across the just-mopped and waxed linoleum floor. But today she wouldn't mind. "I saw one, Mom! I saw a red-breasted robin!"

"Where, Daniel? Can you show me? Is it still there?"

"Out there, in the apple tree. Look! It's still there!" I said, and I pointed out the kitchen window.

Mom stepped over to the single pane of glass, so old that it put a wavy appearance on the outside world, and peered intently out. When the robin came into focus, she clapped her hands and at the same time gave a little bounce of joy. "Oh yes, over there, I can see it now! Spring is just around the corner!"

But I had known since morning. The texture of the air had shifted. I always felt it, and somehow I knew; today spring had staked her claim, and the robin's appearing was the shout of victory.

Growing up in the Flathead Valley in northwest Montana was as close to idyllic as life could get, at least in my wide-open-with-wonder eyes. Each season, after laying claim to its part of the year, brought its own distinctness and offered its own enchantments. And every year I watched a wrestling match of nature as spring struggled to claim her part of the year while I anxiously awaited its triumph. And always, when my hope waned toward oblivion, the sure sign of victory would appear.

Spring brought the most spectacular array of miracles with its resurrection of life.

Mom stopped humming a tune I couldn't pin a name on and turned her brightly lit face toward me. "Let's have some hot chocolate," she said with a long, drawn-out sigh, letting go of held-in hope.

The whole valley breathed a sigh of relief when spring arrived, putting an end to winter and the struggle to survive it. Now we could look forward to the greening of the lawns and the cherry and apple blossoms mingling their perfume with that of the lilac while they robed their hosts with a dazzling display of brilliant colors. Summer hit with an intensity that said, "Brace yourself." But to me it meant playtime, until mid-August, when the stalks of wheat began to bow under the weight of the ripened kernels and it was harvest time at O'Donnell's farm. But that was more of a lark than it was hot and tiring work.

Uncle Frank would stop the combine to empty the newly harvested wheat. It spewed like a jet stream of water out of a narrow chute from the machine into the bed of the truck, and he wouldn't stop until it was a foot or so over the sideboards and the rear leaf springs began to sag. Then my cousin or my brother would roar full throttle into town. I was too young to drive, but the ride was fun, more like being in a boat on the ocean than in a truck on the road. We'd make it to the silo in town, unload the grain, stop to get a cold bottle of Coke, and then bounce and sway back to the farm and make it just in time to load up again. And so went harvest time, sunup to sundown, until the days butted up against September.

Mom's sister Louise had married Frank O'Donnell sometime before my world began. They were the second generation to run what started as a homestead but now was a magazine-cover showcase farm situated between the Lower Valley Road and the north fork of the Flathead River.

The two-story farmhouse was beyond huge. It held a piano, antiques, and cowboy memorabilia and had original Charlie Russell paintings on its walls. Deer and elk heads with trophy racks of antlers were mounted on the walls of the den. The hardwood floors of the front room gleamed, accented by the leather furniture. The north wall was a fireplace and blazed hot in the winter. There were pistols, rifles, tractors, wagons, a bunkhouse, and of course a big red barn, and there was always plenty of remarkably good food.

The Flathead Valley was the Old West defined, except I didn't know it, and to me it was only life as it was. More than the objects, though, what lasts in my memory are the deep feelings of timelessness and settled contentment. They seemed to stretch out from the river and then flow across the fields and through the barn and come to rest in the house, filling it with good cheer and good will.

Fall then *fell,* and with feeling. Autumn is what happens in New England.

Winter came with teeth, and there wasn't a living thing that dared defy its authority. But quite often, as if on cue, it would snow on Christmas Eve, big, beautiful, lazily drifting flakes, glittering like stars in the moonlight, and the feeling was "peace, be still."

And always, just about the time I'd begin to grow weary of winter, the red-breasted robin would appear, and with it, the renewal of hope.

But underneath the seasons lay the land, having a life and vibrancy of its own, unmatched, untamed, undeniable, and holding all the elements of the four seasons, no matter the time of year. For each season I had favorite spots to visit, private places I would go that seemed to invigorate or calm or renew or strengthen me. I don't know why or how . . . It just felt right, and they did. Sometimes it would be under a lone pine tree on the grassy slope of a high mountain. Sometimes it would be on the top of the mountain, where I could almost touch the clouds. Sometimes I would hunker in a hollow carved in the face of a rocky cliff by centuries of pounding winds, or sometimes I plunged in to explore the depths of a mountain lake and feel the stillness only its clear blue water could offer. Sometimes it was the surging power of lightning as jagged bolts would zigzag to bury themselves in earthen motherhood, followed by the rumble of thunder deep in the chest of the dark and lowered thunderheads. Other times it was being still and gazing across fresh fallen snow on a moonlit winter night or watching butterfly wings fluttering against stained-glass windows backlit by a gentle sun.

The binding thread that ran through these special places was the feeling of connection, a connection to all that was, and this sensitivity, developed by nature, gave me my sense of place. I was accepted simply because I was in the world along with every other living thing, some of which did not breathe or have a beating heart. This feeling, this connection, can only be felt and known and not explained. Much can be said in the presence of another living thing without using words. It's called communion. Like love, it is an emotional bubble containing joy and healing. And like love, it cannot be broken by denial.

Chapter Two

With flames of auburn hair plastered to her forehead, eyes tight shut, jaw muscles straining beneath alabaster skin, lips pealed back in a determined grimace, the woman gave an effort that would have made a warrior proud.

"Push . . . push!" the young black nurse exhorted the sweat-drenched woman whose eyes matched the color of sky on a clear autumn morning.

"One more good old-fashioned heave-ho, Mrs. Mercado!" she said.

Easy for you to say, thought the woman, *but I won't scream this time!* "Uh-n-n-n," she groaned against the pain. The woman's shriek pierced the nurse's ears, causing her to cover them with her hands. And then it stopped, the process of life ending the woman's labor pains.

With practiced precision, the doctor moved to his usual place. He was a clinician. A mousy-looking midfortyish man with wispy sandy-colored hair, thin lips—not more than a line in his lower pointed face—he was extremely good at what he did.

"Here it comes. I see the top of its head!" squealed the nurse with pure delight. Always in awe, the young nurse couldn't explain why she felt such joy every time she witnessed the miracle of life; to her, it truly was a miracle.

The doctor handed the delivered, clipped, and made-to-breathe baby to the nurse. "I'm going to lunch," he said and then turned to the exhausted, auburn-haired woman, "You can rest easy now; you have a perfect, healthy baby." Spinning briskly, he strode out the door, the slightest ghost of a smile upon the thinness of his lips. One he would never let anyone see, of course—it would be unprofessional.

"You have a lovely, healthy daughter, Mrs. Mercado!" echoed the nurse, handing the bunting-clad baby to her mother. Gently taking the newborn child into her arms, the new mother gazed lovingly at the beautiful innocence of her daughter's face. The soft brown eyes opened ahead of their time, and the baby gazed back with unmistakable awareness. Held against her mother's breast, the infant cooed in contentment, making that special sound only babies can make, the sound that gives the world a moment's pause and renews its hope to carry on.

A tall, thin, elderly orderly appeared at her bedside and asked in a clipped tone and for the thousandth detached time, "How's the happy new mother? How's the baby? Have you named her yet?"

Not allowing the rapid fire of his questioning to intrude on the sacredness of the moment, Mrs. Mercado smiled serenely at him. "No, not exactly, perhaps in a few moments," she replied.

"All right then. I'll return shortly," he said and abruptly disappeared.

Her brow furrowed in thought, she pried her eyes from her daughter's angelic face and fixed them on a crystal vase holding a bouquet of fresh-cut red roses.

I like the name Crystal, but I've been set on Katherine for so long now, and I told Grandma Murphy that would be her name if it was a girl. But Crystal . . . the name rings like a bell in my ear . . . and in my heart.

After arguing with herself for several moments, her poetic Irish soul took over and she simply combined the two.

"Crystalline," she said to the pen-tapping orderly who had just rematerialized. "Her name is Crystalline Angelica Mercado," she said, spelling it out for him as he transcribed it to the birth certificate.

The woman gazed with adoration into the baby's eyes. "My sweet Crystine," she whispered. The baby cooed, and the world paused for a moment and then continued on, given another reason to do so.

Julie Mercado looked down at her sleeping daughter. *She's beautiful,* she thought, noting the baby's dark, almost black hair, her soft olive-toned skin, and her peaceful lovely features. The memory of the birth pains had completely faded into the mist of once was.

"Crystine," Julie whispered. The baby opened her eyes and looked directly into her mother's. *She recognizes me; she knows who I am,* Julie thought.

She pondered the baby's future and wondered what type of person she would be. She wondered what life would deal her as the years unfolded. That Crystine was special, she had no doubt. Of course, every mother thinks her newborn baby is special. Julie knew that, but Crystine was special special.

Julie was "missus" in name only. Julie and her husband, Juan, were separated, soon to be divorced. She hadn't been able to rely on Juan for much of anything and wouldn't be able to in the future, except for the possibility of more heartache now and then.

The year was 1950, the midpoint of the twentieth century in Huntington, California, a suburb of the growing amoeba known as Los Angeles, and pre-Disneyland, pre-Lakers, pre-Beach Boys Los Angeles had entered its freewheeling mode.

But being a single parent in LA wasn't any easier then than it is now.

Brian Murphy, Julie's older brother, flew out the door of his Chevy sedan, skipped around the front of the car, and flung open the passenger door. Julie slowly swung her legs out, placing them carefully on the ground, cradling Crystine gently but firmly in her arms. Brian lightly took hold of her upper arm and helped her to stand.

"I think they're awaitin'," he chirped. "Take your time though, sis. I'll be your crutch." Julie smiled as he helped her to stand. She looked down the long walkway leading to the front porch of the modest stucco cottage, held in place by a red tile roof.

An elderly lady waited on the porch, rocking in her chair. Crystine's brother Marcus, along with her sister Shelley, paced back and forth in eager anticipation.

It was late afternoon, late August, and hot. They'd moved an overstuffed easy chair onto the porch for the mom and her newborn baby.

How California typical, thought Julie as she and Brian moved up the slightly inclined walk. She emitted a small laugh. Brian gave her a quizzical glance. Looking down at her baby, Julie murmured, "She isn't."

"Isn't? Isn't what?" asked Brian.

"She isn't . . . typical," replied Julie.

"Of course not. No baby is, is it?"

Julie couldn't help but smile once again. *No,* she thought, *but this one goes way beyond that.* She had no doubt at all of this but at the same time wondered why she felt so strongly and thought so much about it.

The two youngsters paced continually. Grandma Murphy was more patient. Marcus, six, and Shelley, five, were Crystine's half brother and sister, and their last name was Hogan. Julie worried a little about that but then quickly dismissed it. This was California, and families with several surnames was becoming the norm.

"What's her name?" Shelley called from the porch.

"Hold on there, sprite," answered Brian, gently helping Julie up the three porch steps. "Let Momma get settled first," he said. Brian guided her to her chair. Cradling the baby, she very gingerly sat down.

Crystine opened her soft brown eyes.

"Oh, Momma, she's so beautiful!" exclaimed Shelley while Marcus beamed. Grandma Murphy simply glowed as only a grandmother can. "Welcome home, baby," she said.

Crystine's eyes moved from person to person, seeming to say hello to each one, making her own special cooing baby sound. She won their hearts in a moment. Julie sighed imperceptibly, offering a silent prayer of thanks. There would be no conflict of jealousy in this house.

Julie worked sixty hours a week to support her family, but she didn't mind. She was accepting of her life but wanted better for her children. Knowing that the means to attaining better lives was education, she constantly stressed the point to her kids.

She would never, barring a miracle, be able to endow them with luxuries or wealth. That wasn't a priority of hers anyway. A wise woman, she knew the true values and treasures of life and knew that love was like a two-edged sword and could bring joy or despair. Her love would bring strength to her family.

She was grateful that Grandma Murphy lived in the house. A widow, a second-generation Irish immigrant, she carried a good portion of the Irish wit and often lightened the hearts of those around her with its use.

Marcus and Shelley adored Crystine. She was the only one to have dark—not quite black—hair to go with her big brown eyes and olive-toned skin.

They were often called on to help take care of her. But it was like playtime with Crystine. Rapidly catching on, she would do what she could to take care of herself, and she did more and more as she grew.

She seldom cried, and never at night, not waking her mother, perhaps sensing the need she had for rest. Her rate of progression impressed even Grandma Murphy.

"Precocious," said Grandma Murphy. Julie looked up from feeding Crystine, who was seated in her high chair. "I'm sorry, Mom—what did you say?" she asked.

"Precocious. I said the child is precocious."

Julie smiled and nodded, not certain Grandma knew the true meaning of the word. But she knew, and yes, Crystine was precocious and so very much more. Her daughter was acutely aware not only of her surroundings and what went on in them but also of the feelings and needs of others.

❦

"Mom, do we have eggs for Easter?" asked Crystine. Julie looked up from the dress she was mending. "Why do we need eggs?" she asked.

"Well, to color, of course, and then to hide."

"And how many eggs do you think we need?"

Crystine pursed her lips in thought. "M-m-m, probably two."

"Just two?"

"Oh no, Momma. I mean two dozen."

"Well, go check in the refrigerator and see if we have enough, okay?"

Crystine turned and scurried into the kitchen. Flinging open the refrigerator door, she stood on her tiptoes to peer into the back of the top shelf where the eggs were kept. Managing to stretch enough to reach them, she removed the cartons carefully and placed them on the kitchen table. Opening the first one, she saw that each pocket held one egg. One dozen. She beamed as she popped open the second carton. Two of the pockets were empty. Her cherubic face fell slightly. Quietly replacing the cartons and closing the refrigerator door, she walked into the front room.

"Momma, we have two cartons; one is full, but the other loses two eggs."

Julie smiled at her choice of words. "So how many eggs do we have, honey?" she asked.

Crystine's face pinched in thought. "Twelve," she said and began counting on her fingers. "And ten!" she exclaimed. "So we have twenty-two eggs!" she stated with certainty.

"Do you think that will be enough?"

— 10 —

"Wel-l-l . . . like you say, Momma, sometimes we gotta make do with what we have, so it'll be okay. It'll be . . . okey-dokey," Crystine quipped with enthusiasm delightful to see.

Then it struck Julie: *More than anything else*, she thought, *this child is just that, an absolute delight.* Julie said to her, "When Marcus and Shelley get home, you can help them color the eggs." Crystine's lower lip extended just a little while the well-oiled wheels in her head turned rapidly. Grandma Murphy, observing from her chair on the other side of the room, chuckled to herself.

"Mom, can I get it started? I know where the coloring is, and the pans, and I can get the water, and . . . and Grandma can help me!"

Grandma Murphy let go a laugh. "Oh, child," was all she could say.

Two hours later, when Marcus and Shelley got home, the eggs were colored and hidden and the mess cleaned up.

"Oh, child," Grandma Murphy sighed with a laugh.

Crystine was not only smart as a whip, but she was a whip of sorts. Well, more like a little director, and she loved to get things done.

She would never be a knock-your-socks-off looker, but she would be a head turner.

Mostly she was just plain cute, a darling in the truest sense of the word, and that's what drew people to her. That and the brightness reflected in her intellect and her energy. Of course all young people have abundant energy—barring a debilitating disease—but Crystine's was super abundant, and she could focus it with uncanny intensity and without effort.

Her mother recognized these things and was grateful for her daughter's gifts. Success, at least in the common view of it, seemed imminent for her. But Julie saw something deeper in Crystine.

She was sweet, and it was the kind that would be very difficult for the world to take away. And she was sensitive, feeling influences most other people could not. Confident that her daughter's sweetness and sensitivity would insulate her from falling into the cold, hard-edged trap of arrogance or into the cutthroat strivings of the world, Julie whispered, as she fell asleep, a heartfelt "Thank you."

And Crystine continued to grow and mature right along with the City of Angels.

Chapter Three

We lived in a spooky, old, unpainted two-story house about a half mile from O'Donnell's farmhouse, across the road from the end of their driveway. It still had a dinner bell on a post in the side yard. Like I said, the Wild West wasn't wild to me; it was home and normal. The lightning in the mountains, the winds on the prairie, the open spaces that were free to roam—this was my place.

We moved out from under the shadow of O'Donnell's farm and into town. The houses had wood smoke curling out the chimneys in the early fall through late spring and around the clock in the winter.

The people I'd run into on the street I knew, most of them for a long time. Well, for as long as my young life anyway. And always their intentions were never anything but friendly. All I knew were the farms, ranches, lakes, streams, rivers . . . and the wonderment of it all. Landscapes and colors were never stagnant but changed with the coming of each season.

There were boots and saddles and county fairs and guns. Everybody had a rifle, more often several, along with a pistol or two. Often I'd see a rancher or a cowboy walking Main Street with a revolver strapped to his hip, not looking for trouble, just in town, looking. Every farm, every ranch had at least a couple of horses, usually more. Some folks living on the edge of town kept a horse right in their backyard. Nobody gasped or objected.

Part of each summer I'd stay at Uncle Frank's farm. He had a buckskin pony named Peanuts. I secretly called him Penis because he was such a little prick. Ornery, he was hard to break and hard to ride.

I'd cringe whenever Uncle Frank would say, "Daniel, go catch Peanuts, saddle him up and stretch him out a little, will ya?"

Well, there was no "will ya" with Uncle Frank. If you ate at his table you did what he asked. I'd swallow hard and say, "Sure."

He'd grin as though he was amused at my apparent agony, and he probably was. He knew full well what a pain it was to catch Peanuts. I'm betting he also knew what the rewards were for catching the little prick. My God that pony could fly! Like the wind, only faster, smoother, and more powerful. Riding Peanuts was like having a surging locomotive underneath me with the pistons pumping at full throttle. And I never felt more alive than when I was atop that pony. So alive that it seemed the gods of myth and legend would welcome me and give me place within their realm.

But I still swallowed hard as I headed toward the barn, a typical big red barn, with two haylofts in the upper part and an open space between them for equipment. Under the lofts were lock bars for milking cows, a few horse stalls, and a tack room. Once in a while, I'd swing on a hanging rope from one hayloft to another, playing Tarzan.

The interior of the barn was always dim, the sunlight grudgingly filtering in through cracks and dust-covered windows. Motes of dust always drifted lazily along in the scattered rays of the sun. But it was a pleasant dimness, never gloomy. A lot of hard work and a lot of good times had taken place in that old barn.

I went into the tack room and removed Peanuts's bridle from off its peg. His saddle, a no-frills brown roper, was slung over the top rail of the stall next door. I pulled it down and hauled it, along with the bridle draped over my left shoulder, to the double sliding doors that faced the pasture. I dropped the saddle there in the doorway. A box of sugar cubes was kept on a shelf just inside the double doors. I fished a couple out. *Maybe I can bribe the little prick*, I thought, dropping them into my shirt pocket as I headed out to the pasture, his bridle in my hand.

It was mid-morning with no wind, the weather pleasant and sunny. The sky was big, big to the point of being all there was in the world.

I spotted Peanuts at the far end of the pasture, gritted my teeth, and prepared for the ordeal ahead. I whistled. "Here Penis," I called. "I got some sugar for ya." He kept grazing; I kept walking with his bridle draped over my left arm. There wasn't any use in trying to hide it; he knew what the game was, and he would make me play it just as long as he could.

"Penis, come here, boy. I got some sugar for ya," I coaxed again. Then I stopped in amazement. The pony had lifted his head to look at me. This was significant, because he usually totally ignored me until I got up close, and then he'd bolt away. He was about half the length of a football field from me.

"My God, he's magnificent," I couldn't help but whisper as I looked at him standing there, his buckskin coat glistening golden in the sun. He stood on the top of a knoll of lush, brilliantly green grass, silhouetted against the big deep-blue sky.

"Magnificent," I whispered again, walking toward him. He remained still, and then he lifted his head and whinnied—at me! Was he glad to see me? That seemed impossible.

Without breaking stride I took the sugar cubes out of my shirt pocket and extended my right hand, palm up. "Come on, boy. I got some sugar for ya," I said once more.

Peanuts tossed his head, his black mane flying back like a flag in the wind. He started walking very slowly toward me, but I didn't trust that. I figured he'd explode into a run any second. I stopped dead in my tracks. Animals are really a lot like people, each one having its own personality and attendant quirks. Peanuts a beast of burden? Hardly. Bambi, his mare, was as sweet and gentle a horse as was ever made. A baby was safe on her back. Peanuts was ornery—not mean, more like mischievous ornery. *But maybe, just maybe, he's had a change of heart, like people do once in a while,* I thought.

He walked straight up to me and took the sugar cubes out of my hand as gently as Bambi ever did. I was so surprised that my hands trembled as I slipped the bridle over his head, easing the bit into his mouth. He took it, just plain took it like he knew he was supposed to, without putting up any kind of a fight. No tossing his head, no skittering to the side, no blowing snot all over my arm . . . nothing, not a single tiny protest.

"Come on then," I said, dumbfounded, and led him across the pasture to the barn doors and then prepared myself for the ordeal of saddling him. First the blanket—he stood still as stone. Then the saddle, and he still didn't move, didn't even twitch. I cinched it up without him filling his lungs like he ordinarily did so later on the saddle would loosen and begin to slip. But I'd learned how to remedy that situation. More than once I'd driven my knee into his midsection, forcing the air out of him. *Maybe he really did have a change of heart,* I thought. Anything's possible.

Turning him toward the barnyard gate, I grabbed the pommel of the saddle with my left hand, hooked my left boot in the stirrup, swung my right leg up and over his back, and settled into the brown roper. No one can tell me animals don't think, or plan, or scheme. I'd climbed atop a live volcano, and it erupted underneath me with the force of a bomb. That buckskin sonofabitch! I hadn't been at all suspicious, let alone expecting it. He'd never bucked on me before. But boy, he sure did this time.

He exploded straight up under me, humping his back in an arc with me at its apex. Then he landed, stiff legged, on all fours, so's he could jar my jaw, my teeth, my spine, and every other bone in my body. He exploded again, this time with just his hind end, twirling it like a cyclone not ready to touch down.

"Pee-n-i-sss," I hollered as I flew off his back, hoping to somehow curse the little prick by hollering that word. I landed like a rag doll in the barnyard.

Peanuts stood like a statue, looking at me as if I were the world's biggest fool, and he didn't run; he just stood there.

"Haw-haw-haw-hee-hee-arghh." I heard laughter from somewhere. I looked up and glanced over by the gate. Uncle Frank was doubled over, holding his belly, his face flushed red from laughing so hard.

"Come on, Daniel, get back up on him. You got to show him who's boss! Cowboy up, young 'un." He guffawed some more, his face still red, but at least he wasn't doubled over.

I wasn't going to show any fear to Peanuts, or pain to Uncle Frank. Springing to my feet, I walked determinedly toward the pony. He stood there, still, and didn't run. I grabbed the reins.

"I'll open the gate for ya," Uncle Frank hollered.

I swung up into the saddle, expecting another explosion. Nothing. He stood there, perfectly still. Turning his head toward the gate, I dug my boot heels into his ribs as hard as I possibly could. Bursting ahead at what seemed near the speed of sound, he shot through the gate as if he'd been shot out of a cannon.

I barely heard Uncle Frank holler out behind me, "Atta boy, Daniel, show him who's boss!"

My God how that pony could fly! And I received my reward, and the gods gave me place, and how I loved that little buckskin! You get bucked off, you climb back on for another go at it. Often times, that's how life works.

Cowboy up.

Every now and then, I'd get to go stay with my grandparents, and I loved being at their house on the edge of Kalispell. By most standards it was a shack. Small, whitewashed, with two tiny bedrooms and no bathtub, just a shower stall in the bathroom. Grandpa's razor strop hung on the bathroom wall, and Grandma's wringer washer was just outside the bathroom set into a tiny alcove.

An old oil heater in the front room kept the place warm, and there was a wood cookstove in the kitchen that Grandma was an expert at using.

Thomas and Anna McDermitt were second-generation Irish immigrants and didn't have much to show for fifty years of marriage and a lifetime of hardship and hard work.

But I knew it was the warmth of the hearts within, not the trappings, that made a house a home.

"Want a bean, Daniel?" Grandpa would ask.

"Sure, Grandpa," I'd reply. Then, very carefully, he'd scoop out one baked bean and just as carefully deposit it on my plate. It was a routine at the dinner table, and we'd laugh as Grandma would scold him for teasing me. It always warmed me from the inside out. And it was the warmth of my grandparents hearts for each other that kept them married for fifty years.

In celebration of that monumental event—as astounding then as it would be now—we gathered at O'Donnell's farm. Grandpa, looking sort of bored, took it all in stride, as he did everything, an accepting attitude he'd learned from life's lessons, some easy, most hard. Every now and then he'd catch my eye and give me a mischievous wink, the twinkle in his eye at full strength. He always let me know he was aware of me. "Never get too stuffy, Daniel. It takes all the fun out of life," he'd tell me.

Galen McDermitt, Grandpa's brother, had come all the way from California to attend and celebrate the anniversary. It was he who planted visions of orange groves dancing in the head of my mom.

"What might your name be, lad?" Great-uncle Galen asked, peering over the top of his wire-rimmed spectacles.

"Daniel," I chirped. "And that's my mom over there." I pointed at her standing by the big picture window in the front room, looking dreamily out at the landscape. She and Uncle Galen had been chatting just a few minutes earlier.

He sat down on the other end of the overstuffed I was seated on.

"How old are you, Daniel?" he asked.

"Six, sir, and I'm in the first grade," I exclaimed.

"You don't say," he quipped. "Where do you go to school?"

"Over there," I said, pointing past my mom out the big picture window in the front room. About a mile away, shimmering in the glow of the late-afternoon early-autumn sun, stood the old white schoolhouse. There weren't any trees near it, and acres of open farmland surrounded it. It stood all on its own, situated a stone's throw off the Lower Valley Road.

"The quintessential country schoolhouse," Uncle Galen mumbled. I pretended that I didn't hear him. I hadn't the foggiest notion what that word meant.

"We all go there," I offered.

Uncle Galen gave me a pronounced look. "All?" he asked.

"Yeah, me, my brother, and my two sisters. There's eight rows of desks, one for each grade."

"Eight grades?" he asked, raising his left brow. "In one school, with one teacher?"

"Yeah, I'm in the first grade, Lauren is in the second, Norris is in the fourth, and Judy is in the eighth!" I exclaimed, rather proud of myself for giving such a detailed explanation.

Uncle Galen let out a low whistle. "Quintessential."

There was that funny word again. I continued on. "There's four of us in the first grade, three in the second, four in the third, five in the fourth, three in the fifth, four in the sixth, five in the seventh, and four in the eighth."

Uncle Galen peered intently at me over the top of his spectacles. "How many students is that?" he asked.

"Thirty-two," I casually replied. His left eyebrow raised again, like Grandpas did when something unusual caught his attention.

"Do you like school, Daniel?"

"Yeah, besides, it's what I'm supposed to do right now."

Uncle Galen chuckled. "I'm a schoolteacher myself, Daniel. Did you know that?"

"No," I replied, shaking my head.

"In California. Do you know where that is?"

"No," I answered, not really interested. Was there anywhere else except here in the untamed west?

"Well, it has beautiful white beaches, a blue ocean, and lots of sunshine all year long. It's south of here. Do you know which way that is?" I pointed. Uncle Galen nodded his affirmation.

"Do you like teaching in California, Uncle Galen?" I asked. He peered at me again, his blue eyes twinkling and dancing.

"Yeah," he said. "And besides, it's what I'm supposed to do right now." He chuckled, and I grinned. Fun. And Uncle Galen warmed me from the inside out, like Grandpa did.

"Keep going to school, Daniel," he said. "The more schooling you get, the better off you'll be." He patted my knee, got up, and joined my mom, who was still standing by the big picture window, looking south.

"I see you've met Daniel," Ellen said as Galen stood by her. "Did you fill his head with visions of sunlit orange groves like you did mine?" she asked.

"No, in fact the lad managed to raise my brow a couple of times."

"He'll do that now and then," replied Ellen, smiling demurely at Galen.

I looked over at Grandpa from where I was sitting. He was seated at the head of the huge dining table. He tossed me a wink.

One year later, I was sitting on the couch next to Grandpa, who was reclining in his easy chair. Wrestling was on his old black-and-white television. Old, as in a twelve-inch screen stuck in a wooden cabinet that stood on the floor.

Suddenly, he went into a coughing fit, leaned forward, leaned back, and wasn't breathing. I panicked and didn't know what to do. Grandma told me to take off his shoes and rub his feet, but Grandpa remained still. Grandma told me to hurry next door and get Mrs. Wilson. I sprinted over and banged on her door.

"Well, hello, Daniel," she said.

"Mrs. Wilson, Grandma sent me to get you. Grandpa's awful sick."

I felt so helpless as I rushed back to Grandpa's house, Mrs. Wilson bustling along behind me. Grandpa hadn't moved. He was gone just like that. I couldn't grasp the idea he would never speak or laugh or tease me again. The idea of death didn't sink in until his funeral, and then I learned how big a hole losing my grandpa tore in me, and how it became a fixed point in my memory, and how life didn't seem as sweet as it had a few days ago.

Chapter Four

Crystine shot her hand up as far as it could possibly go. "I do!" she exclaimed.

"Okay, Crystine, what do you say it means?" asked the balding, gray-haired man as he peered over the top of his spectacles.

"It means divided by," she answered.

"Correct," said the teacher. "A fraction is simply a division problem, usually having an answer less than one. For example, one half means . . ." He trailed off. He knew better than to ask who might know the answer. He pointed, "What, Crystine?"

"One divided by two," she quickly replied and then added, "and the answer, the quotient, is zero point five!" She beamed in triumph, her soft brown eyes bright, inquisitive, and confident beyond her age.

Mr. McDermitt, her fifth-grade teacher, smiled ever so slightly; he was used to Crystine by now; used to the fact that she was not only the brightest student in the class but very likely the brightest he had ever taught in his thirty years in the Los Angeles public school system, the last ten spent in Huntington.

And Crystine was certainly his most delightful student in the last decade. Quick and eager, she soaked up her subjects like they were water and she a sponge. She had a thirst for education, and learning came easily for her. That was the one thing that concerned Mr. McDermitt. Maybe school was too easy for her. He knew the value of being challenged and having to overcome obstacles in order to reach a goal. But Crystine was only eleven, and there'd be plenty of opportunities for life to challenge her, he knew. So Galen McDermitt decided to simply delight in the child and looked forward to the parent-teacher conference coming up. Besides, this was going to be his last year of teaching, and he may as well relax and enjoy it.

He had been lured to California by its endless warmth and the promise of exceptional opportunity. To be honest, he'd been more than a little intrigued by Hollywood, which had rapidly become a mainstay in the fabric of America.

Quite a few of his students had contributed to its mystique, not as faces on the screen but as writers, art and set and costume designers, directors, and a producer or two. He thought about Crystine and wondered if she would end up in Hollywood. She was bright and talented and maybe charismatic enough to do so. She had something else, though, that he had discerned in her. She seemed to feel the pulsations around her with an uncommon sensitivity, which could work for a person or against a person. Only time and circumstance would tell that tale.

But the elderly teacher could read the writing on the wall. The same attractions that had lured him to Southern California, now, along with many additional ones, lured thousands to the place every day. Metro Los Angeles was no longer a balmy, laid-back oasis. It no longer offered the shelter from some of life's harshness that it once had. An undercurrent of danger was growing and gaining strength. Racial divisions, ever-widening economic gaps, and desirable, undesirable, opulent, and outright dangerous neighborhoods were becoming more clearly defined, springing up like cactus in the desert.

Galen could see where it came from and where it was headed. Those who were still being lured to Southern California by the sunshine, the gold, and the glitter could not.

Galen's eyes had been opened when he visited Montana six years earlier. That place was more beautiful than he remembered and felt pure and uncluttered by societal problems.

He'd painted quite the rosy picture of California for his niece while he was there, but the place had changed since then. Naturally he'd added the Irish embellishments to the picture and could tell that she had been quite taken with the then developing mystique of Southern California. He hoped he hadn't done her any disservice. At any rate, it was time for him to retire and time for him to leave sunny Southern California and return to Montana's timeless and unchanging beauty, to where his heart lay.

Julie Mercado pulled her Chevy sedan into the school parking lot. It was late spring, early in the evening.

The sun glowed soft and golden as it made its descent into the Pacific, a beautiful evening by anyone's standards.

She thought stability was an important factor in everyone's life, and so Crystine had attended Parkside from the first grade on. Not a bad place to grow up, Julie mused as she strolled across the parking lot. Her dark hair, showing a few strands of gray, hung loose to the middle of her back. The ocean breeze played with it as she walked. Dressed in white cotton slacks and a light yellow chiffon blouse and with sandals on her feet, she was California casual.

The double front doors were propped open, and she glided through them. The hallway was spotless, the floor polished to a high sheen, with no clutter or open lockers. A single couple strolled her way from the other end of the hall. Other than that, the place seemed deserted, and Julie's footsteps echoed in the emptiness.

She'd never met Mr. McDermitt, but Crystine had mentioned that she liked him, that he was sort of like a grandpa. Near the end of the hallway Julie stopped at the open door of room 11B and peered inside. The watch on her wrist read precisely seven o'clock. Right on time.

Inside the sparkling clean room, the windows were open, letting in the breeze and enough light to keep the overheads off. Mr. McDermitt was standing in front of his well-worn wooden desk at the opposite end of the room. He looked elderly, balding, his fringe of gray hair down a little below his collar, and Julie wondered if there was a bit of the rebel in him. She hoped so. He straightened as she approached. He was trim, about six feet tall, wearing wire-rimmed spectacles, and his blue eyes twinkled a lively dance.

He reminds me of Ben Franklin, thought Julie as she extended her hand. Mr. McDermitt took it, shaking it with genuine warmth. She felt a gentle strength in his hands, hands that had known hard work.

"Mrs. Mercado?"

"Yes," she affirmed.

"You're right on time."

"I believe in being prompt. It seems to help things go a little smoother."

Mr. McDermitt smiled an open, honest smile.

"Crystine is always on time, about everything," he said. "She must have learned that from you. She is never late for class, never late with her assignments. She has no problems in school whatsoever. I'm sure you're well aware of her academics, Mrs. Mercado."

It was Julie's turn to smile.

"Please, call me Julie," she replied. "Mrs. Mercado sounds so formal, and . . . well . . . actually a bit silly. I've been divorced for twelve years and have never remarried."

The news didn't startle him. This was, after all, California, the State of Flux. He thought of his wife of thirty-two years and of how she had suddenly died last spring. He thought of love, both of its longevity and of its sudden evaporation, and decided that how it worked or didn't work was a thing unknowable. *She's a very attractive woman. If I were a little younger . . . well . . .*

"Crystine has never mentioned her dad, as I recall," he said, putting himself back on track. "Mrs. Mercado . . . Julie . . . about Crystine . . ."

"Yes," she quickly replied, a tinge of anxiety in her voice.

"Oh, no . . . nothing on the negative side, certainly not," he interjected. "It's just that, uh, she's being raised very well . . . I mean . . . because you're . . ."

Julie laughed, soft and easy. "I'm not the only single parent of a student in your class, am I?"

And very bright, also. "Oh, no," replied Galen. "It's just that it can't be easy raising children on your own. And on top of Crystine's academic excellence—due in no small part to habits you've instilled in her I'm sure—it's obvious that you're also building a good character in her," he blurted. "Which, in my view, is equal to, if not more important than, acquiring pure knowledge."

"Thank you for the compliments, both to me and Crystine," she said.

"I wouldn't say them if they weren't true. She is an absolute delight to have in class."

Julie smiled again; she knew long ago that Crystine was a delight. "Thank you, Mr. McDermitt," she said.

"You are more than welcome, and please, call me Galen."

Julie couldn't help but smile at how she suddenly felt warmed from the inside out.

Chapter five

Mom rolled down the passenger-side window of the old four-door Lincoln sedan. I thought she was pretty, being Mom and all. Her reddish hair hung loose to her shoulders, and today her blue eyes sparkled with a light I couldn't remember ever seeing, and I was eleven years old. I'm not sure how old she was; maybe her mid-thirties. I never gave it much thought, she was . . . Mom.

"Daniel, hurry please, we have to be on our way!" she urged through the open window.

It was the first week of June. The sky, out of character, was a forbidding gray, which was just as well. It matched my mood and the color of the old Lincoln.

I should have been happy, ecstatic even. It was a significant day in my young life, the last day of school, the last day of elementary school to boot. I had just completed the sixth grade, and next year it would be on to junior high. All the kids from the six separate elementary schools would be gathered there. It meant tackle football instead of those silly flags, basketball against not only other schools but schools from other towns, new friends, and girls. Fun times ahead.

Hesitating after a slow start toward the car, my innards roiling from apprehension, sadness, and anger, I nodded at friends I'd shared five years of school with. Classmates and teammates sharing birthdays and weekends and dreams and discoveries and together facing that freight train coming down the pike—the big change into adolescence. A new world was coming, one I looked forward to, one that made the summer look small and not quite so embraceable. But scratch all that. Add regret to the bag of mixed emotions knotting up my insides.

No need for words now—my teacher had allowed a going-away party in the classroom. I gave my best friend, Jack Hawkins, a weak wave. We'd been in the same classrooms with the same teachers for all of the five years. He returned a weak wave of his own.

I glanced over at Diana, who I decided was going to be my girlfriend, but I hadn't gotten around to her yet. She gave me a sweet smile touched with the sadness in her eyes. I think she would have said yes to my intentions.

Nodding to a few more friends, I turned in dread toward the dismal gray sedan. Pulling open the right rear door, I climbed in and slammed it shut, just to let the world know that I wasn't too happy at the moment. I'm pretty sure the world didn't care all that much.

Looking at me with raised brows, Lauren, my older sister by a year, shrugged her shoulders, a gesture that said, "Deal with it." She always took things in stride better than I did. Dad moved the shift lever to D, and our journey began.

I didn't look back . . . couldn't really. I was losing everything familiar and known and everything yet to be discovered in my world. Watching it fade away would be like letting a whirlwind stir the fog of emotions spinning inside my gut. My sense of place had shifted and was now unknown. Lost and adrift in a sea of blankness, perhaps in mild shock, I stared straight ahead, speaking to no one.

Mom turned around to look at me. She was absolutely aglow—for the first time I could remember—with excitement and happiness. "Don't be so glum, Daniel. We're on our way to sunny California, Disneyland, the Dodgers, the Pacific Ocean, and no more freezing-cold weather. Just imagine! Why, it'll be like heaven on earth!"

Dad just grinned silently. Being more of a realist, I'm sure he knew better.

I smiled anemically at Mom and wondered about that word used when there was no explanation for an unwanted event—fate.

Lauren and I sat in the backseat of the old Lincoln. I couldn't look out the rear window of the sedan until we were a couple of miles out of town, and only then could I look back at the shining mountains receding as we drove out of the Treasure State. Apprehensive about the future, not at all certain that Father knew best, I hoped that between him and Mom, though, together they did know what was best. *At least they might not fight as much*, I thought.

Dad concentrated on driving; Mom was quiet, enjoying the scenery; Lauren was lost in a book. Norris, my older brother, would join us after his annual summer of toil on the O'Donnell farm. My other sisters, Judy and Rene, were already in California.

I rode along in silence, gazing blankly at the passing scenery, wondering if I'd ever see it again or if there was anything in California that could match its raw and rugged beauty. I tried to conjure up images of California in my head but had no feel for it. No feel for the flora or the fauna, for the land or the people. I'd seen it on a map. I knew Disneyland was there. I knew most television shows came from there, in some mysterious, if not outright magical, way. They were mostly westerns—*Gunsmoke, Rawhide, Maverick*, and the like—so I reasoned that the Wild West must be there also.

I wondered what had prompted my folks to painfully uproot us. Maybe the Golden State meant golden opportunities, but I figured the nickname had more to do with sunrises and sunsets than anything else. I pondered fate. I couldn't really put any faith in it, but I thought if it had any influence at all in my life, it was nothing but cruel.

We drove straight through.

The soft gentle breezes in Utah were nice. Las Vegas was just a spot of glitter on the desert, and we didn't stop. In fact, we didn't stop at all except to eat or use a roadside convenience. Dad was on a mission. Mom was in a world of her own, one of excitement and anticipation.

We passed through some mountains west of Las Vegas—I think they were the Sierra Nevadas—and began our descent into Los Angeles. It was huge, gi-normous, gargantuan, and it stunk. A light brown haze hung low in the sky over the metropolis. Hello smog, and the repugnant odor was like nothing I'd ever smelled before, unnatural and alien. Oh boy. I knew right away it wasn't the Wild West or the Land of Oz. Los Angeles was sprawling, and like an amoeba, it was ingesting everything into itself. No synthesizing, no compromising, no consideration of anything but itself and its substance of concrete and steel, asphalt and automobiles, stucco houses and red-tiled roofs, skyscrapers and commerce galore. Even the palm trees were suspect. They didn't really *look* like trees. All I'd known were the evergreens, the maples, the elms, the apple and cherry trees of the north.

Where one city ended and another began was impossible to tell. "Where are we now, Mom?" I'd ask as we drove and drove and drove.

"Downey," she'd reply.

We'd drive on. There were no breaks in the streets or in what fronted on them.

"Where are we now?"

"South Gate."

That didn't register. We never *left* anywhere; how could we have *gone* anywhere?

And I couldn't see. Oh, I could see the unending sameness of the city, and the artificial geography of it, but I couldn't *see*! No land or mountains or forests. No fields of grass or wheat. No cattle, no horses, no blue . . . no big sky. No thunderheads, no water, nothing.

There was no *far!*

There was no Main Street, always the pulse of Anytown, USA.

I felt lost and trapped; I took in a deep breath; I felt sick.

What I experienced could have been the definition of culture shock. It bombed me and then blew me away, firsthand and to the max, without warning and without mercy.

We first landed in Garden Grove, in an apartment. No green grass; everything was fenced and covered with concrete or asphalt. Everything was the same. I felt like I might suffocate.

Later we moved on to one of the beach towns, Manhattan maybe. The ocean was new to me and offered some relief from my suffocation, from the beginning of my ingestion into the Big Amoeba. After a lackluster summer, we ended up in Huntington because Dad got a good job there. I never saw Uncle Galen again. Mom said he'd moved up to Montana. I wished I was with him. He reminded me of Grandpa.

I thought about the day Grandpa died.

I thought about the day my dreams died.

Fixed points, both.

The summer moved along slowly. I had swum in the Pacific but missed the fresh pure clarity of the mountain lakes. I had been to Disneyland but missed the honesty of the county fair. I had baked in the California sun but missed the Thunderheads and the electric light show and crashing symphony of thunder that they offered. There would be no warming chinook wind or red-breasted robin appearing. No unmistakable day when fall fell. No gently falling, moonlight-brightened snow to blanket the earth like a comforter, and say, "Peace, be still." No calves or lambs or foals being born, no crops growing, and no harvest time.

I felt no purity. Not in the land or in the people, and I wondered what the attraction was that brought so many to the Big Amoeba.

Then I felt the buzz, an undercurrent of seeking and perpetual motion in the people. Restlessness was its engine, revved up and never stopping, and that was what propelled Los Angeles, the search for the never-ending party, hope of capturing the ultimate but undefined thrill. And I wondered if I would ever enter the realm of the gods again.

Autumn crept in unannounced and imperceptible, like fog seeping off the ocean in the early morning only to be dissipated by the sun's first strength. But the calendar said autumn, and with it came the start of the school year.

Starting seventh grade at Gage Junior High was a shared unknown by all new students. I was not alone in that boat. The local elementary schools gathered in one place. Okay, that seemed normal, like in the Flathead. As a result, I was able to adjust fairly easily, almost. The school grounds, our playgrounds, were completely covered with asphalt, not a blade of grass to be seen anywhere. A chain-link fence, higher than an average-sized man, surrounded the place. Busy, noisy streets carrying never-ending traffic fronted two sides of the rectangular area. Streets that were not quite as busy fronted the other two sides. A day didn't go by when the air wasn't tainted with the odor of smog, sometimes faint, more often pungent. *This is no nirvana*, I thought. *It's probably closer to hell.*

About half the students were Hispanic. But, for reasons I still can't comprehend, racial tension existed and was building.

Autumn didn't mean football or any other organized sports. No school-versus-school competition. No popular girls in short skirts kicking up their heels and yelling rah-rah-rah. No school spirit, just pissin' around on an asphalt-covered yard.

"Daniel Abrams," the teacher called.

"Here," I called, simultaneously raising my hand. He lifted disinterested eyes to locate me.

Mr. Brewer was tall, tan, blue-eyed, fairly young, and athletic, with short-cropped blond hair, the quintessential Southern Californian and, no doubt, a bachelor. I didn't see any of the marks of marriage on him, like a ring or a growing pot belly. He was my homeroom teacher. The homeroom was where we landed first thing every morning. It was a fancy name attached to a surreal concept, was my best guess, because there was nothing homey about it.

Mr. Brewer wasn't interested in us. I didn't know any of the other students, and I spent less time in homeroom than in any of my other classes and talked to other teachers and other kids more than I ever did or would ever do in homeroom. I never could figure out why they called it homeroom. Like I said, surreal.

School work was schoolwork, the same as it had been in Montana, and it came easy for me. Sometimes it amused me, like "agriculture." Poor Mr. Amerine. He was so earnest and so proud of us for growing anemic carrots in a patch of sandy soil that looked to me like it had come from the beach. I never told him about helping harvest hundreds of acres of prime wheat or seeing acres of lush, green, nutrient-rich alfalfa get baled into hay and loading it into the barn for winter feed. I never mentioned helping with the lambs in the spring, or feeding the "bums"—those without mothers, after the ewe either dies or rejects the lamb—out of bottles, like a baby. Or of covering them with blankets if they were born too early in the spring so they wouldn't freeze from a tail-end blast of winter.

I didn't tell him how I used to eat my fill of fresh apples from off the tree in our backyard, or of pulling up huge stalks of rhubarb that grew wild in the alley behind us and eating it fresh, after first dipping it in a bowl of sugar before each bite. I didn't say how I'd grab handfuls of the lush green alfalfa before it was hayed and eat it like candy or chew on wheat kernels until they turned to gum, or how I'd share oats with the horses. Our neighbors gave us bunches of huge carrots from their garden every year, more than we could use. In the fall, we went up to the mountains to pick wild huckleberries, five gallons of them in a day, and that was after feasting on them all day long.

I never told him what it was like to have a live locomotive called Peanuts surging underneath me, outrunning the wind.

One day I got fed up with the seventh-grade bully, Rocky Snider, so I told him to meet me after school, that we had some things to settle. He hadn't ever picked on me directly, but he'd gone too far with my best friend, and I'd seen enough and had enough of his blustering. He was the bully because he had considerable weight to throw around. I didn't like bullies or liars then, and I still don't to this day. Part of the cowboy in me, I guess.

So after school we headed across the street and into an alley, making sure we were off the school grounds. I started thinking along the way that maybe I'd bitten off more than I could chew, but it was too late to back out now. We stopped and faced each other, and a small crowd circled around us.

"I'll give you a chance to call this off and save yourself an ass-beating," he said to me. I hit him with a right and hurt my hand probably more than it hurt his jaw.

We circled around, flailing away, stirring up a small cloud of dust around our feet. He broke a sweat as he punched down and I punched up.

"Come on, Daniel! You can do it! Bust his chops, Daniel!"

I don't think I heard anybody hollering for Rocky. He started puffing pretty hard. I dropped my hands and stopped.

"Wanna stop now?" I asked.

He nodded and dropped his hands down. Neither one of us had landed a good solid blow after my initial pop to his jaw. I was glad he was a boxer and not a wrestler. Rocky put his arm around my shoulders and complimented me on the fight, and that was that. He never bothered me or any of my friends again. In fact, he and I ended up being friends, not real close, but friends. And so I learned that if you stand up to a bully, or to something that's bullying you, it generally stops. It's happened that way more than once.

The schoolwork, the performance, wasn't a problem, and I was being accepted socially. But it was the place, or rather the lack of one, that I couldn't adjust to. It's hard to feel connected to nonliving matter like concrete and asphalt, chain-link fences and tainted air.

So I got a paper route delivering the *LA Times*. Up every morning at five o'clock, down to the storefront, fold and rubber-band the papers, load them in the bags, sling the bags over the handlebars of my bike, and off I'd go.

Of course, I'd amuse myself. The paper bags were my saddle bags, my bike a pony, and me a gunslinger with the papers as my bullets. The Wild West imagined. I got good at it too. I'd fly along, slinging the papers and putting them right where I wanted, or where the subscriber had specified. I never hit a door unless someone was late with their payment; then I'd rattle one, just as a reminder.

The Sunday edition was huge and unwieldy, and I had ninety of them to deliver. I didn't get home until mid-morning on my first Sunday. The following week, when Sunday morning rolled around, Dad was up and at the kitchen table, drinking coffee. I downed a glass of milk, put on my sweatshirt, and was ready to head out the door.

"Hold up, Daniel," he said. "We'll take the car."

Did *that* ever make my work on Sundays easier. Loading all the papers at one time into the trunk of the old Lincoln, Dad would slowly drive down the street while I scampered back and forth, slinging the heavy papers. It took just a little more time than my regular weekday route did. Every Sunday morning from then on, as long as I had the route, Dad would help me, and it would go "just like clockwork," as he used to say. He'd do things like that, out of the blue and very significant, to let me know he loved me.

Around Christmastime that year, I made more money in tips than I did from my regular collections. That told me I was doing a good job (with Dad's help), and that maybe, just maybe, Christmas was a special time in California also and that people opened their hearts to the feeling of the season. The idea was comforting. But it was still strange. Instead of traveling up to the snow-covered mountains for a tree that could be had for the chopping, plus all the fun involved, we bought our Christmas tree off a parking lot. But at least it was from Montana.

No, there wasn't any magic in the air, or snowflakes drifting down in the moonlight, and there really wasn't a Christmas season, more like just a night and a day.

And the buzz continued uninterrupted.

What I enjoyed most about my early-morning route was the quietness and the solitude. It was a time when *I mattered*, when I didn't feel like I was being ingested. But it all ended one morning when I found out that my boss had lied to me. He had promised me a route coming open that was closer to home, but gave it to someone else. I walked out the door, slammed it shut behind me, and didn't bother to do my route that morning.

Liars and bullies—never have liked either one.

I got an after-school route right away, delivering the *LA Examiner*. I didn't like it as much, given the time of day and with the buzz being at full force.

As nature dragged me along I became more and more aware of girls, especially the Hispanic ones. I thought they were about the most beautiful creatures ever invented.

One day a couple of my friends and I were chatting with three girls, all of us tee-heeing and giggling away, and I ended up staying a little late after school. I was flirting and strutting, putting on my best show, amazed by my intrinsic desire for the girls and what they had to offer. The mystery of it was so intriguing that I lost all track of time. When I glanced quickly at my watch and said, "I gotta go," there was some slight protestation. I was gaining place. It was one week before the beginning of summer vacation.

I flew toward home on my new bike, hurrying to change clothes and get started on my route. A busy, pain-in-the-ass type intersection two blocks from my house was in my path. It had four lanes of traffic in each direction, walk lights, don't-walk lights, honking horns, zipping cars, and the relentless buzz. I couldn't get around it without losing more time.

The light governing the traffic that ran perpendicular to me turned yellow. I set myself, poised in anticipation, at the curb. The sign flashed WALK. I shot forward on my bike, keeping in the crosswalk. Three-fourths of the way across I glanced to my right and saw a car coming straight at me . . . surely it would stop. It had plenty of room to stop.

It kept coming. I looked into the eyes of the old woman behind the wheel. They were unfocused and blank. *She has to see me!* screamed and ricocheted inside my head. *Surely she . . . wham!* The car struck broadside, not slowing down a bit. In fact, she had picked up speed, trying to make the light, which by now was red, of course.

The buzz.

Smashed over, I was at once underneath the car. *My God . . . this isn't happening . . . It can't be happening!* my mind screamed as fear became my shroud and horror my master.

My bike acted as a shield, lifting the car somewhat up and over me, the right front tire hitting my side. I didn't feel any pain right away; I'd been baptized in adrenaline. And then I saw in slow motion, which I thought must be the approach to eternity. Looking up I saw the right rear tire coming at my midsection, and I cried out, "My God!" not in a curse, but in a "If I ever needed You in my life, and You're there, I'm desperate for You now" kind of "My God!"

I tensed myself. The tire hit me square in the stomach. The car hadn't slowed any and continued right over the top of me before coming to a stop. I was halfway underneath it, I crawled out all the way, eliminating any chance of it slipping off the curb and falling back onto me.

Rolling over on my back, my world was now one of pain, and nothing else, at the moment, existed. Then, through bleary eyes, I saw my mom's face framed against an unusually deep, azure-blue sky. With all she had she was trying to be calm, but fear was written across her face. The adrenaline had raised my senses to an acuteness I think only madmen experience.

"I'll be okay, Mom." The words trembled from my mouth.

"Yes, Daniel, you'll be just fine. You'll be all right. The ambulance is on the way." She didn't sound at all confident. She was afraid, and I was too, as I watched the tears fall from her eyes.

Sirens, end of scene, fade to black.

I opened my eyes to a blurred world. I knew I wasn't in the street—the sun wasn't in my eyes and I was lying on something much more comfortable than pavement.

Slowly turning my head to the right and straining to focus my vision, I saw Mom's face come into view.

"Told you I'd be okay, Mom," I said, my voice sounding like it was muffled in cotton. She smiled, calm this time, and lightly gripped my hand.

"I know, Daniel. I knew you would be." She was confident now, and that made me feel a whole lot better.

I tried to move but couldn't. Gasping in panic, I strained against whatever held me down, Mom gripped my hand reassuringly. "It's okay, Daniel! You're all right now!" she exclaimed, trying to calm me.

"I . . . I can't . . . *move!*" I screamed, my voice weak as I strained harder against what held me, not able to feel what it was.

A nurse hurried into the room.

"Daniel, it's okay, honey. You're strapped down, in traction. The doctors have immobilized you for a few days," Mom said.

"W-why?"

She looked away for an instant and then turned to lovingly hold my gaze. "You've suffered a broken back," she said very gravely.

"What does it mean?" I asked in a quavering voice.

"Right now it means you'll be laid up for a time, at the very least for the whole summer."

My heart sank to rock bottom. Another summer spent in the limbo land of no fun.

Four vertebrae in the lumbar area of my spine had received compression fractures. In other words, those about waist high had been crushed. The car had knocked me out and had given me a concussion. The right rear tire had left its tread marks across my midsection. Mom told me later that the doctors weren't sure if I was going to pull through.

I thought about God, the way I was taught to think about him, as God the Punisher. I further pondered fate, the other, undefined God that holds everyone's faith. And right now, He, She, It, or They appeared to be nothing at all except more cruel than I had at first imagined, and on top of that more whimsical, and I was indeed being punished. For what, I had no idea, but I figured that surely it had to be over and done with.

Chapter Six

Nikki Craven skipped through the wide-open double doors of Parkside Elementary, happy about summer vacation starting today and excited about entering Gage Junior High next year.

Her blond hair flopping from side to side as she skipped along, her blue eyes gleamed from the excitement and panned left and right as she bobbed up and down. She stopped in the middle of a skip, raised her arm in the air, and waved it vigorously.

"Crystine . . . *Crystine*," she hollered.

Crystine looked up from talking to a black-haired olive-skinned boy. "There's Nikki; gotta go," she told him. "Call me," she said over her shoulder as she walked away.

She and Nikki had been best friends since the first grade. It seemed an unlikely union, but one of the beauties of youth is that prejudice hasn't yet been learned.

Nikki was from the west side of Huntington, where most houses had a swimming pool in the oversized backyard, two cars in the double garage, and two parents in the house, quite often one of them a step-parent. Nikki had a stepfather.

Crystine lived on the east side of town in the same house she'd lived in since she was born. Her mother drove a seven-year-old

Chevy sedan, parked it on the street, and had never remarried since her divorce. The only major change in her life had been the death of Grandma Murphy a year ago. The hole left in the fabric of the home, though smaller now, could still be felt.

Crystine was envied by the other girls because of how easily she attracted boys. They claimed that her well-developed breasts gave her an unfair advantage, but she knew all about that, and boys, and didn't think much about it one way or another. Confident beyond her years, her attractiveness was that she was simply *there*, present in the moment, and she never moved from *there*.

Nikki was the insecure one in their friendship, although Crystine had never given her any reason to feel that way.

"Well, girlfriend, we made it!" exclaimed Crystine, raising her right hand high in the air and then slapping Nikki's upraised palm with a loud smack.

"Yeah baby," said Nikki with an unusual show of enthusiasm.

"On to Gage," Crystine proclaimed. "But first we have the whole summer in front of us to enjoy," she said and winked conspiratorially at her friend.

"Too bad about that boy who got hit by a car. He won't have much of a summer," remarked Nikki.

"What boy?"

"Didn't you read about it? It was in last week's newspaper."

Thinking it was obvious that she hadn't, Crystine didn't bother to answer. "Is he okay?" she asked absently.

"Yeah, he'll live, I guess. His name is Daniel, uh . . . Abrams, or something like that."

Crystine's mind was elsewhere. "Hm-m-m-m," was all she said, curious about the sudden fluttering in her stomach. Turning her head, she stared pensively through the open doors of Parkside Elementary. "Be right back," she said to Nikki and started toward the doorways.

The hallway was empty and still, last year's echoes of youthful exuberance archived to nostalgia. She reached the end of the hall after a slow walk and stopped in front of room 11B. The door stood open. She poked her head inside and, finding the room empty, went in and made her way across the gleaming floor to the large oak desk at the other end. She lightly placed her fingertips on the edge of the desk. Dreamlike and very slowly, leaving her fingers on the edge of the desk, she began to circle it, much like a dance, trying to feel some residue of presence or some aura etched upon the ether. She felt compelled to do so, although not sure why or what it was she was looking for.

She thought of Mr. McDermitt and the last words he had spoken to her.

"You're a very special young lady, Crystine, and I'll bet there's a special someone out there just waiting for you."

Kind of strange words for a teacher to say, she'd thought and then quickly dismissed it as she remembered her mom saying, "I really like Mr. McDermitt. It's funny how he made me feel . . . warm from the inside out. But, of course, he's no Tyrone Power." Crystine's mom compared all men to Tyrone Power, and it had become a standing joke in their house and always brought on a giggle.

A sudden warm feeling flooded the inside of her, and she stopped circling the desk. At the same instant a gentle truth penetrated deep into her being. A vital *something* was missing from her life.

"Did you forget something?" Nikki asked Crystine as she came walking up to her.

"No, I wasn't looking for anything, just one last walk for memories, I guess, but I did find something."

Nikki gave her a puzzled look. "What? You're not carrying anything."

Crystine paused and looked left over the school playground. A puff of wind ruffled her hair and then dropped it to lie on her forehead. "I found out that something feels like it's missing."

"Well sure, we're leaving six years of our childhood behind. All we gotta do is discover what comes next, don't we?" said Nikki.

"Yeah, that's all," said Crystine, knowing it would take something out of the ordinary to fill the *something* that was missing.

Chapter Seven

Mom drove me in the old Lincoln to see Dr. Hickey for our weekly visit. She pulled the lumbering gray beast to a stop in front of his office. I was hoping that this would be my last visit but half expecting that it wouldn't.

Dr. Hickey was an elderly, white-haired gentleman, small in stature, who loved life and didn't take it too seriously, except for his work, which he seemed very good at. He had my trust.

"Well-l-l, hello, Daniel, how are you feeling today?"

"Fine, doctor. I'm walking every day, sitting up more of the time, not lying around hardly at all."

The doctor glanced up at Mom, and she nodded her affirmation.

"Let's take the brace off and have a look at you," he said.

I removed my T-shirt, deftly unhooked the laces—the contraption was a lot like an old-fashioned corset—and handed it to Mom.

Dr. Hickey told me to turn around, and I did. He ran his fingers gently over my back. "Keep your legs straight and try to bend over and touch your toes," he said, so I did. I felt his feathery fingers exploring the lumbar area of my spine. He'd taken x-rays of it last week. "Okay, Daniel, straighten yourself up." I did and didn't have far to go—my fingertips hadn't gotten anywhere near my toes.

"Now fix your fists at your shoulders and hold your arms parallel with the floor," said the doctor, demonstrating the position he wanted. I followed. "Now twist at the waist, very slowly, first right then left." I did. "Any pain?" he asked.

"No," I answered.

He glanced again at mom. "Has he had any pain during the week, Mrs. Abrams?"

"No, he hasn't mentioned any at all."

"A little faster now, Daniel," he said. I upped the speed of motion, taking each twist a small degree further into its angle. Doctor Hickey watched my eyes. It felt so good to move that I further increased my speed, making myself dizzy with the rapid movement.

"Okay, Daniel, that's all," he said. I stopped. "Are you having any pain now?"

"No, sir," I replied. He hadn't seen a wince on my face or in my eyes but only the beginning of a rapturous delight at being able to move again.

A slight smile crossed his face, and his own eyes lit with delight. "All right, Daniel, that's all," he said.

I looked at Mom. She held the back brace out to me. But before I could take it, Doctor Hickey intercepted it.

"No, Daniel, I mean, that is *all*. You've healed up and won't be needing this," he said, holding out the brace.

I couldn't believe my ears. The interminable caution and endless restrictions were over! Done, with a capital D. Free! Free to play, to ride my bike, to shoot a basketball, to run . . . and to swim! The exhilaration of hope, tempered by necessary caution, had returned to me. I knew I'd have to take it slow and easy at first, but at least I could finally do something. I wouldn't be at full strength in a week, maybe in a couple, but certainly not before school started.

I hadn't seen much of my best friend, Tim, all summer. At that age, sitting around talking is about the last thing young men want to do. But he came over that evening. We went to the local park to stroll around in mild celebration of my release from constriction.

"You be sure to see that Daniel takes it easy, will you, Tim?" Mom asked him as we left the house.

"Sure will, Mrs. Abrams," he replied. Mom knew that he would, and so did I. Even if I felt like a newborn colt, Tim would rein me in. He kept his word.

We walked and talked, about our summer, about football, about the coming school year, and about girls.

"I learned to surf pretty good over the summer," Tim stated, as if it were an established fact. "My brother gave me his old Dewey Weber."

"Really?" I said. "You mean Greg actually gave you something? He didn't ask for blood or demand that you be his slave or anything?"

"No, believe it or not, he didn't ask for a thing," Tim replied. "He really did just give it to me. Of course, he'd gotten a new one for his birthday and didn't need it anymore."

We laughed, and it was the icing on the cake of what had been a glorious day. I hadn't felt this buoyant in a long time.

"It won't take me long to get better than you," I said.

"Better than me at what?" he asked.

"Surfing."

He gave me his left-eyebrow-raised, right-eye-squinted look, and we guffawed again. Oh, how sweet it was just to be out and moving and laughing and anticipating good times again.

The Beach Boys blasted out of Tim's transistor radio. We stopped our jabbering to listen. Surf music was getting big, and as teens are wont to do, we adapted our life style to the current rock and roll craze.

Surfin' bop-dip-da-dip-da-dip.

We wore white Levis, Pendleton shirts over white T-shirts, low-cut black Converse tennis shoes, and our hair dry and loose. We were little mini Beach Boys. Counter to the "Surfers" were the "Greasers." They wore die-hard Elvis-style pompadours, khaki pants, and long-sleeved tucked-in shirts. How or why the rivalry had come about was beyond me, but it was there and real and serious.

The sun was setting on a day in which I felt reborn, and I didn't want it to end. But Tim reminded me that I'd promised to be home around dark, so we headed that way. But before we got there, the sun gave way to darkness.

Tim's a big, raw-boned, athletic, happy-go-lucky kind of guy, so I couldn't figure out why his face was all swollen and bloodied, why my right arm was up over his left shoulder, or why his left arm was around my waist.

"Wha . . . a-a-what the hell happened, Tim?" I mumbled, my mouth not working right.

"We were jumped," he said flatly, "by five high-school Greasers. They beat us up pretty bad."

I tried to move. Pain screeched like a banshee bitch, shooting through my left shoulder. I staggered. Tim's arm tightened around my waist.

"Take it easy, Daniel. Come on. I'll help you get home."

My head was engulfed in a swirling fog, a mist filled with black shadows darting back and forth, featureless vapors of malignant intent. My mind splintered. My senses were twisted askew, and I couldn't grasp the situation.

"C'mon, Daniel. I've got you. It's not far now."

The soft light of the living room hurt my eyes. Mom gasped and covered her mouth with her hand to stifle a shriek. Her eyes were wide in shock and disbelief.

"Oh God, no! Norris . . . come quickly!" she shouted over her shoulder.

Tim and Mom helped me hobble over to the sofa, Mom gently seating me.

Dad hurried in from the kitchen and immediately picked up the phone.

"We got jumped for no reason," I heard Tim say.

"Oh my, my," Mom said, taking a closer look at Tim. "I'll have Norris give you a ride home as soon as he's finished with his call," she said.

"Oh no. I mean, I'll be all right. I'll be fine. Daniel probably needs to get to a doctor right away," he said as he stood up. Tim looked at me. "Call me," I think I heard him say. I think I nodded that I would. I think I thanked him and said good-bye. I was tired, exhausted, and all I wanted to do was lie down and fall asleep. Mom wouldn't let me, and with good reason.

Dad had called Dr. Hickey, made the arrangements, and then drove us to his office. Doc was waiting for us when we arrived. The pounding had left me with a broken left collar bone, a concussion, and a bruised and battered face.

It was Thursday night, and school started Monday. I began it with my left arm in a sling, my face swollen and discolored, and a creeping uneasiness settling deeper within me. Welcome to another year; keep your guard up.

I got to thinking that maybe I really was being punished for some unknown sin or some atrocity committed in another life. It seemed that fate hit me hard and frequent. But what about fate? *If it was a predestined ordering of events in my life, who set them in place?* I asked myself. I couldn't come up with a definitive answer. I decided the hell with fate.

Tim and I never talked about that night. That we'd both suffered a beating was evident—his face was as puffy as mine on the opening day of school. But years later, as Mom and I talked about it, she swore up and down that I'd come home alone that night, and she never once wavered from the story. I, of course, thought that was too bizzare and that she'd been in shock from seeing me all beat to hell. Maybe she was right; then again maybe she wasn't, strange happenings in my life seemed to becoming the norm.

Chapter Eight

It didn't take long to get caught up in the buzz. Surfers, surf bands, beach bunnies, and the discovery of beer—the search for the ultimate party was on, and schoolwork meant little to me, which was reflected in my grades. I didn't care. I was one of the "cool" guys, and I had place, but it was a place not even close to the realm of the gods.

Girls aroused more than curiosity in me, and I had one goal in mind, to satisfy that arousal. I knew what I wanted, and it was all glandular. Then I met *her*, and it was no longer *what* I wanted, but *who* I wanted.

One of those teen parties with a shadowy chaperone whom you never see but know is there was going on at someone's house. Slow, romantic music filled the air in the dimly lit front room. She was sitting on a blue corduroy sofa with some black-haired boy whom I didn't know. When I first laid eyes on her—Ka-whump!—I was hit by Cupid's arrow and then some, a whole lotta and then some, a brand new world of and then some.

I locked in on her. Doubt was banished to another universe; it had no place in mine. She was who I wanted. An unfamiliar something fluttered inside my chest, and I liked the feeling. I felt as if I could walk on air, and perhaps I was. She filled my awareness so completely that I thought I had become invisible. I probably was to her, I thought, relegating my chances with her to those of a snowstorm happening in hell.

"Fight!" someone hollered through the open front door. I bolted through it to check it out.

Two guys I didn't know were flailing away at each other; the rest of the party gathered around for the show. Scanning the crowd, I saw the boy she was with but not her. I figured she wasn't interested in watching a couple of knuckleheads trying to land a punch. I thought that was way cool and maybe my chances had gone up a little, to more like a rain-storm in hell.

The fight brought the chaperones out of the shadows, and the party was over. Tim and I strolled along toward home, keeping a wary eye out for any sign of an attack, a learned response to the Big Amoeba.

"Do you know that girl who was sitting in the front room?" I asked, trying to sound oh so casual.

"Maybe. There were a lot of them—which one?"

How could I tell him the one with the angel's face? The one bathed in grace? He'd think I was beyond corny for sure. But that was how I'd seen her.

"Uh," I stammered, searching for some locating point. "She was sitting on the couch . . . uh, just before the fight broke out . . . with . . . I think this guy named Delgard, or something like that."

"Oh, yeah, sure, I know who she is. Her name's Crystine . . . Crystine Mercado."

Her face was before me until I fell asleep that night. Sweet dreams, all night long.

"Nikki, did you see him?" Crystine asked over the phone.

"See who?"

"Daniel Abrams, at the party."

"Oh, yeah, of course I saw him. He was with Tim, wasn't he?"

"Do you know Tim?" asked Crystine.

"A little."

"Well enough to talk to him?"

"Yeah . . . why?"

"Find out what they—him and Daniel—thought about the party. Find out if Daniel . . . well . . . noticed me, will you, please?"

Nikki knew what Crystine was up to. That she was interested in Daniel didn't surprise her, and the little director had gone to work. Yes, she'd be more than happy to talk to Tim, she said as she hung up the phone. Nikki smiled; she couldn't wait to talk to dreamboat Tim.

The following Tuesday morning, I caught Crystine's eye for the first time ever. We were between classes, and our paths happened to cross. Surprised at my own shyness, I flashed her a weak smile. She smiled back, and it beamed with such force that if it had been malevolent, it would've knocked me off my feet. But it was far from malevolent, and I basked in the sweetness of it.

Her beautiful brown eyes were bold and fearless and at the same time, soft and welcoming. We locked in on each other. Stunned, I couldn't speak or move; enchanted, I forgot to breathe. Time suspended itself and engraved the moment.

Fixed point.

"Hey Daniel," somebody called.

With great effort I broke the moment, looking away from Crystine and glancing around irritably, I located Tim coming toward me. I looked back at Crystine. She was no longer there but was moving on to her next class. I stood, like an awestruck statue, and watched her walk.

"Hey, hayseed!" Tim hollered, referring to my Montana roots. I cringed and hoped Crystine hadn't heard, afraid that if she did, it would hurt my chances of winning her heart. From the first moment I saw her, she was who I wanted, and knowing her heart would be like heaven.

"Didn't you say anything to her?" Tim asked.

"No . . . well-l-l . . . I was going to until you crashed in like a renegade wave."

He ignored me. "Su-u-u-re you were. Why, you're still tongue-tied," he said as he slapped me on the back.

I made sure not to let him see me wince. Tim was the jovial kind of person who didn't know his own strength.

"Well, I talked to Nikki this morning," he stated.

"Nikki?"

"Yeah, Nikki . . . Nikki Craven; you know, Crystine's best friend. Jeez, I'm starting to think you really are a hayseed."

No, I was just stunned, but not for long.

"And all this California sun has finally baked your brains," I countered. Still, my pulse raced. Why would he be talking to Crystine's best friend?

"Yeah, she said she likes you."

"Wha-a-at . . . Nikki likes me?"

"God Daniel, are potatoes growing out of your ears? I said—now listen carefully—Nikki told me that Crystine likes you. Her favorite color is yellow, her favorite song is, "He's So Fine," and her and Nikki are going to the dance this Friday night. Oh . . . and she'd like to meet you. Need to hear any more?"

"Uh, no," I peeped, my heart racing, my feet off the ground, butterflies fluttering in my stomach, and my thoughts flying off to a mysterious wonderland called Crystine.

"So, we're going to the dance Friday night, right?" Tim asked.

"Well, yeah, of course," I replied, trying to appear nonchalant.

He grinned big, not at all fooled. "Gotta make my next class. See ya after . . . hayseed," he chortled as he walked away.

If I'd ever have to be in a foxhole, Tim is the guy I'd want in there with me.

Checking myself in the mirror, making sure everything was in place, I tucked the yellow and white short-sleeved checked shirt into my white Levis.

"Bye, Mom!" I hollered toward the kitchen as I headed for the front door.

"What time can I expect you home?" she asked from the kitchen doorway. It wasn't an open question; I knew my boundaries. Mom worried about me more than she used to. She'd seen the real LA and didn't like what she saw.

"Eleven-thirty at the latest," I replied. The dance ended at eleven.

The sun cast its rays on the gym at Alameda Park, making it shimmer golden against a knoll of green grass. Above, the sky was pink, orange, and lavender. A Pacific breeze sweetened the air.

We poked our heads through the door, decided the place was lively enough, and walked in onto the dance floor. The windows, high up the wall near the ceiling, were open, letting in the cool ocean breeze. The place was rapidly filling up. I took a deep breath, trying to calm myself for when Crystine arrived. The DJ was ambitious, spinning a lot of fast tunes in between his attempts at clever banter.

Impatient to get the show on the road, Tim started circulating. I took a strategic seat on the top row of the bleachers, giving myself a clear view of the entryway doors. The sun was finished with the day, and the dance floor dimmed with the loss of light. The entryway into the gym was brightly lit in contrast to the interior dimness. With my attention fully focused on the bright entryway, all else faded into a blurred background.

Then she suddenly appeared, framed between the light and the shadow, a mysterious silhouette. I couldn't exactly *see* her, but I knew. Her body shape, how she moved, how she carried herself, how she walked, and her presence were all etched in my memory, and I had no doubt it was her.

Butterflies danced in my mid-section as I wove my way down through the now-crowded bleachers. Stepping onto the dance floor, my senses, my awareness, and my energy were heightened to the level of obsession, maybe beyond. Crystine, of course, was the object of my focus. I kept her in my sights as I moved across the floor.

"I don't see him," said Crystine anxiously.

"See who?" asked Nikki.

"Daniel."

"Oh, he'll be here all right. Tim's over there," Nikki assured her, pointing over at the DJ listening to Tim talking in his ear.

"I still don't see him," said Crystine, even more anxious.

For the first time in their long friendship, Nikki thought she detected a slippage in Crystine's confidence, a flicker of doubt in her usual self-assurance.

A blond-haired boy approached the two girls and asked Crystine to dance. That was normal; it was always Crystine first, but Nikki was used to it and it didn't bother her in the least. What did surprise her was that Crystine politely refused the offer. She was usually off and running as soon as she could and, like any young woman, liked to flirt. To wait for one young man was out of character for her.

The lights dimmed further, and Tim moved away from the record-slinging DJ. Catching my eye, he gave me his patented big grin. The song "He's So Fine" began to play.

With my eyes again fixed on Crystine, I floated across the rest of the dance floor to her and with all the charm I could muster asked, "Wanna dance?" She smiled up at me, a velvety luminescence emanated from her, and she offered me her hand.

I took it. My knees went weak. I wasn't sure if I'd be able to dance, at that moment not really wanting to. What I wanted was to hold her tight against me and kiss her, right then and there.

Moving hand in hand out to the center of the dance floor, we danced apart, but not far, to the in-between fast and slow song. She flowed like liquid as she moved to the music. The room grew dimmer, and she seemed to grow brighter. The music stopped, and I took her hand in mine. My mouth went dry. I wasn't sure what to do next. She smiled so sweetly and so knowingly at my shyness.

I was saved. "Harlem Nocturne," a slow instrumental with a strong sax riff and a guitar back, began to play. Crystine melted into my arms, her head snug against my shoulder, her soft, burnished bronze hair caressing my face. I wanted to breathe deep of her, of all that she was. We danced very slowly, rocking and swaying and holding each other. I tingled way beyond blossoming sexuality. She was much more than just a girl, she was . . . Crystine.

We touched and flowed, me into her, her into me, until we flowed as one and danced the night away.

She fit. She was so . . . right. I once again had place, and it was with her. My long season of winter was over, and the iciness that had begun to encase my heart quickly melted away.

To my surprise and dismay, the music stopped, the lights came on, and the dance ended.

Still holding Crystine's hand, I walked her to the entryway. "Thank you, Daniel," she said.

"For what?" I asked.

"For being you," she replied. Not for the dance, not for a wonderful evening, not for being polite and not trying to fondle her, but for being me. Not truly understanding all the implications of what Crystine had just said, I replied with impressive insight, "Can't be anything else, I guess."

God, she's so lovely, I thought.

"Hayseed, ya ready to go?" Tim asked. He was standing right next to me. I hadn't noticed him come up. Crystine and I had been talking, about what, I'm not sure.

"Do you want me to walk you home?" I asked her, hoping with all my heart that she'd say yes.

"Oh, Nikki's mom is coming to get us . . . but call me tomorrow . . . please!" she said. Nikki handed her a scrap of paper and a pen. She hastily wrote down her phone number and handed it to me. Then she kissed me lightly on the cheek and said, "Good night, Daniel." She smiled her melt-your-heart smile and then turned and walked away. I watched her go. I loved to watch her walk.

"Ya ready to go?"

"Huh?" I answered, turning dreamily in Tim's direction.

"Ya ready to go?" he repeated. "I can't be late or I'll be grounded. Then we can't go to the beach with Greg tomorrow, remember?" he said.

Tomorrow? All I wanted to do tomorrow was call Crystine and hear her sweet voice. "Oh yeah, tomorrow," I answered with little enthusiasm. I scanned the parking lot for her, but she was gone.

Chapter Nine

The early morning sun peeped around the curtains of her window, awaking Crystine. Stretching languorously, strains of "Harlem Nocturne" drifting through her mind, she snuggled deeper into the warmth of the covers, realizing that the warmth she was feeling didn't come close to what she'd felt last night in Daniel's arms. *Nothing could,* she thought, smiling demurely.

Her room was small but adequate—a dresser, a single-door closet, a single wood-frame, double-hung window, light yellow painted walls, and a beige rug on the hardwood floor. It was expertly clean and tidy; Crystine took good care of the few things she had. She had no doubt that one day she would have everything she wanted. But that was far away, and today it didn't matter. She was happy to wake to a promising new day, and what she wanted out of it was to hear Daniel's voice and maybe see his face.

She got up, stretched once more, drew her long hair back, pinned it in a bun, and proceeded into the kitchen.

Her mom looked up from reading the Saturday morning newspaper, a steaming cup of coffee in her hand.

"Have fun last night?" she asked as Crystine sat down at the table and poured herself some cereal.

Slicing a banana over the top of it and then drenching the cereal and fruit in milk, she replied, "I met a new boy last night!"

"Oh?" her mother said, taking a sip of her coffee. "Does this new boy have a name?"

"Tyrone Power!" she blurted, bubbling over with laughter, her mother joining her.

Crystine was the apple of her mom's eye, but she wasn't treated like a doll to be dressed up and put on display. Julie was wise enough to know that her daughter would lead her own life someday, and she always tried to prepare her to that end. But first and foremost, they were friends and could talk about anything Crystine was comfortable with, and the list of subjects grew longer as she grew older.

Julie was acutely aware that her daughter was entering womanhood. And she knew that the rapid-paced, ever-changing, ever-growing environment—Los Angeles—that she was being raised in was not all glitter and happiness. That Crystine could intellectually handle the fluff and the gruff of her environment she had no doubt. Julie's concern was for her emotional well-being, her happiness, and her contentment.

"Come on now, did you really meet a new boy . . . friend?"

"Mom!" gasped Crystine in mock embarrassment, her eyes dancing with delight.

"What's his name then, and don't you dare say Tyrone Power!"

"Daniel," answered Crystine.

"Does he have a last name that you know of?"

"Abrams."

"And . . ." goaded her mother.

"Well . . . he's cute. Wait till you meet him!" Crystine grinned. "He'll make you forget Tyrone Power."

"No!" Julie blurted, feigning shock. "Why, that would be unthinkable . . . impossible!" she exclaimed.

"I gave him our phone number. I hope he calls today, I asked him to."

"You asked him to? Sometimes, Crystine, I think you are a little too bold."

"Well, Mom, how else are we supposed to get what we want?"

Good point, thought Julie, *too good to argue with.*

"And besides, Daniel is different," continued Crystine.

"And how is he so different, other than being the heir apparent to Tyrone Power?"

Crystine put her spoon down and looked at her mother. Her eyes were lit with an intensity Julie had never seen before, and Crystine had her mother's absolute focus on what she was about to say. With an overwhelming earnestness, she said, "I can't really explain it, but somehow, he makes me feel warm from the inside out."

Julie didn't blink as she set her coffee cup on the table, appearing slightly stunned.

"What?" asked Crystine, noticing her mother's look.

She didn't answer. Her mind blazed, illuminating the memory of Crystine's fifth-grade teacher, Galen McDermitt. *How odd,* she mused. *Mr. McDermitt affected me in that same way.*

"Where is Daniel from?"

"Montana."

Julie picked up her coffee. Her eyes dropped to the newspaper on the table, but that wasn't what she was seeing.

"I'd very much like to meet Daniel," she said without looking up.

Crystine finished her cereal, took her dishes to the sink, and washed, dried, and put them away. She immediately set about her weekend routine, stripping her bed, getting her laundry going, sweeping and mopping the floor in her room. It was her natural bent to be organized and efficient, and to take the initiative.

But today was different, Julie noticed. Usually Crystine chattered, laughed, and talked to her mom about her plans, her future, and things within her comfort zone. Today she was quiet, pensive.

All day, when the phone jingled, Crystine would stop her chore and listen for her mom to call and say, "It's for you." And up until now, disappointment prevailed, because that didn't happen. The day dragged on. She felt as if her feet were mired in mud, each motion requiring an effort to do what was normally effortless.

It wasn't that Daniel might not call, though she desperately wanted to hear his voice. She knew he would be at school the day after tomorrow and that they could talk then. The anxiousness she felt was way out of proportion to the situation, and she knew it. The reason for her uneasiness was stubbornly elusive. Then she nailed it down. What she felt was a strong sense of danger. But why? She was safe in her own home.

The phone rang.

"Crystine, it's for you," Julie called from the front room.

She dropped what she was doing. Her heart raced, her breath stopped, and anticipation propelled her into the front room. Her mom handed her the phone, smiled a knowing it'll-be-all-right smile, and graciously left the room.

She drew in a deep breath. "Hello," she said, straining to sound casual.

"Hey, girlfriend," came a chipper voice across the line.

"Nikki?"

"Yeah, it's me. Are you all right?"

"Huh? Oh, yeah . . . fine. I'm fine. I just thought you might be Daniel is all."

"Daniel? Is all? Are you sure that's what it is . . . is all? I've never seen you like this before," said Nikki.

"Like what?"

"Like you not even talking to me during the dance last night. Like you being in the arms of only one boy and dancing every dance with him. Like you being in a daze during our ride home, and like you not calling me this morning when you promised that you would."

"Oh, Nikki, I'm so sorry. I didn't mean to ignore—"

Nikki cut her off. "It's okay, but don't try to fool me. You've never been stricken like you are right now. Don't try pretending your feelings are *is all*. I know you way better than that." Nikki giggled over the phone.

Crystine smiled inwardly.

"So call me later, okay?" said Nikki.

"I will, and this time I'll remember," Crystine said, slowly hanging up the phone. *Nikki was right—I've never felt this way before. It's like a missing part of me has been put in place.* And she knew what that missing *something* was that she didn't understand while alone in Mr. McDermitt's empty room.

Chapter Ten

Shortly after daylight, Greg pulled up in his light metallic blue '55 Chevy Nomad station wagon. It wasn't a woody, the coolest of the cool surf wagons, but it was next in line.

Two surfboards were strapped to the carrier on top—Tim's old Dewey Weber and Greg's new one. I didn't own a board, so Tim and I would share his, either on a time basis or on alternate rides. We hadn't decided yet.

Tim stepped out of the wagon, letting me into the backseat. "Hayseed, we got some real surf coming up today," he said in his usual cheery manner. Greg grunted some form of greeting at me and we were off.

Surfing was the farthest thing from my mind. My thoughts were on Crystine as I gazed out the window at the endless parade of glop. *What's happening to me*, I thought to myself. *Here I am, doing the* in *thing, and I'm not the least bit in* to *it.*

I hoped I'd be able to call her today. I hoped she wouldn't be anxiously waiting for me to. I hoped I wouldn't disappoint her when I did reach her.

I caught and rode some good-sized waves with only one severe wipeout. Riding a powerful ten footer I was cruising along and doing fine. For some (foolish) reason I decided to stick my arm in the wave wall, which caused me to lose my balance. Out of the corner of my eye I saw the board fly up into the air just as I went under the surface. Although I am a strong swimmer from my early training in the placid mountain lakes, this was a different world altogether. This water seemed alive and roiling with frightening purpose, which was to keep me under and pulverize me while I was there.

The ocean spun me along on its sandpaper bottom, turning me into a circus acrobat doing front and back flips and somersault after somersault. I couldn't get my legs under me so I could push up toward the surface. Spinning and tumbling further out to the open sea, my lungs burned for air. Fear crept cold into me. Panic screamed at the edge of my fear.

Suddenly, mercifully, it stopped. My feet touched bottom, and I exploded up through the surface of the water, gulping in the smelly California air, which right then was as sweet as the spring chinooks of Montana.

I looked around, dazed and disoriented, trying to get my bearings. "What the . . ." I said out loud after realizing that I was standing on the ocean floor. Tim's board was sloshing up against the beach not more than forty yards away. I could've sworn I'd been carried at least a half mile out into water hundreds of feet deep! Sometimes a few seconds can seem like an eternity.

I learned a lesson of nature that day based on the broad notion that for every action there is an equal and opposite reaction. If big powerful waves come in, big powerful undercurrents go out. They're called riptides and are nothing to be trifled with.

My right shoulder and knee were scraped up but not bleeding. I could move everything, so no bones were broken as far as I could tell. And so standing in the Pacific Ocean, nearly drowned, bruised and battered with waves crashing over me, I suffered a new panic attack.

Staggering to knee-deep water, I stopped to run my fingers over my face. What if my eyes swelled shut and I couldn't see her? What if my mouth puffed up and I couldn't talk to her? Or worse yet, couldn't kiss her? What if I'd broken an arm and couldn't hold her? I felt all around my face; there was nothing painful when I touched it. Okay. Pulling away my hand, I didn't see any blood. All right, big relief.

Was I obsessed? Probably. Did it matter? Not to me, and it wasn't worth considering further. What did matter was that I wanted more of Crystine, more of her body, her soul, her being. More of what was in her that turned butterflies loose within me and conjured visions of her purity and loveliness in my head. More of what was in her that touched me to my very core. It seemed beyond the realm of possibility that I could ever get enough of her. Puppy love? Some would say so, but I think not. By nature's own design we were ready, and therefore able, to have our lives melded into one.

I retrieved the Dewey Weber and carried it up the beach to where Tim was lying on a beach blanket soaking up some sun.

"Ready to go, Blondie?" I asked.

"Soon's Greg gets in," he murmured from out of his drowsiness.

Laying the board down, I sat in the warm sand by him, gazing out at the relentless waves curling into silver pipelines, one right after another.

Greg was coming in, riding a twelve footer. I shaded my eyes against the late afternoon glare, looking past Greg and out at the smoother surface of the water. A few surfers out there straddled their boards, waiting for the Big One. Just beyond the breaking waves, to where they began their swell, I noticed a surfboard drifting along with it's steering fin up and moving toward the beach pretty fast. It seemed odd, flipped over like that, with its scag up and cutting the water like it was.

I poked Tim in the ribs. "Here comes Greg," I said.

He propped up on one elbow, shaded his eyes, and looked out to where I was pointing. "What is that behind him?" he blurted as his jaw dropped open.

"That . . . Oh, just a loose surfboard, I guess."

Tim jumped up and ran down to the edge of the water, motioning frantically at Greg to come in. Greg casually waved back at him. Tim splashed further into the surf, cupped his hands around his mouth, and began hollering at the top of his lungs for Greg to hurry.

At first I didn't understand his urgency. Then it struck me like a hard-swung sledge hammer. Oh, God . . . this couldn't be real.

"Shark!" Tim screamed. "Shark!" he screamed again, "Shark!" he hollered for the third time, pointing out to the swelling surf. I ran down beside him, and both of us frantically waved at Greg to come in. "Shark! Shark!" we both screamed as the dorsal fin of the creature picked up speed, leaving its wake in the water.

We finally got through to him, and the grin left his face. He took the top of the wave and looked back to where we were pointing. Seeing the dorsal fin coming fast at him, his tanned face suddenly turned ghostly pale. He dropped on his belly and began paddling for shore like a man chased by a demon, which was pretty much the case. Breaking out of the waves' angle, he cleared the pipeline just ahead of the crashing curl and paddled furiously toward Tim and me.

We quit screaming. Silence engulfed the scene, and all we could do now was watch it play out. The shark *exploded* out of the face of the wave with huge powerful jaws agape showing horrendous razor-sharp teeth gleaming bone white in the sun. Its lips were twisted back in a demonic grin, and it came straight at Greg. A great white; oh my God! Its cavernous jaws thundered closed, snapping down on Greg's new board, taking off the back end of it. My breath was caught in my throat. Tim was screaming, his eyes wide and white with fear. I didn't see a flood of red on the water, and Greg was still paddling like a madman on what was left of his board.

The board stuck in the sand, and he was off it quicker than I'd ever seen any cat move. He ran right past us and far up on to the beach. His trunks were wet, and I don't guarantee it was only from sea water. I know I'd nearly pissed mine.

We went up and sat with him. He was shaking like a freezing man, his face still whiter than the shark that nearly got him. Tim put the beach blanket over his shoulders. None of us talked—we couldn't; we were in shock. After an hour or so Greg said to Tim,

"Don't tell Mom and Dad, okay? They'll never allow me to go back into the surf again." Tim simply nodded his head.

We had pretty much composed ourselves. The day was over, and that was the end of my surfing career. I didn't want my last thought in this life to be, *Oh no, I'm going to turn into shark shit!*

On the way back to Huntington my only thoughts were of that mysterious wonderland called Crystine. It was nearing sundown when Greg wheeled to a stop in front of my house. We all said, "See ya later," and that was the extent of our conversation from the beach to here. Tim pulled the door closed and they drove off, the old Dewey Weber on top of the new bitten-in-half one.

"You're home earlier than I thought you'd be," Mom said when I opened the screen door and went through it. "Did you have fun today?" she asked

"Oh sure, a ton of fun, at least," I said. I think that's about what a great white weighs.

I took off down the hall and skidded to a stop at my bedroom door, yanked it open, tossed my stuff on the bed, and almost pulled the top drawer of my dresser off its tracks. I scooped up the scrap of paper hiding among my socks, ran out of the room and down the hall, and raced to the phone. I unfolded the paper on which was Crystine's phone number along with a quick note that read, "Please call." Even her handwriting was beautiful to behold.

That anything could jolt me after my day at the beach was impossible to believe, but I had to believe it. It felt like bolts of electricity were shooting through me. My hands trembled, my knees weakened, and my breath came in shallow spurts. The day's events thus far paled in comparison.

"Daniel," Mom called from the kitchen, "are you all right? How was your day at the beach? Are you hungry?"

"Yeah, mom, uh . . . fine . . . fun, no . . . um, I mean . . . not hungry . . . no," I replied.

"Well, dinner will be ready in twenty minutes, in case your appetite returns."

I couldn't stop my hands from trembling. My fingers refused to work as I tried dialing the phone. Concentrating my effort, I finally succeeded.

"Hello," a pleasant woman's voice answered.

"Is Crystine there, I mean, home . . . please?" I thought I heard a slight tinkling sound, like the disguised laughter of delighted amusement.

"Why yes, she just happens to be home," the woman replied.

The day's events sifted into a dream as my palms got sweaty.

"Hello." Her voice flowed into my ear like cool water flowing into a dry and thirsty land.

"Crystine?"

"Yes."

"This is Daniel."

"I know. I know your voice, Daniel."

She knew my voice? I was overjoyed at the thought.

"I'm sorry I didn't call sooner. I just got back from the beach with Tim and his brother," I said.

"Oh, I didn't know you were going to the beach today!" she exclaimed.

"Uh-oh, I forgot to tell you last night."

"At least now I know why it took you so long to call me," she said teasingly, her daylong uneasiness fading away. "Well, did you have fun? Did anything exciting happen while you were there?" she asked.

"I don't think you'd believe me if I told you," I replied.

"I trust you," she said. Those words were like music sounding in a bell tower, ringing and echoing off distant hills drenched golden by the sun, resounding over and over somewhere deep and unfamiliar within my heart. "Well, what happened?" she asked.

"Oh . . . uh, I wiped out and was nearly dragged out to sea and drowned. Then Greg, Tim's older brother, had a great white shark track him and then attack him. It blasted out of the face of the wave, chomped down, and took a bite—"

"Oh my God!" Crystine interjected.

"Out of his surfboard," I concluded.

"Oh, Daniel, are you all right? Did you see the shark?"

"It was only thirty feet away. I could look right into its open jaws and see its huge razor-sharp teeth. Scary!" I added.

"Are you all right? Is everyone all right?"

"Yeah, I'm fine. Greg is okay, but his brand-new board is wrecked. He was pretty pale all the way home, though."

"Wow," she sighed. "That's quite a story. Really, Daniel, all that happened today?"

"I would never lie to you."

"Can you come over?" she asked.

"When?"

"Right now . . . tonight . . . as soon as you can!" she implored.

"I'll be there as soon as I can. If I can't make it I'll call, okay?" I started to hang up the phone.

"Daniel," I heard her say.

I put the phone back to my ear. "Yes."

"Do you know where I live?"

"No . . . Well, not exactly," I replied, feeling a little foolish. She giggled as she gave me her address. She lived eight blocks away! Did fate finally smile on me? It seemed so.

Twenty minutes later, as the western sky clung tenaciously to the last rays of the sun, I was knocking on her door.

It opened, and Crystine was *there*, her smile reflected in her soft brown eyes, bold and inviting. Her burnished bronze hair hung loose to her shoulders, like strands of gold in the setting sun.

"Hi, Daniel." She greeted me with her voice and her smile and her welcoming look. It was music in the bell tower again. My senses went spinning, and I had no doubt, at all, about Crystine.

"Come in," she offered. I did. She guided me over to the sofa, and we sat down together, lightly touching. I can't describe the room because I really didn't notice it. Her mom came in from the kitchen.

"Mom, this is Daniel. Daniel, this is Mom."

"Hi," I managed to say.

"Nice to meet you, Daniel," she said with undeniable sincerity, helping to put me at ease. She looked at Crystine. "Tyrone Power?

Maybe," she quipped, giving Crystine a wink and a smile and then graciously leaving the room.

Crystine smiled at me with that special smile of hers that could melt an iceberg. It certainly melted my heart.

"Want to sit out on the porch?" she asked.

"Sure," I replied. Anything. I felt like putty.

"I'll get us a couple of Cokes," she said as she stood up and went into the kitchen. I was transfixed as I watched her walk.

The night was warm and velvety, the sky remarkably clear for Southern California. We sat on the front porch swing, gently rocking back and forth. Crystine was sitting up against me, and she was the most wonderful thing I had ever been up against.

"I like it when you are next to me," I told her.

"And I like being next to you," she replied, taking my hand in hers. I looked deeply into her eyes, and that was all she wrote. I was lost, gone, almost dissolved. Crystine had become my world and my only desire. How or what exactly happened at that moment I cannot explain, but it doesn't matter, it's about the heart, and you know or you don't.

"I want to kiss you," I said with surprising boldness. She tilted her face up to mine, inviting my kiss. Our lips touched lightly at first and then crushed into a deep pool of hunger and passion. We stood, locked in our kiss. She pressed herself into me, like cool clear water, and I was the parched and barren land. It wasn't for this moment that I was born, but in this moment I knew that I was born for her and she for me. We were a perfect fit, and our souls were being knit together.

Our lips parted. Her breath, warm on my cheek, was the breeze from the oasis that was her. "Daniel," she whispered, and the sound was like a symphony played by love and tenderness. I wasn't able to stand. We sat down on the swing. And as if by a miracle, all the uneasiness in my life was washed away. I hated to leave her that night. She was now my world and I was hers, and we were complete.

Yes, we were young, young enough to feel and to know and to trust, young enough to be able to abandon ourselves to the encircling enchantment and to each other. No analysis required. Yes, we were young.

After that, I spent more time at Crystine's house than I did at my own. Sometimes we'd go off to a party or a dance, but just being alone together was what we wanted the most, and that was how we spent a lot of our time. We'd talk about anything and everything and nothing at all. We never talked about our future. There was no reason to. It seemed our world had been ordained and would not or could not ever end.

We would spend our youth, our maturing, our middle age, and our aging together, evolving through the white heat of passion to parents loving and guiding our children to partners establishing ourselves in the world to friends caring for and nurturing each other and finally to being warm and constant companions, amused at the world and ourselves. And always lovers with our souls knit in comfort and completeness.

Chapter Eleven

It was a late springtime Friday evening, and Nikki was throwing a party at her folks' house, a two-story, four-bedroom, white stucco Spanish type with oversized yards in front and back, an in-ground swimming pool taking up most of the backyard, and the rest covered with concrete ringing the oval-shaped pool. Along the side of the concrete ring was a driveway leading to a two-car garage with an apartment on top of it. Leading up to the apartment, on the pool side, was a flight of wooden stairs. A railed landing offered a reprise from the climb just outside the entry door to the unoccupied apartment.

The upstairs landing almost hung out over the deep end of the pool, making a perfect diving platform, and I wasn't the only one to notice it. As the party progressed, some of the other guys saw it as such and began jumping off it into the pool, cautious at first, and fully clothed. But as they got more used to it, reckless abandonment increased.

I didn't consider joining the horseplay. I had my girl with me and had no need to play Tarzan games to try to impress one.

But having Crystine with me was more than just a prize to be gained, although she certainly was that and more. We were not transient, a product of the party, looking for kicks, and that was the difference.

Reclining side by side on a couple of chaise lounges, we watched the antics unfold, sometimes laughing. It was like watching kids at play. Their games were all right and were probably thought necessary by those engaged in them, but we had no reason to join in. She'd look at me now and then and smile and squeeze my hand, knowing that my heart belonged to her.

As it grew darker, the party grew louder. All my friends were there, as were Crystine's and Nikki's. Some of the people neither of us knew.

I heard rumors that someone had brought wine to the party, and as I continued to watch, more and more guys leapt into the pool with all caution thrown to the wind. I figured that the rumor had congealed into fact. Rowdiness being what it is, I thought it only a matter of time before someone got seriously hurt, as in cracking their skull open on the concrete or due to a fight breaking out for any number of meaningless reasons. I wasn't in the mood for rowdy; I was in the mood for something else—I wanted to be alone with Crystine.

Nikki rushed by on her way into the house. Crystine reached up and grabbed her by the arm. "Don't you think things might be getting a little out of hand?" she asked her friend.

I looked up at Nikki's unfocused eyes.

"It's a party!" Nikki exclaimed. "My folks will be home soon anyhow."

Her folks had gone out to dinner and let Nikki start the party early but would soon be the shadowy chaperones. But maybe not soon enough.

"Look at them," Crystine pointed out, directing Nikki's attention to the stairs. Guys were running up and down half naked, jostling each other as they went, getting more and more daredevil as they jumped into the pool, and sneaking drinks of wine under the stairs in between the jumps. Of course, Tim was the ringleader of the circus, and Nikki wouldn't confront him.

Crystine didn't push me to do anything—she never did— but she shot me a quick glance before turning back to Nikki, and I knew that she was thinking maybe I should do something.

"What if somebody gets seriously hurt?" she asked her friend.

"Oh, don't be a party pooper," replied Nikki, trying to make light of an escalating and potentially dangerous situation.

"You know me way better than that," Crystine shot back, ready to give up the argument. After all, it was Nikki's party. But I could tell that she was genuinely concerned, and with good reason.

Tim was standing at the bottom of the stairs, feeling his oats and basking in his glory.

Crystine was still engaged in conversation with Nikki. I squeezed her hand gently. She shot me another quick glance and the flash of a smile. Releasing her hand, I stood up and sauntered over to Tim.

Now Tim was one of the most, if not *the* most, popular guys in school, for several reasons. He was blond, good-looking, athletic, and exuberant; he laughed readily, was honest and friendly, and had a heart of gold. But mainly it was because he could fight his way out of a sack of wildcats. Except when we got jumped, of course, but we didn't see them coming.

Why we were best friends, I had no idea.

"Hey, hayseed . . . you old stick-in-the-mud," he said as I approached. I ignored him. "When you and Crystine getting married? Hell, you might as well be already!" he exclaimed.

That we would be one day, I had no doubt.

I walked up to him. "Crystine's getting real anxious about someone hurting themselves. Nikki doesn't want to throw a wet blanket on the party and won't do anything, so I thought it a good idea if you could put a stop to the guys jumping in the pool."

"Damn, Daniel, are you getting pussy-whipped already?"

Rage like the fury of a caged tiger let loose and sprang up in me. Rage that anyone, even my best friend, would dare to reduce what Crystine and I had to such a base level of commonality. I took it as an insult and an affront, as something close to sacrilege.

I hit him flush on the jaw with my right hand. I rocked him but didn't knock him down, and it hurt my hand. Tim staggered back a step and gave me a stunned look. The party got very, very still. *Here goes*, I thought. *I'm in for a whipping now.* Tim brought his right hand up in a fist, more as a reflex than anything, and then he lowered it down to his side and *grinned* at me.

"Jeez, Daniel, if it means that much to ya, we'll stop," he said. But I think he knew the real reason I'd hit him. He never once referred to me as being pussy-whipped again. And how could I be? That was something about Crystine I didn't know, and it had nothing to do with how special she was to me anyway.

"What was that all about?" Crystine asked as I plopped down on the chaise lounge, my adrenaline pumping so hard I feared my heart would pound out of my chest. My senses tingled as if pricked by thousands of tiny needles. But I acted cool.

"Oh, I asked Tim to ride herd on the boys and keep them from jumping in the pool," I replied, which was more or less the truth.

"That's not what I'm asking, Daniel, and you know it," she said. I looked deep into her eyes and she into mine. I couldn't fool her—might as well not try.

"He said something I just couldn't let slide," I answered. She didn't press the issue. But I'm sure she had an inkling of what it may have been about. Crystine was instinctively perceptive, along with being gracious.

"Are you and he still friends?" she asked. It wasn't an idle question. She knew how close Tim and I were, how we'd hung together almost constantly before I'd met her. She knew I'd hurt if I lost him as a friend.

"Oh . . . sure . . . I guess. I hope so anyway." I mumbled.

She placed a gentle hand on my forearm. "Look," she said, pointing toward the stairs. No one was climbing up and down them. No one was jumping into the pool from off the top landing.

I looked over at Tim lounging near the bottom of the stairs. He gave me his patented big grin. Yeah, we were still friends.

Crystine looked at me and gave me a smile of reassurance, her face aglow from the love within. If my heart had calmed down at all after my encounter with Tim, it started up all over again and beat strong inside my chest.

"I want to be alone with you," she whispered. "Nikki's folks are here, in the front room," she said, assuring me that the party would be held under control. I guess we had started to mature, being worried about the safety of others and all that.

"Let's go," I said and stood up. I reached my hand down, helping her off of the chaise lounge. Not that she needed it. Among her many obvious and more subtle qualities, she was athletic, fluid, and I loved to dance with her.

We danced one slow dance before we left, soft, romantic music playing out of something from somewhere.

She was wearing light tan-colored shorts, a low-cut sleeveless yellow cotton blouse, and leather sandals on her bare feet. Her hair curled around the back of her head; she'd pinned it in a French bun. Her skin was tanned to an olive hue. Her soft brown eyes like liquid that would take a lifetime to fathom. I had a lifetime to give.

We stopped dancing, and I pulled her close. She pressed up against me, hard, insistent, urgent, and she took away my breath. We kissed, deep and slow and wet and hungry. She pulled back, looking at me with an honesty born from the depths of her soul. "I love you," she breathed. My chest opened up, allowing the soft wind carrying Crystine's love to blow gentle across my heart. And I would not have traded the three words she had just spoken for anyone or anything the world had to offer. Their preciousness to me was beyond price, and our knitting together was completed in that one singular moment.

Being the suave person that I am I asked, "Wanna go somewhere and get a Coke?" forgetting there were plenty of Cokes at the party. We may even have drunk one or two; I couldn't remember.

She smiled. "No, we can go to my house . . . Everyone's gone and won't be back till midnight," she said.

"Let's go," I said, wrapping my arm around her waist and guiding her toward a side gate that would allow us access to the street out front. She didn't hesitate after waving a quick good-bye to Nikki.

The night was balmy and quiet. Crystine and I were on foot, strolling easily along, holding hands. It wasn't far to her house, but we had to walk a short distance on one of the busiest boulevards in town. At the moment, it was empty of traffic, and no other people were out on foot that I could see. The world seemed still, and ours, and we were alone.

We ambled along, enjoying the evening and each other's company, anticipating what the night still held for us, though not quite sure what it might be.

A car appeared two blocks away. It wasn't speeding or careening, and no cops chased it. Just another set of headlights, and nothing unusual caught my attention.

I walked on the outside of the sidewalk, nearest the curb. The oncoming car pulled up to the curb and came to an abrupt stop next to us. Curious and alert, I fixed my eyes on it. Four punks in their late teens or early twenties were in the chopped and lowered Chevy sedan, two in the front and two in the back. Fear seized me, more for Crystine than for myself. If they had serious bad intentions, I wouldn't be able to do much about it, and I didn't know whether to tell her to run or to stay by me. Then the one in the front passenger seat, nearest to us, shot his arm out the window and flipped his wrist, and something like a small coil of rope came twisting at us as the car sped away, stupid laughter dribbling out its open windows.

The coil of rope spun through the air until it landed at my feet.

"It's a snake!" I hollered, jumping back and spreading my arms out wide, feeling for Crystine, finding her, moving her away, closer to the storefront windows, all in a split-second, my eyes never leaving the serpent on the walk. "Take off down the sidewalk!" I shouted at her.

I looked closer at the creature as it uncoiled its sinuous self and started to slither toward us in the dim lamplight. Crystine gasped behind me. What was she doing still there?

"It's okay; it's harmless," I said as I turned and looked at her. Her face had paled, and she couldn't move, frozen by fear.

"Are . . . are you sure?" she asked, looking past me and down at the sidewalk. The snake had lost any interest in us and had turned to slither away.

"Yes, I'm sure. It's called a garter snake. They're all over in Montana. They like to hang out in gardens and grass. I've never heard of anyone getting bit by one, but even if they did, they're not poisonous," I said as I pulled her to me. She was trembling. I held her closer and tighter.

She looked up at me with misted eyes. "Are you my gallant knight, my noble sir?" she whispered.

"I am. I will be," I replied, and I meant it. I felt ten feet tall, having her think of me as her gallant knight.

My dad had taught me to always walk nearest to the street when walking on the sidewalk with a lady. I asked why, and he told me it was in case a car drove by through a puddle, so the lady wouldn't get splashed. Or, in this instance, get struck by a flying snake. I was grateful for his good advice.

Crystine grasped my hand and said, "Let's hurry to my house," and began pulling me down the sidewalk. She didn't have to pull very hard, and we arrived at her house within minutes.

Being in her house was always comfortable and cozy, but we never had much time to be alone. Tonight was different—we had a lot of time.

I sat on the sofa as Crystine glided around the room, opening windows to let in a cool cross breeze. She put on some music and swayed to it, her natural sensuousness fluid and hypnotic. All of a sudden she was next to me on the sofa, sitting tight up against me, resting her head on my left shoulder. The soft yellow light from a lamp on the far side of the room highlighted her burnished bronze hair, turning it to the color of molten gold. I put my hand on her knee. She covered it with her own and drew it upward along her silken thigh, stopping at the hem of her tan-colored shorts.

"Crystine," I whispered as she turned her face up toward mine. I got lost in her kiss, lost in her and all that made up her being. I could stay there forever, and deep within myself I knew that I would, and that she would stay with me.

"I love you, Crystine," I breathed, but those few words didn't seem adequate to express what filled my heart. But no words could.

"And I love you with all my heart," she whispered. We kissed. I picked her up and carried her into her bedroom. When our bodies entwined and joined as our souls had done, when I exploded and lost myself to her, and her to me, our total melding into one was completed. I had been baptized into her and she into me, and we entered the realm of the gods on the plane of the sacred.

We sat back down on the sofa in the front room. Midnight rolled around as we listened to soft music, basking in the wonder of the lightning and the thunder that had belonged only to us.

Mrs. Mercado walked in through the front door.

"Hi, Mom," chirped Crystine.

"Hi, Crystine. Hi, Daniel," she replied with a smile.

"Hi, Crystine's mom," I said, and her smile broadened. Crystine squeezed my hand, assuring me that everything was all right.

"Been to see an old Tyrone Power movie?" Crystine asked her mom.

"No," she replied, "and come to think of it, I haven't been to see one for a long time. I guess I don't really need to." She paused and looked at Crystine and then at me and then back at Crystine. "I doubt you'll be needing a Tyrone Power either," she said, smiling a secret sort of smile before turning and heading for the kitchen. Before entering it she turned her head to the right. "G'night, Daniel," she called. That was my cue.

Crystine came out on the front porch with me. We kissed once more and once more, and I got lost in her sweetness again. We forced ourselves apart and said good night, and it had been just that, a good night.

As Crystine became sweeter and sweeter, life followed along. How either continued to increase seemed impossible and amazing, but I accepted it with an abiding gratefulness. My love for her would never die, and that we would eventually marry and have kids, or have kids and eventually marry, was a given. The order of the events really didn't matter. What did matter was our love. It was all we knew, all we wanted to know, all we needed to know. Its immensity swallowed us up. Bigger than the both of us, I believe is how the saying goes.

The words commitment and relationship were around at the time, but I never heard them used much in everyday speech or ever read them in magazines or newspapers. I did hear them in the classroom once or twice. Like history: "He was committed to the cause of . . ." Or math, like, "What is the relationship of these two triangles?"

We didn't talk of the words or the concepts behind them because they never occurred to us. The love between us was not something to be feared but something to be embraced and cherished. Love is a matter of the heart, and our youth allowed us to trust and revel in the glory of that truth.

Love often begins white hot and then reverses to burn and leave scars. Love can be the ultimate joy and the fulfillment it brings beyond comparing. Or it can be the ultimate despair, its loss extinguishing the spirit, causing cold mistrust or quaking fear if it should approach too close ever again.

A great English poet stated, "Tis better to have loved and lost than never to have loved at all." Some may agree; some may disagree. One can only respond out of one's own experience and from one's own heart.

And yet love cannot be denied, nor will unbelief in its existence bring about its end.

Chapter Twelve

I can't remember exactly when it happened, but I do remember the shattering devastation.

It was a few days before or a few days after I graduated the eighth grade and school let out for the summer. A summer with Crystine, a summer to explore and to grow with nothing to interfere with the sweet, sweet time we would spend together, endless summer days and boundless summer nights. The anticipation had me in a state of bliss. If heaven existed, I was about to step into it.

I had spent an enchanting and magical day with Crystine. No silly games existed between us—never any over, under, besting, or worsting. We were in love, and simply being and being together was enough for us.

Then it happened, the annihilation of my senses and the shattering of my mind. A white-hot blade, wielded with unerring force, utter and irrevocable, pierced to the depths of my soul.

I touched down at home that evening long enough to gobble down some dinner. When I was nearly finished, Mom looked at me with extreme intensity. "Your father and I have decided to return to Montana. We'll be leaving in a week," she stated with flat finality.

"What . . . what?" I stammered, not believing my ears, her words not registering.

"Montana . . . We're returning to Montana," she answered.

"No! You're kidding, right? You don't . . . you can't mean it, do you? What about . . . *me?*"

"Daniel, we've given it a lot of consideration and have decided that this is not a good place to live," Dad interjected.

"Yeah . . . but . . ." I started to protest. He cut me off.

"Don't yeah but," he said with more than a note of finality. No arguing, end of conversation. A darkening despair sank its fangs deep into me, spewing its unrelenting venom, saturating me with poison. I felt sick.

"Excuse me," I mumbled, pushing away from the table. I had to escape the source of shock, flee the horror of what I'd heard, afraid I might fragment and shatter or explode like shards of glass, with no one able to pick up the pieces. *Crystine—I have to reach her now* was all my seared mind could think to do.

I found my way out the front door just as the sun was setting. "Go down, stay down, and don't ever rise again!" I wanted to scream at it as the blackness began taking over. I floated a ways down the street until I found a phone booth. Fumbling for change, I fed the machine and then dialed her number.

"Hello," she answered. Her voice gave me some relief. I wasn't sure I could speak coherently, if at all.

"Oh, Daniel!" She was bubbly. "I'm so glad you called! I have the greatest news!" She didn't pause for breath. "You've met Sally, Nikki's aunt? Well . . . she and her husband run a summer camp, right on Big Bear Lake. Do you know where that is?"

"Sort of," I replied, my voice barely audible. She was flying along with excitement and didn't notice my lack of enthusiasm. My sense of loss had only deepened.

"Anyway, in a couple of weeks it'll be open. There's the lake and the mountains, canoes and boats . . . maybe even horses to ride. We'll have picnics and cookouts and campfires, all the things you've told me about, all the things you love. And guess what else . . . we can be alone . . . a lot," she said, her voice lowering. "It will be so-o-o fun! It'll be glorious for a whole week and at no cost. Can you go? Oh, Daniel, I love you so."

The darkness deepened and grew blacker, enveloping my soul. My heart might as well have been cut out. I feared I would succumb at that moment and scream in anguish.

"I . . . I won't be here," I said, straining against a chest-heaving sob, tears flowing freely now.

"Wha . . . what?"

"I won't be here," I repeated.

"Are you going on vacation or something? Can't make it to Big Bear? I won't go either if you can't go!" she exclaimed.

I didn't know what to say, let alone how to say it. How was I to tell her that our hopes and dreams had just been shattered? How was I to tell her that her heart was about to be broken along with mine? How could I say that our souls were going to be wrenched apart? How could I explain that what God had joined together was now being torn asunder?

"We're going back to Montana," I sobbed, unable to keep it in check.

Silence.

"Wha . . . Oh, no, God no . . . Daniel, you aren't . . . you can't. Oh, please no; say it isn't true. It's too cruel. Daniel, please . . ." Crystine's voice was cracking. What was left of my heart shattered completely.

"We are, Crystine. Dad just told me at the dinner table tonight."

"Whe . . . when?"

"In a week."

More silence and then sobbing.

Maybe they'll change their minds. Maybe it'll be okay and we won't go. Maybe . . . I was grasping at straws.

"Oh, Crystine, you are the breath that I breathe, and I love you more than life itself. How can this be happening?"

"Daniel, come over, right now, please. I need you."

During the next week we spent as much time together as we possibly could. We talked, we loved, we tried to rise above it, hoping against hope that the imminent would not materialize.

Mostly we just held each other, trying to make some sense of that cruel and capricious god we have named fate. We couldn't even come close.

"Until I see you again, you will always be in a special place in my heart," I whispered to her.

"And you in mine," she murmured. "And what happens to one of us, happens to the other, Daniel," she said. I didn't understand, didn't need to; I believed her.

Parting was an obliterating sorrow, and it was only the ice covering my heart that held the shattered pieces together. The poisoning of my soul had taken root and began to fester, and there was the darkness. I hated heaven and I hated hell and didn't give a damn what either one might do to me.

My only desire, my only hope, lay in Crystine, and somehow I would endure the time until I could get back to her.

※

I hardly remember the trip back to the Flathead; the only state I was aware of being in was the one called numbness.

After our arrival, Mom and Dad were trying to get set up and settled. Dad was having trouble finding suitable work, and I ended up out at O'Donnell's farm for another summer of aloneness.

After I got an address, the first thing I did was write to Crystine, and every day after that. She did the same, and her letters kept me somewhat buoyed up.

The mailbox was a little more than a quarter of a mile from the farmhouse, so Uncle Frank taught me how to drive his old Ford pickup. Every day I'd drive out and get the mail. That was my job. That and he had me painting his big barn red. I was glad for something to do, something to keep me busy, something to occupy my time. It helped keep the pain at a distance.

The days drifted by, and I'd just go through the motions of being involved in them. Crystine's letters were always the highlight of my day. Her handwriting was adorable, and her letters like water that quenched my thirst. On Sundays I'd read all the letters again that she had sent me during the week even though I had read every letter twice to begin with.

Aunt Louise, Uncle Frank, my cousin Dennis, and anybody else in the house all thought it was so cute, me and my letters to and from Crystine. I'm sure they believed it was a bad case of puppy love and would soon pass. I let it ride.

Late summer arrived, and with it came the wheat harvest. It was as usual a busy and exciting time, a break from painting, and I was ready for that. I even got a cold beer now and then during this harvest season. School would be starting soon at Flathead High. I thought I'd try out for football, maybe have a shot at making varsity someday. At least that dream was still alive.

Chapter Thirteen

rystine sat alone in the front room, lights off, the sun just setting, darkness creeping into the room and into her mind. She was in a quandary, faced with a dilemma of the kind life throws at us and is always unwelcome, the struggle between the heart and the head, the head usually winning by convincing us that what is felt in the heart is fantasy, or wishful thinking, or, at the very least, unrealistic.

She'd moped about all summer. Her only expression of life was the anticipation of receiving Daniel's letters every day. Nikki frequently came over to try to cheer her up, succeeding for short periods of time, but still couldn't talk her into doing much of anything, like going out to a dance or to the beach. Down to the local hangout for a Coke was as far as they got, and that was always lackluster.

Her mother did all she could to comfort Crystine and to insulate her from despair. But she couldn't let it continue. She couldn't sit by and watch her withdraw herself, losing the exuberance for life she once had. Somehow she had to pull her out of the doldrums. It was of utmost importance to Julie that her daughter understand the advantage of acquiring education beyond the public offering, that she understood the need to establish goals and objectives that would give her ample opportunity to lead a happy, productive life, one in which she'd be able to stand on her own.

How to deal with the situation would be a very delicate operation. She knew that Crystine was extremely vulnerable and couldn't handle any more hurt. Julie wouldn't—couldn't—scoff at it or dismiss it as puppy love with a trite "You'll get over it." She was aware that what Crystine and Daniel had known ran much deeper than that, and it broke her heart to see it gone.

In a strange way Julie missed Daniel also. He'd been in her home enough to have established a welcome presence. She couldn't explain why she missed him, but it helped her to understand the depth of loss her daughter must feel. Then she understood that the same thread that had briefly mingled her life with that of Galen McDermitt also ran through Daniel. That was what she felt and inexplicably missed. Both men, old and young, had left a lasting impression on her. She could only imagine how her daughter must feel.

"Crystine, you need to snap out of it."

"Snap out of what?" Crystine replied in honest innocence.

"The doldrums, your pining over Daniel."

"Mom, I love him. I always will!"

Julie's heart was breaking for her daughter. She hoped, she prayed, for just the right words to say to her.

"What if you never see Daniel again, honey? You're both so very young. Will he wait for you? Will you wait for him?"

"Mom, don't say that please . . . Don't even think it. What happens to him happens to me. What happens to me happens to him. How can we not wait for each other?"

"And in the meantime, darling, will you just drop out of life?"

"I won't. I haven't," Crystine replied. But Julie knew better. She knew the love that had blossomed in the young couple was the kind dreams are made of, the once-in-a-lifetime-if-ever-at-all kind, and her heart broke even more.

"You already have, honey, a little bit, and you know that," Julie said.

Crystine was silent as tears welled up in her eyes. "Oh, Momma, I miss him so; I just do!"

Julie didn't press the issue any further, she just held her daughter, held her while the anguish in her heart let itself out, saturating her mother's shoulder with wetness. But Julie didn't give up.

Slowly Crystine saw that she would have to get on with her life. She couldn't let the dying hope of future happiness rob her of present happiness. To her, Montana may as well be a foreign country, and Los Angeles was . . . well, Los Angeles . . . the Big Amoeba, absorbing everything and everyone into itself.

Hypnotic and seductive, the buzz was impossible to ignore.

Crystine's quandary was over. She signed the completed letter, "Your Friend, Crystine," sealed it, stamped it, walked out the front door, dropped it in the mailbox, and sent it to Montana, the anguish in her heart pouring out through her eyes.

Chapter Fourteen

The old Ford pickup had a four-speed transmission. I put it in reverse, backed out of the shop, spun it around, ground it into second gear, spewed gravel, and headed out to the mailbox.

It had been five days since I'd gotten a letter from Crystine—an eternity.

I roared down the lane, raising a larger-than-usual trailing cloud of dust. Skidding to a stop, the dust cloud catching up to me, I reached out the window and opened the mailbox. There it was, and my heart soared. I eagerly opened her letter, my eyes hungering to see her handwriting, to devour her every word.

I could not believe what I had just finished reading. I read it again; sure enough, it was a good-bye letter, signed: Your Friend, Crystine. Friend? *Friend?* How could we be friends? We were in love! We were lovers! She belonged to me! I belonged to her! How could this be? Friends? How was it possible for love to slip into friendship overnight? This was a decision she weighed and made, not something felt in her heart. I did not, could not, understand it. I refused it. I read it again.

Your Friend, Crystine.

Fixed point.

My vision blurred, and my heart turned to ice, my world to black. The thump of my now-frozen heart was like the hammer of a blacksmith pounding red-hot iron on his anvil. Denial screamed, echoed, and rebounded inside my skull. My soul spiraled downward, caught in a vortex toward utter despair and devoid of hope.

I ripped the letter to shreds, tossed the pieces out the window, threw the truck in gear, and blindly roared back to the house, a roiling cloud of dust following me. Screeching to a halt in front of the shop, I shut off the engine, leapt out of the cab, ran into the house, threw the rest of the mail on the kitchen table, and bolted back outside, glad I didn't see Aunt Louise.

I ran as hard and as fast as I could. I ran the mile out to the river. I ran back again. I ran out to the mailbox, stopping long enough to stare in disbelief at the pieces of Crystine's letter remaining on the road. I ran to the barn, went in out of breath, sweating, my chest heaving. I wasn't tired. The rage against the pain shot me through and through with an unholy energy called fury, and now I not only hated heaven and hell but threw out a challenge to both: *give me your best fucking shot.*

I pulled the saddle off the top rail of the stall, slung it over my shoulder, grabbed the buckskin's bridle, and draped it over my left arm. Dropping the saddle at the double doors, I headed out across the pasture, marching with furious purpose toward Peanuts.

He looked up from his grazing and then tossed his head up and down as he snorted and whinnied with an ear-piercing pitch. He began to stomp his front hooves into the ground, prancing back and forth for a minute or two. Suddenly stopping dead still, he stared at me with bold and challenging eyes, a proud and untamed stallion. I kept marching. "Run, you son-of-a bitch. Just try it," I muttered under my breath. He snorted again, flared his nostrils and came at me at a fast trot, his intentions hard to read, maybe dangerous. He stopped, stood as unmoving as a stone, and stuck his muzzle in my face.

I stepped quickly to the side and slipped the bit into his mouth and then the halter over his ears. He bowed his head a little and flattened his ears, making it easier to get it done. Holding his reins in my left hand, grabbing a handful of mane with the same, I swung my right leg up and over, mounting him bareback. I figured he was up to some deviltry and would buck, maybe buck me clear to the moon—I could only hope. And then, all on his own, he took off across the pasture toward the barn at an easy lope.

I tossed the blanket and saddle on him, cinching it tight without having to knee the wind out of him.

Then I ran him, out to the north fork of the Flathead River and back, out to the mailbox—Crystine's letter now scattered by the wind—and back.

I ran him past the barn, across the stubblefield that had held the summer crop of wheat, across the hayed alfalfa field. Out to the river and back again, out to the mailbox and back again.

I ran him.

He was Peanuts, a surging locomotive clad in buckskin hide with four legs for pistons. I ran him and ran him, and he was tireless and ran with the force of a hurricane, my rage the fuel that drove him. I wasn't exhilarated; I wasn't welcomed by the gods. I tried to lay siege against their realm, take it by force of storm and fury.

"Take your best fucking shot," I screamed at heaven and hell and the realm of all gods.

I ran him. I wanted him to stomp and grind the world into submission. I wanted him to outrun my pain. I looked down with blazing eyes from staring at the sky. Peanuts was covered with a lathered sweat, his nostrils flaring in and out like a dragon's, breathing fire. I reined him in with all my might. Reluctantly he slowed. I have no doubt he felt my intensity and wanted to help me outrun the pain, but it was no use.

The sun glowed golden in the west, and I stared into it as I rode him at a slow walk the last quarter mile to the barn, hoping helplessly that there was a Sun God, one that would shine down on Crystine, causing her to have a change of heart. Or go down and stay down forever, covering the earth with a blanket of darkness.

I walked Peanuts into the barn, once a place of friendly warmth after the neighbors had gathered to help build it, a place families depended on for their own and the livestock's sustenance, a timeless place where kids learned how to play and how to work, a place now forbidding and gloomy. I rubbed Peanuts down, curried him, gave him some oats, and then turned him loose to pasture and water. He walked slowly away, stopping about halfway between me and his customary far corner of the pasture. He looked at me, snorted, tossed his head, pranced for a while, and then stood . . . still.

I turned back into the barn, slung the saddle over my shoulder and bridle over my arm, and went into the tack room. Uncle Frank was waiting there for me.

"Maybe that was something you had to do, Daniel," he said, "and I'll give you that. But if you ever lather Peanuts up like that again, it'll be the last time you'll ride him." He wasn't angry, just matter-of-fact. Maybe he knew the what and the why for.

I didn't say a word, just nodded my head slightly and put away the gear. Uncle Frank went about his business. I climbed up on top of the barn and stared into the setting sun, my hopes fading along with the remaining daylight of this, the blackest of all my days.

Peanuts stood where I'd left him in the pasture, looking up at me. He tossed back his head, whinnying loud and long, and I could swear, mournful, as if he could feel my pain. Then he sprinted off to his far corner. It's called communion, and I loved that buckskin.

The most unusual thing happened, though. Whenever I wanted to ride him all I'd have to do is go to the edge of the pasture and call him. He'd come running. Of course, I'd whistle and holler, "Here . . . Penis," just for fun, but he didn't seem to mind.

I spent the next couple of weeks painting the outbuildings around the place and riding Peanuts in the evenings, with restraint. I couldn't run from the pain, so I kept to myself to keep it hidden. I tried not to let it eat me up alive or make me bitterly useless and was mildly successful. But the ice continued to thicken around my heart, and darkness became my only desire. Yeah, paint it black.

My folks got a place in town, and a week before school started I left the farm. Dad wasn't having any luck finding work. We were up against hard times and struggled in the Flathead.

Crystine thought the siren song of LA would draw her into the buzz and she could lose herself there in numbness. It did, but she couldn't. She sent a letter to the Flathead Valley signed "I'm sorry. I love you, Crystine."

Aunt Louise pulled out the day's mail and saw a letter addressed to Daniel Abrams from Huntington, California. By now she recognized Crystine's handwriting. *Oh, how cute,* she thought to herself, intending to get the letter to him on Thanksgiving, after dinner, a couple of months away.

Chapter Fifteen

My old school friends in the Flathead had drastically changed, establishing their separate cliques and circles, none of which I was interested in meeting the requirements of joining. I didn't give a damn about the Flathead Braves or school and ran with a rough crowd, inflicting pain on whomever, wherever, and whenever I could, but it didn't ease mine any, and after I realized that, I pulled back some.

The school year moved along like an ice-filled river, but I showed up. Fall went around the corner toward winter, and Thanksgiving was a week away. We didn't make it out to O'Donnell's farm. Aunt Louise had suffered a mild stroke the previous week and wasn't up to preparing dinner. It was just as well, as Mom and Dad weren't getting along, and I was morose and didn't feel thankful for a damn thing anyway.

The river of life began to move more swiftly, and all signs, along with the calendar, said summer was coming. I had no enthusiasm for it, no plans, and nothing to look forward to except maybe earning a few bucks to help out a little and to get myself some beer.

Then Dad landed a job in a sleepy little hamlet nestled in the mountains ninety miles west of the Flathead Valley. We'd be moving at the beginning of summer once again, another summer alone. But this time it didn't bother me; instead, I was relieved to be leaving. It would only have been a matter of time, and a small amount of that, before I'd gotten in serious trouble with the school, or with a girl, or with the law. Just a matter of time—the train had been roaring full speed and dead center down the track, headed for the inevitable wreck.

Situated in a deep valley carved out by the Kootenai River and ringed with mountains, the town of Libby sits on the southern edge of the river, a hardworking, blue-collar, beer-drinking town with third-generation families firmly entrenched.

To the south and west of town rise the Cabinet Mountains. The word magnificent falls short in trying to describe them. Maybe the term awe-inspiring comes closer. Not only are they true wilderness, but they are officially classified as such; grizzly bears like living there, and many do.

The tamarack tree, also known as a larch, dominates the surrounding mountains. In the fall they turn to a golden yellow color, and if the setting sun hits them just right, they'll draw the breath right out of you in open wonder. On rare but very special days the river born from ice will appear turquoise in contrast to the yellow of the tamaracks or the white of the snowcapped peaks or the sapphire blue of the sky that covers the valley.

The town had been a sleepy little burg for several generations with about the same population running on the same economy, logging, a huge sawmill, a vermiculite mine, the US Forest Service, and the ever-present merchants, a good deal of whom owned bars and taverns. The same last names were always mentioned in the local paper, and the same last names were always popular in the local schools, year after year after year. Good old boys and . . . sleepy. Until now.

I could feel a strong undercurrent . . . a buzz.

Construction had just begun on a huge dam spanning the Kootenai River, ten miles upstream from town. The lake to be created would stretch ninety miles to the north, reaching into Canada, and was to be named Lake Koocanusa. Can you say Boom Town? Libby was about to explode.

It was exciting, and I realized that I missed the feeling of excitement in the air. The Big Amoeba had ingested a part of me after all.

Dad had landed a pretty good job. We lived in a nice house as a result, not that anyone paid attention to that sort of thing up in that neck of the woods. Status symbols, fancy neighborhoods, and the so-called prestige bestowed by position on the economic scale simply didn't exist.

I actually looked forward to a new start in a newly built high school. Maybe my life would return to something approaching normal, whatever that was.

The depth of the valley and the surrounding ring of mountains seemed to act as an insulator of sorts from the rest of the world, and now my world consisted of the town, the valley, and the goings-on in them, viewed from a renegade high schooler's perspective, of course. Life was almost good again. Maybe someone would come along to help me forget Crystine, or at least take the edge off the vivid memories. Maybe ease the pain of losing her, or erase it altogether. At least I had a small amount of hope.

It was getting close to winter. I ran through the door in my usual impatient rush of youth, threw my school books on the kitchen table, and hollered, "Hi, Mom. I'm home." I opened the refrigerator door, scrounging for a snack.

Mom walked slowly in from the front room. I didn't really see her, just glimpsed her out of the corner of my eye.

"Daniel," she started, and I knew right away something was up. There always was when she prefaced what she had to say with my name. "Your dad left."

"Huh . . . uh, where'd he go?" I asked, quite detached.

"No, I mean . . . he *left* . . . went away . . . for good . . . won't
be coming back. He, he . . . left a note . . . I don't know where he
went."

I closed the refrigerator door, my appetite having flown away,
replaced by nausea churning in the pit of my stomach. Numbness
crept back in, and I felt like a dead man walking. I managed to ask
Mom if she was okay. She tried to smile and managed a weak one,
"We'll be fine," she said without much conviction, trying to hide
her hurt.

"Yeah, we will," I replied without much conviction, trying to
show courage. The best we could do was hug. And I had to wonder
at that point if reincarnation was an actual fact. Surely I had driven
spikes through the hands and feet of Christ or done some other
heinous act in some ancient past. Surely there was some reason that
life not only refused to treat me kindly but continued to severely
punish me.

Beer drinking wasn't an occasional indulgence in Libby; it was
an established culture. I dove right in, and it welcomed me with
open arms. Two things happened: it increased the buzz and it eased
the pain. For a while.

I went to work after school and sometimes on weekends as a
bagger in a grocery store. We all went to work. My older sister,
Judy, showed up about then just to help out. She did that sort of
thing quite often, without complaint, and asked nothing in return.
I didn't realize until much later that saints do exist in this world and
she was one.

Life went on, and I did the usual high school thing out on
the edge more than most; faster cars, heartier beer parties, lots of
girlfriends, seeking freedom without knowing what it was, pursuing
happiness without having defined it. An airhead, more or less. But
I did manage to finish school. Out of a graduating class of ninety, I
ranked number forty-five. You could say that my distinction was in
defining the word mediocrity. But a deep vacancy inside me where
my heart should have been continued haunting me, and I wondered
how it was possible that I could still hurt. God, I missed Crystine

at times. No one had come close to replacing her; probably no one ever would.

I kicked around the idea of trying to find her in LA and then talked myself out of it. Maybe she wasn't there. Maybe she had changed. Maybe she wouldn't remember me. And maybe, worst of all, she'd reject me once again, a possibility I could not face and would not survive.

Most of the recent graduates went to work at the sawmill or plywood plant. I signed on with the US Forest Service to fight forest fires, thinking it would be more exciting, up in the Cabinet wilderness. It was hot, grueling, dirty dangerous work all summer long, but neither one got me, not the fires or the Grizzly bears. Deep down I suppose I was hoping one or the other would.

All good things must come to an end, the saying goes, and that included the fire season. Time to return to civilization and become a responsible adult, and that prospect would surely give me an opportunity to define dismal. Besides, I hadn't noticed very many satisfied or happy adults along the way to becoming one, and I already knew what "Can't Get No Satisfaction" and unhappiness were like; they'd been my companions for years.

So my best friend Roger and I decided to beat the draft to the punch and joined the army. Vietnam was at its peak; glory hallelujah.

The recruiter mentioned joining under the "buddy system." Well, Roger and I didn't go to boot camp together, didn't go to 'Nam together, and didn't go through any of the war together. The recruiter made it a point to tell me I'd do a tour in 'Nam, though, and that I'd be ducking bullets while I was there.

"I don't intend on ducking anything," I replied. He shrugged his shoulders, gave me the standard US Army you're-a-body-in-a-bag look, shoved a paper at me, and grunted, "Sign here."

Vietnam was, and still remains, an enigma. I'm not certain that the historians have it properly categorized to this day. Was it a war? It hasn't really been decided yet, and I don't know how to answer the question. What I do know is that young men got killed over there . . .

all the time, their faces or their arms or their legs blown off to go flying through the atmosphere, chests ripped open, guts torn out and spilling on the ground, screams of terror and agony permeating the air, pounding relentlessly and hopelessly into your ears.

Tension, fear, terror, psychoses, depression, mania, hate, rage, mistrust, and confusion took turns imprisoning each man's mind. Drugs and alcohol and blood soaked the land. Suicide and murder were an everyday occurrence. Death and dying and tanks appearing out of the dust, like iron-clad, fire-breathing dragons intent on killing. Mines and bombs and machine guns popping up out of nowhere; air strikes and guerrillas and liberated villages laced with land mines or sprinkled with their own version of tortuous booby traps, and agent orange, and napalm, to add color and flavor to the grisly scene—a constant bloody peril.

And soldiers going crazy—for a minute, or an hour, or a day, or a week, or a month, or forever—gone irretrievably insane, never to return from the world of shock secreted deep within their shredded mind.

The blood. The redness. Everywhere. Always. Blood seeping, and flowing, and spewing, and pooling on the soil, the soil drinking it in with an unquenchable thirst.

And the blood lust.

And the thrust of bayonets.

And the killing.

Most often it was simply cold-blooded, but sometimes reluctant, sometimes with purpose, sometimes with wanton savageness with blood boiling in a furious rage. Manic, psychotic, enraged blood lust in the jungle. There was no glory, just gut-level instinctual survival, terror or rage its driving force.

I felt alive for the first time in years because I could identify what was out there waiting to hurt me or kill me, and I could do something about it; I could fight back. And I didn't have time to dwell too long on Crystine or any of my past; if I wasn't in the moment I could be dead.

Was it a war? That debate hasn't been settled. But I know. I've settled the question. It was a nightmare trip through hell, a hell

I'd challenged, and it rose up to meet me. No use going into the politics of war, Vietnam in particular. No use discussing the clash of ideologies. They're always slanted, containing lies of commission or omission manifesting endless opinions and are better left to the self-proclaimed intellectuals residing in ivory towers. And in complete safety, I might add.

But . . .

. . . experience can't be argued with.

. . . experience is irrefutable.

. . . and if war is hell, I experienced war.

Not having a clear objective was the norm. Just slog along through the jungle and the swamp and the slime and the mud and the heat and the steam and the insects and the Viet Cong, hoping you didn't shit your pants or get a leg blown off or have a fifty-caliber machine-gun slug rip through your chest. A drink of cool sweet water was a touch of heaven.

I was a soldier, assigned to infantry, a grunt. My training was to kill and to be so good at it that I had a chance to save my own life and possibly those of others. I know I took a lot of lives. Indirectly I probably saved a lot of men's lives. Directly, I remember only one.

I had aged fast. Everybody did who survived. The aging wasn't due to the passage of time, which moved two ways: on a clock linked to geologic changes or in suspended split seconds where an eternity could pass. It was the split seconds that brought about the aging.

The entrance in and out of our platoon was a revolving door. Still, we were always careful to take a wide-eyed wild recruit and teach him as best we could. But the main part of training always came under fire, and after they'd finish puking their guts out and shitting their pants, they'd be ready for some serious instruction. Maybe get to the point where if they had an enemy in their sights they could squeeze the trigger, maybe. It's a spooky and a powerful feeling to look down the barrel of your rifle, pointed at another human being, and decide whether he lives or whether he dies. The decision is always there, and you've got a split second, wrapped in eternity, to make it.

The training for all new recruits was progressive and predictable. Like the saying goes, nothing gets you in shape like playing the game under fire.

I'd made sergeant, mostly because I was still around. We'd get freshly trained college kids, second lieutenants, for platoon leaders, scornfully or affectionately referred to as ninety-day wonders. They got that label for a couple of reasons. One, they got their official US Army officers' training in ninety days, and two, if they managed to survive in 'Nam for more than ninety days, it was a wonder how they did it. They had to train those boys fast because so many of them needed replaced. A new arrival would strut up to me and say, "Sergeant, I'm Second Lieutenant Candy-Ass-So-and-So, the new commander of this platoon!" He'd be crisp and clean, ramrod straight with his jaw clenched in a determined set, his eyes ablaze with fire and fear, and let's just say that he was unseasoned.

"Welcome to the 101st Airborne Rifle Platoon, sir!" I'd reply, saluting him sharply and crisply.

"Anything to report, Sergeant?" he'd snap.

"Yes, sir!" I'd fire back. "When you are up to your ass in alligators, sir, it's hard to remember your primary objective was to drain the swamp, sir!" I'd shout.

The grim set of his jaw would slacken, the thin line of his mouth drop open a little, and a blank look would come across his face. Happened every time.

I'd draw up to my full height and more, on my tiptoes, and salute him with precision crispness. He'd almost be recovered by then.

"Uh, thank you, Sergeant . . . that will be all."

"Yes-s-s, sir-r-r," I'd fairly shout, spinning on my toes, marching the other way, the grins in place on my men's faces, mostly with tongue-in-cheek. It was a little comedy relief we could count on now and then.

Of course, the lieutenant had no idea what I was talking about until later, provided he survived the ninety days, that is. But we'd take them under our wing, give them as much room as we could, not allowing any unnecessary endangerment, and go from there. Some made it; some didn't. None of them got murdered that I know of; I never saw any that were back shot. We got this one from Southern California. He reminded me of my long-ago buddy Tim, except this guy's eyes were brown instead of artists' blue. I went through my usual routine about alligators with him, and that was that. Time would tell. I considered getting to know this one a little more than most, him being from the LA area and all. Maybe by some quirk of fate he'd run across Crystine. It was possible. I had a lot of faith in that cruel and capricious god by now, but I set the idea aside.

To Crystine I was probably as good as dead. And the odds of accomplishing that eventuality increased daily. Besides, I might get to liking this "second looey," and that would for sure increase his chances of getting killed. My faith in fate and how the sonofabitchin' thing worked was strong.

This second lieutenant received orders to lead us on a routine recon mission, just south of the demilitarized zone where a lot of men got their asses shot off, just southeast of the coastal town of Hue. We were being sent to scout the area for a possible hammer-anvil maneuver. That's when one company entrenches and another gets behind and on the flanks of the enemy ahead and drives them into the teeth of the entrenched company for slaughter. Oh, the glories of war, or in this case, police action, uh-huh. Just a leisurely stroll through the jungle, out and back in one rising and setting of the southeast Asian sun. We weren't as high-strung as nervous cats but had our guard up just the same.

We'd nicknamed our lieutenant Wild Bill. It wasn't because he was reckless or out of control—just the opposite; Wild Bill was "cool under fire." He used his head and we knew it, so he almost had our trust, except his instincts hadn't been tried yet.

We halted at the edge of a good-sized clearing, Wild Bill in the lead. The clearing was nearly circular, with dense foliage and trees surrounding it. It was noon and there were no shadows, no breeze, it was unbearably hot, humid, sticky, and sweaty.

I scanned the clearing and the perimeter foliage first with my naked eye and then with the field glasses. Wild Bill did the same. I continued to try to detect anything unusual while he used the field glasses. I noticed no shadows, no glints of sunlight off reflective surfaces—metal usually—no fresh dirt scattered or mounded, no leaves or bushes or shrubs moving in the mausoleum-like air. Nothing out of the ordinary; nothing I could put my finger on anyway.

Satisfied, Wild Bill signaled for us to move out ranger file, which is army lingo for single file. The normal platoon size for a rifle company is forty-three men. Today we had twenty-six. Like I said, a revolving door.

We moved out to the middle of the clearing. And then it hit me . . . hard, and the hairs on the back of my neck stood up. The zone, it's like a sixth sense or the hyper sharpening of the ones in place. It brings acute awareness and sharper, clearer vision; inaudible tones and sounds become audible; tense muscles suddenly relax, like those of a cat, ready to spring in less than the blink of an eye; and there's an extraordinary surge of adrenaline.

I put my finger on it: no birds, no sound, no nothing!

"Hit the dirt!" I bellowed, reaching up to grab Wild Bill's right shirt sleeve as I fell toward the ground. A fifty-caliber machine-gun slug slammed into his left shoulder where his heart had been a millisecond earlier, exploding in a crimson fountain, spattering his shocked and ghostly face with a spray of blood. I kept hold of him, and we hit the ground together.

One eternity passed; another coming up.

His eyes, like full moons, widened by fear, pain, and confusion, told me he was going into shock, and fast! Machine gun fire whizzed over our heads like angry wasps whose sting was deadly.

"Snakes!" I yelled on instinct, meaning crawl on your belly lower than one if you could. Wasn't any need to tell the men that; they were seasoned and crawling back for the cover of the jungle foliage, a few of them already at the perimeter. At intervals of fractions of a second, an M-16 would raise up above the tall grass to return fire in the direction of the machine gunners. To stand would have been suicide, and nobody was inclined that way right then.

I slipped my knife from its sheath, cut off a strip of my shirt tail, and wrapped Wild Bill's left shoulder as best I could. We couldn't stay put.

"Lopez!" I hollered at the nearest soldier crawling away. He looked back, saw the situation, and immediately turned around to help.

Another eternity passed.

We grabbed the back of Wild Bill's shirt and, leaving his rifle and gear behind, started dragging him to cover. The men who had reached the perimeter cover were returning fire. I noticed that there weren't as many wasps buzzing overhead now. Along the way I visually checked a couple of shot-up soldiers. They had no chests and were dead.

The remainder of the platoon had reached cover and was returning fire with a vengeance, relentlessly raking the area behind us. We got Wild Bill to relative safety, all in about two minutes real time; in combat time . . . at least three eternities passed.

The radioman was at work, calling for a chopper with a medic and a few rockets to fire into those "goddamn VC machine gunnin' bastards." His buddy was one of those lying back along the trail with his chest blown open.

Wild Bill was lying on his back, his head propped on my helmet. He was in shock all right. The blood splattered on his white-as-fresh-fallen-snow face was beginning to dry. I took a kerchief from his pocket, wetted it with water from my canteen, and washed his ghostly features. The radioman flipped me a first-aid kit. I cut away my makeshift bandage, replacing it with a compress from the kit. His shoulder had been shattered; there wasn't a lot of blood loss, but for sure there was a lot of pain. He was done with this war for a while. It was just as well; I was starting to like the guy.

He looked in my eyes then, long enough to focus and say, "Thank you, Sergeant."

"You'll be all right, sir," I replied. "You've cut your tour of duty a little short, though, I'd say." He managed a weak but genuinely thankful smile. I grinned back. It made me feel good for a moment, even though what I did was just a natural reaction.

I heard the w*hump-whump-whump* of the chopper blades beating the air. A couple of rockets screamed into the clearing, slamming their targets. The firing of the machine guns and the rifles abruptly stopped.

"The medic'll be here shortly, sir. Won't be long you'll be on your way back to the states," I said.

He let out a sigh of relief through his pain and then closed his eyes peaceful-like. He'd be okay.

I'm not sure what became of Lieutenant William Hopkins. I saw the medics put him on the chopper. I suppose from there he eventually made it back to California, in geologic time.

I wasn't proud of Vietnam. I was extremely proud of my men, though, and of myself a little. Maybe we did some good. A lot of young men died over there, and for no particular reason, other than someone else's cause, undefined as it was. I suppose that could be said of any war, though.

One form of government exists in the world. It's called a plutocracy, and any other name is a smoke screen. "Make the world safe for democracy," uh-huh.

I think a whole lot of folks got rich off Vietnam. Here lies GI Joe, slain in battle, died in vain, take it to the bank. I suppose that could also be said of any war, though.

※

I was used to constant adrenaline and relying on my instincts. The only thing that mattered was the next minute or two. I was used to making split-second decisions, hoping they were right, hoping they didn't get me or someone else killed. I thought I had served my country. My country had used me as cannon fodder.

I didn't lose any pieces of my body over there. I wonder sometimes if I didn't lose a few pieces of my soul. I had entered the realm of the gods several times again, only these times were chillingly different. These gods were dark and menacing and as cold as ice.

The adjustment returning home was jarring. I had no idea how deep the unrest and protests ran, and I almost took it personally, but in the end I decided that a lot of it was just a fad and was blindly done, the "in" thing to do, and now and then got out of hand, like a few protesting college kids getting killed, slain in battle, died in vain.

I returned to Libby to visit Mom. I got word that my good friend Roger was driving over from eastern Montana to see me and was killed in a one-car accident on the highway. This, after he had done a one year tour of duty in 'Nam.

But somehow, perhaps for some reason, I had survived.

Drive on.

Chapter Sixteen

Elbows on the table-top, chin resting in her cupped hands, Crystine looked imploringly at Nikki.

"I don't know what to do," she uttered, tears of anguish welling in her eyes. Nikki reached across the table, covering her friend's hand with her own, offering her comfort and understanding without words. They had gone through school from the first grade and were still best friends in this, their last year of high school.

"Your mom will understand. She's cool, way cool," said Nikki. She was like a second daughter to Julie and probably spent more time talking with Crystine's mom than she did with her own.

"I know she will," Crystine replied. "I mean, I don't know what to do now, about this . . . about my life. I feel . . . trapped, Nikki." The dam broke, the tears flowed, and Crystine began to sob. She sobbed at the loss she felt, sobbed at the cruel twists of fate, and sobbed because the baby growing in her womb wasn't Daniel's.

She liked David Diaz well enough and had almost convinced herself that she loved him. He loved her and had told her so many times, both in and out of the throes of passion. He was the only one able to come close to subduing Daniel's memory. It would never be erased altogether, Crystine knew, and in times when she needed to feel safe, or comforted, or at peace, his memory became all the more vivid, all the more poignant, and then the pain of losing him would become all the more acute—a paradox hard to live with.

It was two months until graduation. At least she didn't have to face the dilemma of whether or not to finish school. That would happen.

She gazed through dry eyes out the kitchen window at Nikki's pool, remembering that night when she and Daniel could no longer confine their love and had soared upon the plane of the sacred and would for all their lives. She remembered Daniel by her side, locked in place, the piece that completed her. But he was gone now, and to remember him any longer was too painful. She decided to try not to . . . if only her heart would agree with her head.

She became Mrs. David Diaz one week after high school graduation. But she was still Crystine and *there* and in six months' time was as fully prepared for motherhood as was possible.

As the birthing time neared, though, her energy went down. Her mother's, however, increased exponentially. Julie was *so* excited! Her first grandchild, and she fussed and fidgeted over every little detail almost to the point of being underfoot, but Crystine appreciated beyond words that her mother was near. She would have been okay without her, but just barely.

She and her mother were, first and foremost, friends. Love was never in question and was boundless from the day of Crystine's birth. And now a grandchild to love! Julie could barely contain herself, often making her daughter laugh at her fussiness. Love is boundless and sees far, and Julie saw what may come. She knew that Crystine had made what she thought to be the proper and noble choice; certainly, at the time, the socially acceptable one. Whether it was the right choice or not, only time would tell.

Crystine gave birth to a beautiful healthy daughter near Christmas time and named her Holly, in part because of the season, but mostly because that had been Grandma Murphy's name.

She and David and Holly Julia Diaz remained in the same neighborhood Crystine had grown up in. That way, her mother, at her insistence (as close as she'd ever get to insisting on anything from her daughter) was near should she be needed, or even if she wasn't, which was most often the case.

But more importantly, Crystine's sense of place was in that neighborhood, an anchor she needed to hold on to, a feeling sometimes that all would be well or that Daniel was near or would return some day to find her. But deep down inside she had to admit that she was a little apprehensive, if not downright scared, of the future.

The change had been so damned abrupt.

David was a hard worker and reliable in bringing home a paycheck. But being a recent high school graduate, his opportunities for advancement were severely limited, and Crystine saw why her mother had always stressed the importance of education.

It didn't take long to hone the routines of baby care to precision, giving her plenty of spare time. With a return of her normal high energy levels, Crystine sought a new challenge in her life and decided to enroll in a local college. Grandma Julie was more than happy to watch Holly a few times a week, especially since David's absences from home were becoming more and more frequent.

Two years after Holly had entered the human race, Crystine gave birth to David Diaz Jr. Fifteen months later, with toddlers in tow, she returned to her mother's home, a divorce from David pending.

Not sure what had happened, thinking she had loved David, second thoughts had crept in. Maybe it had been only a flare of passion. Though easily mistaken for love, its inevitable destiny is to always, if not die out, at least fade to the miserable state of gritty tolerance or grim acceptance. Crystine recognized that probable future and settled it, right then and there, deciding to never let it happen again. Falling in and out of love, real or imagined, was not something she wanted to go through every few years. She wasn't convinced that falling in and out of love was a real state anyway; *there had to be something missing to begin with,* she mused.

Love at first sight rarely, if ever, happened, she'd heard. But she knew it did and had happened to her and Daniel; that had been, without question, real.

Her soon-to-be-former husband had thrilled her, had made her laugh, had pleased her, and had almost made her forget. But he had never made her feel warm from the inside out.

A tear trickled down Crystine's cheek.

"Welcome home, baby," Julie said as Crystine came through the door, holding Davey against her breast and Holly's hand in hers.

"Mom, I'm hardly a baby anymore. I'm twenty-one now, you know," she said.

"Of course I know. But you'll always be my baby. That never changes. You'll find out some day," she replied with a knowing smile.

Marcus and Shelley had moved out and Grandma Murphy had been gone a long time, so Julie was glad for the life that had come into her house.

The night was balmy. A soft cooling breeze whispered across the front porch. Crystine sat down in the swing where she and Daniel had spent so many evenings glorying in the rapture of simply being together. Julie was seated in a chaise lounge at the other end of the porch, drinking her customary cup of coffee as Crystine sipped a Coke. The babies were asleep in their rooms inside the house, the front door left open to hear them should they cry.

"I'm all tangled up inside, confused, like I'm drifting without direction, not knowing how I'm going to take care of Holly and Davey," Crystine said.

"Don't think about it right now. Give yourself some time to recover," Julie said. "Then think things through, slowly and thoroughly, considering not only your obligations but also what it is you want out of life." The Irish twinkle entered her eye. "Maybe find a rich old man, reel him in, and marry him," she winked.

"Mom!" Crystine protested. "I'd have to love someone before I could marry him, and I'd need a lot of time to even make certain of that!" Then the Irish twinkle got the best of Crystine too. "Besides," she added, "I happen to have my own Tyrone Power."

"Who could that possibly be," asked her mother.

"Daniel Abrams," Crystine replied unexpectedly.

Julie looked somberly at her. "Oh, baby, I'm so very sorry. Will you ever get over him?"

"I don't know . . . I don't think so."

"Well . . . a rich old man it is then!" quipped Julie, succeeding in lightening up the situation a little. But, oh, how she would have taken away her daughter's heartache, if she only could. "How about David? Do you miss him? Is he going to help out?"

"I don't miss him. It's over, and just as well. Staying together would have been hurtful to us and to the kids. As far as him helping out, I don't even know where he is."

Julie thought about Juan Mercado, how she hadn't seen or heard from him since Crystine was born. She wondered if all men were alike; just out for fun and not willing to accept any real responsibility. But deep down, she didn't believe that; she always believed in the best in people, until they proved otherwise.

They fell into silence, and Crystine rocked back and forth in the swing, the memories of rocking in that same swing with Daniel overtaking her.

"Education."

"What?" Crystine replied, jarred from her reverie.

"Education," Julie repeated. "It's the one thing you *can* count on to help you get what you want, to help you take care of the kids," Julie said.

"I know, Mom. I've thought about it a lot. I'm not sure yet, but somehow, someway, I'll get it done," Crystine said.

"That's my girl. I'm here to help, honey; always will be."

"Mom?"

"Yeah baby."

"I know I'm supposed to be grown up and all, but I really don't know what I'd do without you sometimes . . . most times," said Crystine.

Crystine's mom didn't burden her daughter with the fact that she had been diagnosed with breast cancer, and six months later Julie Mercado passed away.

Crystine cried. She screamed, she denied, she fought, she cursed, she sobbed . . . and sobbed . . . and sobbed until her tears ran dry and she succumbed to exhaustion, but not to the relief of sleep, only to the restless shadow zone between there and wakefulness.

"No . . . It can't be . . . It just can't, not Mom . . . moms live forever, don't they? Not Mom . . . anyone . . . anything . . . Oh God . . . not her," she whispered to no one there as her tortured soul tossed and turned her on a bed of anguish.

Crystine was familiar with deep and abiding sadness from the loss of Daniel, but this was a searing grief, a white-hot pain from which there was no escape, a stark and icy realization that she was now all alone in the world, and its truth hammered her heart with near crushing force.

"Oh, Daniel," she whispered into the dark, "where are you? Where is the comfort of your beating heart?"

❧

While I had been taking lives out of the world in Vietnam Crystine had been bringing lives into the world in California.

❧

Crystine continued to live in her mother's house. It offered her some comfort and sustained her most cherished memories.

She went to work as a secretary to support herself and her children. Her boss kept asking her out, but at the risk of her job, she firmly declined. Not about to get caught up in the web woven by the games of power and control, she stood her ground, kept her job, earned her boss's respect, and got promoted to office manager.

Empowering.

Her phone rang.

"Hey, girlfriend!"

"Nikki!" exclaimed Crystine, taken by surprise.

"Listen, you need to get out. I've got it all set up, Friday night at the Whiskey-a-Go-Go! Whadda ya say, kid?"

Still my best friend, thought Crystine, her heart grateful. She'd had to lean on Nikki constantly in the six months since her mother's death, and Nikki never minded. She was single, afraid to marry—she'd seen the heartaches—but she wasn't afraid to have fun.

"Carol . . . you know Carol, my little sister? She'll babysit Holly and Davey for you at no cost! C'mon, what say?" urged Nikki.

"Sounds fun, Nikki. Okey-dokey . . . Let's do it!" she exclaimed, a touch of her former boldness resurfacing.

They arrived at the latest LA hotspot in Nikki's black '68 Chevy Malibu SuperSport, the car and the women polished and all aglow.

"Ever been here before?" asked Nikki as they walked through the early evening and across the parking lot to the entrance holding an intimated promise of fun times.

"Of course not. With the kids and work, I don't have the time, and actually, not much interest either," replied Crystine.

"Well, tonight, girlfriend, it's going to be let-our-hair-down time!" Nikki said, laughing. Crystine joined her.

A precursor to disco, the club had loud, DJ-infested music, multicolored lights swirling overhead, and gyrating bodies filled with various substances, longingly lonely, momentarily happy people, predators, and prey.

Taking it in with a single glance, *Nothing new*, thought Crystine as they seated themselves at a table on the edge of the dance floor, offering them a view of the patrons on the floor and of the other tables.

A cheerful, chirpy waiter, dressed in unusually bright colors, materialized at their table. Nikki ordered a martini, Crystine a glass of merlot wine.

The man stood at the edge of the dance floor, his eyes glued on Crystine. Her burnished bronze hair, flowing like molten metal to the middle of her bare back, had captured his attention. The rest of her he found just as captivating. He was in his mid-twenties, and his dark brown medium length hair was parted on the left. About six feet tall and 175 pounds, he was lean and trim. His off-white jeans were accented by a pastel blue pocket T-shirt that matched his oceanic blue, penetrating eyes, which alternated between hard and soft, punctuated by a high sheen.

He moved lithely across the dance floor toward the girls' table with an easy graceful gait, like a tiger on the prowl. Nikki saw him coming and knew immediately that he was making a beeline for her friend. Crystine always got asked to dance first. It had been that way since they'd started going to dances in junior high.

He stopped at the table with his right hand extended toward Crystine, his eyebrows raised inquisitively. "May I have the pleasure of this dance?" he asked with an unnecessary attempt at suaveness.

Crystine reached her hand to his in acceptance, flashing the required polite smile as she rose from the chair, wondering if she could do this. She had not danced, hadn't even considered it, in a long, long time.

Her natural fluidity hadn't deserted her, and she danced and twirled and swayed with the best of them until the young man escorted her back to the table, his ice blue eyes aglow at the wonder of her lithesome beauty and grace.

He thanked her politely and sincerely. Crystine returned the thank you, seated herself, and thought no more of it.

"Crystine, you looked wonderful out there!" exclaimed Nikki.

"I did?" She hadn't thought much about that either. "I just danced," she continued, a little out of breath. "Did you?" she asked Nikki.

"Oh . . . yeah, a couple, just to warm up. I saw a whole lot of eyes on you, girlfriend."

"Really?"

"Really."

Crystine danced and twirled for the rest of the evening, forgetting her troubles, forgetting her world, forgetting herself.

"Having fun?" Nikki asked.

"A blast," replied Crystine, taking a sip of wine. "More than I thought I would."

"We should do this kind of thing more often," suggested Nikki.

"It probably wouldn't hurt. In fact, it would do me some good just to get out and let my hair down, as you put it."

"That's my old friend," replied Nikki.

"Hey! I'm not old yet; speak for yourself!"

They laughed, having a good time.

Sudden quietness. The room lights dimmed to a soft glow, and the silver orbs above the floor stopped spinning as their lights went dark. A slow instrumental with a strong sax riff and a guitar back played soothingly across the room.

Crystine set her glass of wine on the table and became quiet and still and listened, her senses and awareness heightened. Yes, it was so. The strains of "Harlem Nocturne" filled the room.

It seems a lifetime ago since I danced to the sweet refrain, safe in Daniel's arms, and yet it feels like yesterday, she thought, as she stared pensively into the glass of red wine.

Looking up, she saw the man with the ice-blue high-sheen eyes approaching. He stopped at her table, hand extended, eyebrows raised not quite as far as before, as if to say, "Well . . . ?"

Crystine hesitated, not sure of herself for a fleeting second, wondering if she could dance to the melody she held on the plane of the sacred. She glanced at her friend. Nikki sensed what the hesitation was about and encouraged her with a go-ahead nod.

Crystine reached out, placing her hand in that of her suitor's. Inundated with emotions conjured by the memories of beauty and bliss, she glided to the middle of the dance floor.

Could she? Should she? How?

They danced, not too close, not too far, and not too fluid.

He's not Daniel, she thought, *but then no one ever will be, except Daniel.* She knew that, but he did feel comfortable and easy to be with. *Perhaps a flame has been kindled,* she thought. But having been saddened and hurt and crushed, she was aware of the need for extreme caution to go along with the kindled flame.

"I'd like to know your name," he said to her as the dance came to a close.

"Crystine. And yours?"

"Jim . . . Jim Wheating," he answered. "Crystine, I'd like to call you . . . uh . . . take you out to dinner or something. Would you mind? Would you mind giving me your phone number?"

Feeling very flattered, almost blushing, she replied, "No, I wouldn't mind, and the answer is yes to the dinner or something."

The high sheen in his eyes matched the glow of her smile.

A year later she broke her never-marry-again vow and became Mrs. James Wheating, leaving Huntington behind, which Nikki said was probably a good thing for her, and moving north with Holly and Davey to Riverside.

Chapter Seventeen

My thoughts of Crystine, only seeds at first, were beginning to take full bloom, and I wondered how she was, or if she was. Almighty death had been the closest thing to me for over a year, and I'd done nothing but wait for the cold touch of its hand while I watched it go about its grisly work. Nothing can stand against its power, and I could not dismiss the fact it may have claimed her by now. As far as I was concerned, fate, the servant of death, was only cruel.

But I couldn't face the glut of glitter in LA right then. I'd had enough sensory and adrenaline overload and needed the peace and solitude of the mountains to help focus my mind on life and what it had to offer instead of death and what it took away. And underneath? The fear of finding her and being rejected, a possibility I could not face, knowing that if it happened I would drift away forever, captain of a rudderless ship. I told myself that she'd likely have forgotten me, being twenty or twenty-one by now, and the chances of finding her in that megatropolis were the equivalent of finding a raindrop in the ocean.

The buzz phrase in the states was "tune in, turn on, drop out," and so I did. It was that or let the bitterness of the war twist into unrelenting hate that would drive me somewhere in my mind to someplace on the globe and I would never return from either, like the vets who lived and survived in the woods of Washington and Oregon, real-life Rambos. Mental toughness is a necessity of surviving war. No one prepared us for the aftershock.

I enrolled at the University of Montana, its culture 180 degrees from Vietnam and attempting to keep in step with the University of California, Berkeley. I had aspirations of studying law, still naïve enough to believe that justice was a viable, living concept that somehow worked itself out, and left to itself, perhaps it would.

My psychology class required a couple of labs. I chose one where a guest was going to demonstrate hypnotism by putting the whole group under. It was winter, and the lab was at night on the other side of campus, almost a half mile away from my dorm.

As I walked along and alone in the cold and dark with the wind knifing through my clothing trying to put frost on my bones, I told myself I wasn't going under and would expose the hoax if I could, angry for picking the lab in the first place and wondering if I'd make it there without freezing. I had never felt the cold come at me with claws that stung and burn my legs while I pressed against the wind as the ice pellets drove into my face.

About thirty others were in the room, some warmed up, some still red in the face and shivering. I sat and let some feeling return to my hands before removing my coat, thinking I should allow myself to be hypnotized so I could make it back to the dorm pain free. But I didn't really believe it could be done, and my anger doubled.

The class instructor introduced the guest, a very tiny red-haired fortyish woman, and she started in. It was mesmerizing to watch. I don't know how she did it, but it only took a moment before she had people shivering, sweating, swatting at flies, and crying tears. And yup, "When I count to three, you will all wake up. One, two, three." The people looked around stupefied with silly grins on their faces.

My mind was swirling as I considered the possibilities and what-ifs of group hypnosis in the military arena, or in any arena for that matter, like advertising, or propaganda, or brainwashing, or at the end of an evening with a reluctant date. I didn't believe it possible until now, but I remembered someone came up with the idea of group-think a while back, and of course, there was Hitler. But I was just a college freshman, doing a little philosophizing of my own on the walk back to my dorm.

❦

Summer arrived, school ended, and I went to the little town of Seaside on the north coast of Oregon to help my brother fix up and run an old motel a friend of his had bought. We did enough fixing and painting on the place to make it passable and opened up for business. Sort of.

A lot of people were gallivanting around the country, and we developed a reputation as a good place to stay, especially since we'd trade lodging for grass, or hash, or mushrooms, or mescaline, or LSD. We weren't experimenting with drugs—hell no. What we did was conduct full-scale research all summer long, catching the people traveling between San Francisco and Seattle.

But we damn near drowned. It was the rain. It never quit pouring. I didn't know the sky could hold as much water as the ocean. It seemed that way at times, in fact, all the time, until the middle of July. Near August I got contemplative and made an attempt at becoming spiritual, or at least trying to ascribe some meaning to life other than fate being the bastard of death.

Our motel was a couple of blocks from the ocean. A promenade ran parallel with the beach from the north part of town to the southern part of town where it was forced to a stop by Tillamook Head, a lush green tree-covered mountain that jutted out into the Pacific. It always had a cloud sitting on top of it, like a mystic misty crown.

Every day after mid-July I'd end up on the beach at sunrise or sundown or anytime in between. I had a favorite little sand dune I'd sit on and try to engage in meditation, contemplation, or annihilation. Most of the time it made my head hurt because I was looking for answers to universally unanswerable questions: What am I? Who am I? Why am I?

I must admit some of the most spectacular and beautiful sunsets I have ever seen occurred right there on the north Oregon coast while sitting on that little sand dune. Maybe if I were more artistically inclined they would have inspired me. But never anything poetic or dreamy came of those sunsets, no undeniable desire to try to capture a small part of their unmatched beauty with words or oil paints or watercolors. I just couldn't reconcile the fact that all the waste from all the cities west of the Continental Divide drain into the vast indigo ocean in front of me, not to mention what goes on in the ocean itself, with any ideas of romanticism. So I reached the conclusion that, in all reality, the ocean is one gigantic cesspool.

Works for me.

One evening I strolled to the beach to check out the beauty of the sun kissing the sky good night. Trying to look spiritual and a seeker of cosmic truth, I sat on my customary sand dune; no shirt, no shoes, wearing only cutoff jeans and gazing wistfully out over the ocean. Seaside was mainly a resort town, and in the summer people flocked there by the thousands from Portland and the rest of the Willamette Valley. On this particular Friday night, a handsome young couple came strolling down the promenade toward me, their arms locked around each other's waist, swaying to music I could not yet hear. The woman was gorgeous, glossy-magazine-cover gorgeous. They stopped on the prom, not far from where I was perched, to revel in the magnificence of the shifting masterpiece in the sky. A ten-foot-wide sidewalk, the promenade is raised up about three feet at the back of the beach. An ornate concrete railing runs along the ocean side of the walkway, about two and a half feet high, with access ways down to the beach spaced intermittently along its length.

Without warning, this young woman turned a ghastly pale and began swerving while she stood in place. I realized that they hadn't been swaying in a dance as they approached me; they'd been staggering in an early evening drunk. And then this glossy beauty leaned over the railing and puked profusely, sound effects included, over and over, into the sand below. She finished up with the dry heaves and then slowly straightened, her eyes watering, her mascara running like black rivers through her makeup, snot hanging from her nose, hair disheveled, a mortuary shine on her face, and then went limp and collapsed into a heap, her friend easing her down alongside the railing.

I did have a revelation that evening while I was sitting on that sand dune on that lovely beach: it's what's inside that counts.

All summer our clientele had been transient hippies, which was fine, except no matter what substance I ingested, I was unable to attain a constant spiritual state, excluding the gorgeous lady puking; but that was only momentary and funny to the point of ludicrous. But life had to be more than pain and sorrow, death and dying, gaining and losing advantages and opportunities or tallying ledger sheets.

"The just shall live by faith!" proclaimed the exuberant young man in the motel courtyard. This young man had a buoyancy, a light, and a joy about him I had never seen in anyone, most notably myself. He was preaching holiness. And peace. And joy. And love, the kind not selfish. He was preaching Jesus.

For the first time in my life I chose to attend church on a Sunday morning. I went devoid of any substances, except coffee, which is acceptable everywhere. It didn't hurt any, was enjoyable, and I met Lynn Hopkins. Holy cow, holy guacamole, holy whatever. I'd never heard angels sing, but I'm pretty sure they'd have a hard time matching the velvet purity of Lynn's voice ringing like silver bells echoing off golden mountains, filling the valleys below and the sky above. And what came through that angelic voice was heartfelt every time and would bring tears to my eyes. The hardest thing for me to believe was that a woman like her lived in this world. Open, honest, truthful, kind, fearless, and guileless, she knew her ground and stood on it.

Everyone in her family went to that church. Mom and Dad, three brothers, and a younger sister. They were the happiest bunch I'd ever run across, and before long Lynn and I were close friends.

But it wasn't just she that would invite me over for dinner or to watch some football or to hang around; anyone one in the family would. They all knew that I was no saint—Lynn especially—but that didn't bother them. They were just themselves and accepted me as such, and as a result I had gained a little faith that life had something to offer.

And it occurred to me that spirituality may not be any more complicated than being happy, relaxed in who you were, and content in life. That is what I saw in Lynn, and she somehow quietly and slowly filled up the holes and put back the pieces in me that I had lost along the way. It's called, I believe, gentleness.

Her dad, Smokey, was a logger, had been all his life, except when he'd been fighting in World War II.

"Ever work in the woods, Daniel?" he asked.

"Fought forest fires in Montana."

"Well, that's nothing like logging in the brush, setting chokers on the downed timber."

"Chokers?"

"Twenty-five-foot-long one-inch line with a bell and a nubbin at the end, hanging from the butt rigging. You shove the nubbin under the log, throw the bite and bell over the top, put the nubbin in the bell, and cinch her down. That's all there's to it."

"Is that what you do?"

"I started there—everybody does—but now I'm a hooker."

These loggers have some strange lingo, I thought.

Lynn looked at me from the other end of the couch and smiled and then turned to her dad. "Maybe you should explain," she offered.

"Well, what I do is pick the roads and then hang the blocks from real sturdy stumps; gotta make sure they're real stout or Tony Z. up in the yarder will pull 'em right out of the ground. The haulback runs through these two blocks at the end of the road, bringing back the butt rigging. The rigging slinger stops the butt rigging, and the three choker setters hook a log. When they go to a safe spot, Smitty gives three toots on the gun and off they go, all day long," he said, his blue eyes twinkling, set deep in his tan, leathered face.

That explained it.

"How long you been at it, Smokey? I asked.

He pulled out an unfiltered Kool cigarette and lit it. "Eileen!" he hollered toward the kitchen. "How long we been married now?"

"Twenty-four years."

"Been at it twenty-five years," he said to me. "The only thing ever happened was a swinging choker bell hit my shoulder and chipped the bone. Want to give it a try? They're hiring right now," he said.

Fall was coming on, the motel was no longer fun, my brother was heading off to somewhere, and Smokey wasn't any bigger than me, so I figured I could handle it.

"Sure," I said as Eileen brought us fresh-baked apple pie.

"Go on up first thing Monday then and apply. Crown-Zellerbach's been around a long time and owns most of this county. Steady job, good benefits, good for raising a family," he said.

"I'll do just that," I said, wondering about the family part. Maybe he knew something I didn't.

🜚

The show, the area of downed timber, was usually a partial circle around the mountain the tower sat on. My first day out we were at the tail end of finishing a show. No trees, no foliage, no green, just stirred-up dirt and scarred and splintered stumps. It threw me into mild shock at first, and this was after 'Nam and bombs and napalm. The ghastly sight looked like the aftermath of Armageddon, but before long I got used to it and it became normal. Funny what we can get used to.

One day I was having trouble getting the nubbin under a log tight to the ground and with no choker hole anywhere. I managed to dig and shove until I got a loop of the choker line to poke out the other side.

"Abrams, need some help? My grandma could have that choker set by now," hollered Smitty the rigging slinger from somewhere out of sight.

"Be there in a minute. Don't get your panties in a bunch."

I vaulted over the log and could just get a grip on the choker line. I halfway stood, braced my legs, and reefed like hell. The nubbin sprang out like a striking rattler, hit my left canine tooth, and broke it off at the gum line. But I got the goddam choker set and hustled out of there.

"What you got in your hand?" asked Smitty.

"My tooth," I said and grinned, showing the gap.

"Let's see it." He looked. "Well, now you're not only slow like my grandma, but you're getting toothless like her too." Everybody laughed, and Smitty blew the go-ahead whistle. Jabber went like that all the live-long day.

Lynn was always doing surprising and unusual things, kind and helpful and selfless things, for me and other people; that's how she was. One time I'd been out on a forest fire on company land for three days. We'd gotten it under control, and only a few men were needed to keep an eye out for flare-ups, which weren't likely since it had started raining, the week-long type of pour down, which seemed to happen every week once summer ended.

The crummy, the loggers' bus, dropped me off at my one-bedroom cabin just as it was turning dark. I noticed that the lights were on. I didn't recall leaving them on, but I could have. I opened the door and found Lynn standing in the kitchen beaming as bright as any lighthouse on the Oregon coast, her blond hair tied back in a ponytail, her blue eyes sparkling and all aglow. She looked more beautiful in her jeans and long-sleeved flannel shirt than any glossy magazine cover girl I could remember.

I was black with soot and dirt, and the sweat that once soaked my clothes had dried to a vague crust, I smelled and looked like I'd aged ten years, my voice croaked, and my joints felt shot through with fire. I tottered on the verge of collapse.

The cabin was sparkling clean, warm, and inviting.

"Lynn!" I exclaimed, unsure of what I was seeing and not used to this kind of treatment.

"Hi, Daniel. They called my mom from camp and said you guys would be home soon," she explained before I could ask. "I thought you'd be tired and hungry, so I came over to fix you dinner. Had to climb in through a window, though." She giggled.

"There's hot water for a bath, if you want," she continued.

A hot bath waiting, the mouth-watering aroma of roast beef and apple pie, a cheery house, and Lynn. Near heaven, and something easy to get used to.

I looked at myself in the mirror before settling into the bath and wondered why she hadn't run away. The returned reflection shocked me. But she was like that, not concerned about outward appearances, only about what was in a person's heart.

In all the times I went to her house there was never any drinking or drugs, no cussing or fighting, not a hint of hostility. In fact, I think they even liked me, and after a while I felt like I wouldn't contaminate Lynn or her family.

She was sweet and pure and true, and I fell in love with her. It wasn't the all-consuming fire, eat-me-up-alive kind of love I'd known with Crystine. Lynn was a slow, sweet burn, a patient journey, a long-term trust, and I knew my heart could rest with her.

We were married not quite a year after we'd met. We put up a plaque in that little cabin and in every house we lived in since. It read: "Don't walk in front of me, I might not follow. Don't walk behind me, I may not lead. Just walk beside me and be my friend."

Worked for us.

Chapter Eighteen

With a new husband and work and night school and Holly and Davey rapidly approaching their teens, Crystine often wondered how her life would have been with Daniel. The answer lay unrecognized at her feet, vibrating up and all around her, and as the LA lifestyle, piece by piece, absorbed more and more of her being, those thoughts, in rare quiet moments, came along with more distance between them and carried less poignancy with each arrival.

Just stay busy; you'll be all right, she told herself.

Her mother had left her with two lasting impressions: the importance of education and the magical world of movies, and she took Crystine twice a month to the theater from the time she was able to understand speech. The movies were never a disappointment, always a thrill, and she grew up and watched Hollywood take over the world, a brilliant rainbow to be followed with a sure pot of gold at its end. Behind the magic, she understood that making movies was a business and tailored her education with the idea of working in that business. She was rewarded with a permanent position at ABC in the programming department. And she was on her way.

As always, Crystine was just . . . Crystine, acutely sharp, ever present, ever aware of her goals. She moved into management on her own merit, long before corporations were forced to establish equal-opportunity hiring practices.

She had a BMW convertible and designer sunglasses, and she and Jim had purchased one of the finest houses in an upscale neighborhood. Holly and Davey were progressing easily through school. She made it a point to stay away from the drugs flowing like a swollen river through Southern California. Whether they came under the guise of "flower power" or "ecstasy," she stayed away, allowing nothing to cause her to veer off the path toward her goal, which was to attain everything she wanted, though much of it as yet undefined.

But she was certain of what she didn't want.

She didn't want to ever feel her back against the wall again. She didn't want to ever feel the depth of grief as it overpowered her when her mother died. And she didn't want to ever, ever feel her soul wrenched asunder as it was the day Daniel had been taken away. Pouring her energy like water from a bottomless jar, she sought to insulate herself from future shock by wrapping herself in wealth and luxury and traveling and busyness.

Just stay busy.

So life was good, and busy, and held a denied emptiness that moved to deeper and deeper levels.

Jim burst through the front door, slamming it behind him. He reached to his left, grabbed the drapery cord and pulled them closed, and leaned his back against the closed door. It was midafternoon on a Saturday. Crystine looked up in surprise. "What are you doing? What's going on?"

He put his forefinger up to his lips. "Shhhh."

She set her book down, got off the couch, and parted the drapes to peer out the window. She grabbed the pull cord and opened the drapes.

"No, don't!" he shouted.

"What's wrong with you, Jim? There's nothing out there I can see."

He slid along the wall far enough to crane his neck around to see. "They . . . there will be," he stated with a slight stammer.

Crystine took hold of his arm, "Come with me to the couch. You need to settle down, and we need to talk."

She had noticed some bizarre behavior from him lately, bordering on paranoia. He hesitated and then nodded his head and took one step with her toward the couch. Then their window to the world outside exploded inward with the sound of thunder booming and the sudden screeching of tires. Shards of glass like thrown daggers sprayed the room. Crystine screamed, letting go of Jim's hand. He bent at the knees, getting low and looking out the window frame, and watched as a black sedan sped down the street, smoke billowing from the rear tires.

Davey came running down the hall and saw the floor covered with broken glass, the pieces like ice cubes or triangles or daggers. "Mom! Mom! Are you all right?" he hollered.

She had dropped to her knees and turned her tear-streaked face to him. "I'm not cut," she said. "Call the police." Davey went to her and gently helped her up, guiding her to the couch.

"No!" said Jim.

"What do you mean, no?" said Crystine.

Davey headed for the phone. "I'm calling," he said. "Someone shot out our window, and Mom could have been hurt, maybe killed, or didn't you notice the bullet hole in the wall over there?" He pointed. "I don't care what you think . . . or say."

Crystine had thought that she and Jim were on the same wavelength, moving along the same track.

He had nonstop energy, nonstop ideas, grandiose plans, and he sometimes carried them out. But he was beginning to wear Crystine down with his incessant energy. She'd met her match.

Way beyond ambitious, he was a man driven, on a mission known only to him, and seldom home. With Crystine establishing herself in the corporate world and Jim operating like a tornado, they were the proverbial two ships passing in the night. But they were acquiring things while losing sight of their chance at happiness.

"I don't know," he told the officer when the police arrived. "Someone drove by and shot the window. That's it; that's all I know."

The officer snapped his notebook closed. "You done, Fred?" he asked his partner, who was busy digging the slug out of the wall.

Fred gave the pocketknife a twist, and the bullet fell into his left hand. He dropped it into a small plastic bag. "Yeah," he said and turned to the other officer. "Anything else?" he asked Jim.

"No, sir."

"Mrs. Wheating?" he asked Crystine, seated on the couch next to Davey.

She shook her head slowly, "No, nothing," she whispered.

"All right. We'll try to find out what we can." He took a long look at Jim and then turned to Crystine. "Do you need to see a doctor, Mrs. Wheating? I could call an ambulance for you. I imagine this is quite a shock."

"No thank you, Officer. I'll be okay." Davey put his arm across her shoulders.

"All right, then," he said and, after examining the window frame one more time, softly closed the door behind him.

Jim stood in the middle of the room. Davey removed his arm from his mother's shoulders.

"All right, Jim, tell me exactly what's going on," demanded Crystine as she stood up. "Nothing random like this ever, ever happens in this neighborhood. It isn't the ghetto." Jim remained silent.

"It's drugs, isn't it, Jim?" said Davey.

"You stay the hell out of this," he said.

Crystine whipped around and looked at her son. "Do you know what you're talking about?" she asked him.

"Yeah, Mom, I do. They teach us about them in school. All the signs are there . . . in him." He jutted his chin toward Jim.

Crystine turned to face her husband. "Is it true? Have you gone far enough to jeopardize our lives?"

Jim raised his left arm and gestured toward Davey. "Who you gonna believe, me or the kid?" he asked.

"I am going to believe my son, and I'd appreciate it if you'd clean up this mess and get a new window installed," said Crystine. "Before dark."

No, Crystine didn't do drugs and didn't know anything about them, so she never recognized the high sheen in Jim's eyes. She thought at first that he was just really excited to be a family man and settling down, and she admired his boundless energy. But he was an addict. Cocaine had him, and his bizarre erratic behavior, as she thought back on it, confirmed the fact.

Six years after her second marriage, Crystine was finished with her second divorce. This time it was different. She wasn't in a hard place, with her back against a wall. Her career was on the upward swing and she could make it on her own. She didn't hurt or miss Jim at all, because in retrospect, she realized she didn't know him at all.

She wondered briefly if the marriage would have lasted, had they worked at it or if Jim hadn't become strung out or, better yet, had just been honest. And she understood at that moment that honesty was essential. Trust isn't possible without it, maybe not possible at all.

She wondered if working at a marriage was a valid concept or just an "en vogue" of current social philosophy, easily changed by the next blowing wind. Work at love? She supposed it could be valid, almost. But deep in her heart she knew better, for she had known love in its purity and knew that it flowed like electricity, having no choice but to travel to its attraction.

Love wasn't a decision, or a choice, it just *was,* and it required no analysis. She had known love pure and absolute, and to diminish it from that apex of creation was impossible to do. She knew this in that secret place in her heart where she still carried Daniel.

Chapter Nineteen

Our daughter Jenna was born ten months after Lynn and I were married. A blond blue-eyed darling, she took after her mother.

Ready or not, I was a father, and along with that came a new responsibility, the need to settle down and settle in. It was easy to do. Lynn knew how to be a mother, and that took away a lot of my anxiety. I wasn't sure if I was up to taking care of a brand-new person, never having had any previous training.

We talked about life, ours in particular, what we wanted, what was important to us, how we were going to handle the things to come. We decided that as long as we could make ends meet, keeping our needs basic, Lynn would stay home with the children and I would bring home a paycheck. It worked out fine. We always had more than enough of the necessities of life and never had any unpaid bills.

Of course, we didn't have two new cars or a big house on a hill in the middle of its own acreage. We didn't take vacations to exotic places around the globe or have a cabin on a lake or a beachfront condo, but we didn't care—we had our health and were content.

A high lead logging crew is made up of a hook tender, also known as a hooker, a rigging slinger, and three choker setters.

My father-in-law, Smokey, was the hooker of our crew. Sometimes he was like a ghost, spending all day in the back of a tough show, figuring out where, and sometimes how, to hang the tail blocks for the next road. Other times, he was an out-and-out pest, offering suggestions, pointing out a "better" way to do things, or simply barking orders and taking over. But he did know all the tricks and pitfalls of the trade, having worked in the woods all his adult life, and was always there if we got in a tight spot. He had a sense about the woods, and as a crew we developed this sense, a rhythm in working with each other, a mutual trust and respect acquired over time, an eye out for danger, all good things to have, as someone's life could depend on any one of them.

Sometimes in the winter the wind would blow with near hurricane force, and we were stuck with one of those days. The clouds hung nearly on top of our hard hats. Rain by the bucketful, driven horizontally into us by the fierce and relentless wind, coupled with the temperature hovering around the thirty-two degree mark, made for an all-around gloomy, miserable day. To top it off, we didn't have any lift on this road; that is to say, the butt rigging came back dragging on the ground. So now we had to yank the chokers free of the entangling brush before we could set them, doubling our work, doubling our sweat, and doubling our straining and aching muscles, ankles to shoulders. A tough and miserable day.

We'd hooked a turn of three good-sized firs, each about three foot in diameter, and Smitty, the grizzled old rigging slinger, sent 'em on their way, the yarder grunting and groaning with the effort to get them up the hill. Must have been too much of a strain for the old girl, because the butt rigging didn't come back right away. We waited, and a couple of guys lit cigarettes; one took a dip of chewing tobacco. We waited. Ten minutes went by. It was silent up on the landing.

"Looks like we got some ass time, boys," Smitty quipped. I didn't like the idea much, not in this weather, but I took a seat on a spruce stump. Bart sat on a log. Darryl plopped down on another log.

We waited a few more minutes, hoping the yarder engineer would signal us to come in. No luck. We sat. The wind and rain continued to hammer us out of a gun-metal gray sky, threatening to snow. We're beginning to stiffen up from the cold.

And that's part of logging, folks. Don't forget that both the toilet paper at the store and your house, all cozy and warm in winter, are built of wood.

Across from me on one of the logs sat Darryl Rudtke, a third-generation logger with no other aspirations in life. He was a little shorter than me, built like a bull and a hot shot by nature, and he loved working in the woods.

Today, though, he was just a tad bit sullen; maybe it was the weather, or that the butt rigging was on the ground, or maybe it was because his wife had been screwing the neighbor. In any case, he hadn't spoken a word all day, contrary to his usual bragging motor mouth.

It was still silent up on the landing.

With the lightning quickness of a surprised cat, Darryl leapt up on top of a huge fir stump. Standing as straight and tall as he possibly could with his face turned into the wind, he removed his hard hat and held it limply with his left hand down at his side. Raising his right arm up in the air, pointing his index finger at the low-hanging sky, he began twirling his arm in a broad circle. After a couple of complete turns, he threw his head back and hollered at the top of his lungs into the gray and dismal day, "Verily, verily, I say unto thee . . . *Get fucked!*" The rain beat his face into a reddish hue. Laughing maniacally, he put his hard hat on and sat down once again in silence. I damn near fell off my stump; thought I'd bust a gut laughing. Darryl didn't say another word the rest of the miserable day, which we had the good fortune to finish out.

I've never claimed to be a religious man. I've always thought of religion as one group of people pitted against another group of people, each group defining God and then setting up rules and rituals about how to please that definition in a most smug and self-righteous way. I could be wrong, but I think the gospel is about grace.

Anyway, that's the story of the "Sermon on the Stump," and old Darryl the Preacher (as he was naturally now called) never did get struck by lightning, as far as I know.

❧

We were nearing the end of the big timber. Even so, four-, five-, and six-foot diameter logs were not uncommon. Often three logs would bring a highway truck to its 78,000 pound net weight capacity. That's thirty-nine tons.

The fallers and buckers would run across a huge fir that had been down for eons, the wind having done its work in the dim and distant past. Fir would last forever in this wet climate and cedar nearly so, but spruce didn't fare so well.

They'd buck these giant fir blowdowns into log size. Some we'd load out; others we'd keep for wood logs. Many of us heated our homes with wood in the winter.

We came across one of these old blown-down firs on a sunny, early autumn afternoon, just lying there in plain sight at the back end of the road. We had plenty of lift on this show, and this old fir was sitting on top of the back-end mountain, level with the landing. We could look straight across and see Gunnar, the chaser, and Tony Z. at the controls of the yarder.

It was good enough that maybe they'd load it out; it certainly was a prime wood log, and big. Big enough to call for the inch and a quarter diameter bull choker. It came back by itself on the butt rigging.

Smitty blew the stop whistle, the single bull choker dangling from the butt rigging swinging back and forth. Darryl the Preacher and I went barreling in to hook the log and send it on its way. In and out, one log, one turn, done deal. I grabbed the bell of the choker, slid it up the line, and tossed the nubbin over the log to Darryl so he could poke it through underneath the log from the other side.

"Holy shit!" I hollered and dropped the bell, taking off at a dead run away from the old fir. Darryl peered over the top of it from the other side and wasn't far behind me in about the blink of an eye. A whole new world of possibilities had presented itself to us, and we sat for a minute discussing the best course of action.

A hive of honey bees had been prospering in this old log for more than a few years.

Smokey convinced us that the honey bees weren't too likely to sting us, as they'd been peaceful and dormant for quite a few years. If we were quick, we'd be okay, so Darryl and I snuck up on the log from the back end of it. I grabbed the choker and flipped it once more over to Darryl, keeping a wary eye on the bees, staying upwind from the hive. Here came the nubbin under the log, and I slipped it into the bell and strategically placed it near the hive. We sauntered back to a safe spot and nodded at Smitty, who then gave three short blasts on his whistle. The yarder started the pull as we sat on some stumps, ready to watch the show.

The yarder strained against the weight of the log as it pulled it up the mountainside. To compound the problem, its nose acted like a plow in the soft ground, all the while twisting and turning, slowing down, speeding up, moving herky-jerky, like a Brahma bull in its eight seconds of glory. It took several minutes for the behemoth to get home, riling up the bees but good, we supposed.

Finally, Tony slammed it down on the landing with a jarring thud, raising a cloud of dust that obscured the log. Gunnar didn't wait for it to clear. As soon as Tony slacked the line, he went hell bent in there, leaping on top of it like a man leaping onto the back of a bronco. Prancing forward a few steps, he bent to unhook the choker, his back to us.

In different weather we might have thought he'd been struck by lightning, maybe a bolt intended for Darryl the Preacher. Gunnar jerked straight up and kept on going, his boots about two feet off the surface of the log, landing a couple feet back of where he'd started. Waving his arms wildly in circles over the top of his head, gyrating his torso like a puppet with a loose hinge, he spun around toward us, turning the air blue with the curses he threw our way.

Taking a flying leap off the log, he ran like a demon was after him, arms flailing wildly, flinging more curses as he went, and ended up hiding behind the yarder, hollering and cussing at us so loud it echoed off the mountain side. We couldn't help it; we were rolling with laughter.

He certainly had a dilemma up there on the landing.

We recovered from our laughing spasms and settled back down to watch the rest of the show unfold. Tony had to climb down out of the yarder he was laughing so hard, the double-you-over kind. Gunnar cussed all the louder, perplexed as to how he was going to unhook that bull choker and escape the wrath of the bees, which by now had calmed down some.

Tony walked slowly up to Gunnar and placed his right hand on the poor fellow's shoulder. He had worked in those north coast woods for forty years and seen about everything there was to see, so we figured he was consoling him, laying out a plan to get the choker loose. Gunnar nodded, and Tony waddled back to the short ladder leading up to the cab of the yarder. Climbing it, he set himself down at the controls, still grinning. Revving up the diesel engine and then lifting the old fir so it was about thirty degrees from the horizontal, he cut it loose. That ancient giant slammed into the earth, causing a shudder we felt clear at the back end. Another cloud, only this time it was made of bees instead of dust.

Tony slacked the butt rigging down to the ground, leaned his head out the cab window, and hollered, "There ya go, Gunnar; you can unhook her now."

We near fell off our stumps guffawing as Gunnar waved his arms and gyrated around on the landing once again. He'd lost his hard hat during the first encounter with the bees but had picked it up when he ran behind the yarder. Now he lost it again, only this time he ripped it off his head and slammed it to the ground, turning the air even bluer than it was before. We didn't know if we could take any more, our stomachs hurt so bad by then.

The swarm of bees returned to the hive. We watched Gunnar sneaking up on them. This time he didn't mess with the working end of the bull choker; he just slipped the other end from out of the butt rigging. Taking a couple steps away, making sure he was in the clear, he stopped and turned toward us. Thrusting his right arm high into the air, he saluted us with the international high sign— the middle finger fully extended. We figured we had it coming, but it was well worth it as it induced another fit of laughter.

Paul Hakanson, better known as Hacksaw, another old-timer in the north woods, ran the log loader up on the landing. He was generally an ornery cuss, but every now and then he'd have a streak of mercy, and that day was one of those days. He got Gunnar's attention, waved him away from the bee log, and with the delicate touch of a piano player, gripped it with the loaders' grapples. Gently, but not easily, lifting it, the bees not noticeably disturbed, the bull choker still wrapped around it, he swung it around and set it down as gently as any mother putting her baby to bed.

Gunnar wasn't the type to hold a grudge, and by the end of the day he saw the humor in the whole scene. To show that he held no ill will, he managed to extract the honey from the hive by quitting time, enough for the whole crew to have a smacking, gooey, sticky good sample on the trip back to camp. It was the sweetest and purest I had ever tasted.

And the sweetness and the pureness of that raw and wild honey brought a pang to my heart, for it brought up the sweetest and purest memories of Crystine. And I understood, riding to camp in that dirty old crummy, way up in the north woods, that she lived in a tender secret place in my heart and always would, a truth I could not deny.

Chapter Twenty

Working on the landing as a second loader, I'd have time between trucks to read a little, if the logs didn't need a lot of trim work and were good sized. This was one of those times. I was sitting on a log, doing some reading.

The drivers got some free time too. Poking his face through the open window of the truck's orange cab, Old Leroy asked, "What ya reading there, Daniel? A love story?"

"Might turn out that way. I just started in on it."

Hacksaw gave two short blasts on his whistle, and Leroy started backing under the grapple. Time to go to work.

I have often wondered about authors. What makes one? Not colleges; they make technicians. So what makes a person sit down, set aside a piece of their life, and then risk it by writing a story that others may or may not find worth reading? Stories about anything, stories born out of the imagination or that fly out of fantasy, stories that create new worlds or new galaxies or a parallel universe, fixing them forever in the fabric of the human psyche. Like *Star Wars* or *Lord of the Rings*. Stories of heroes like Tarzan or James Bond that go on forever. Timeless stories like *The Wizard of Oz*, *Alice in Wonderland*, *Peter Pan*, and *Huckleberry Finn*.

What could be the makeup of these people who dare to enrich or expose or satirize the world? Madmen or Madwomen? Geniuses? Poets? Dreamers? Lovers? Haters? Jesters and clowns? All of the above? But I do think that one word could be consistently applied to the makeup of an author: eccentric.

And such was Ken Kesey, an author living somewhere south of Clatsop County in Oregon and most noted for *One Flew over the Cuckoo's Nest*. But I was reading his *Sometimes a Great Notion*, in between the trucks, the story of a logging family facing the challenges of everyday, workaday life. Not what you'd call mainstream stuff. The eccentricity was that the upheaval of the hippie Vietnam War era was still lingering and fresh in the social consciousness. He also had a psychedelically painted bus loaded up with his "Merry Pranksters," and they'd go on periodic jaunts across the country, just, can you believe it, for the fun of it. Eccentric, I'd say.

What captured my attention was that it nearly paralleled my life at the time: a logging family—Lynn and me, my father-in-law and his wife, my brother-in-law and his wife—living in the same neighborhood in the same small town, working high lead logging together, getting by.

It was made into a poignant movie, with major stars in the lead roles, filmed a few counties south, on the Siletz River, and it caused me to wonder. For a time I chalked it up to coincidence, until I could see that it was the first thread of a mysterious tapestry being woven into my life.

Chapter Twenty-One

At the very outset of her marriage to Jim, Crystine was determined to strengthen her position as a professional woman, able to provide good lives for herself and her children if it came to the point of them being alone. It had come to that. She was on her own and had no one to rely on, no one to help with hard times, no one to offer strength and comfort to, and no one to strengthen or comfort her. But she was used to that.

Over the last year she had felt as if she'd been in a heavyweight fight and was the one still standing. She didn't miss Jim and wondered if men were all alike. Once you became the "old lady," they lost interest—quickly—expecting all the fun while accepting no responsibility. She'd had enough and thought that maybe love was just another of life's many illusions, a dead-end twist in an endless maze.

A vivid image of Daniel drifted slowly and easily across her mind. She wondered if he would have lost interest and wished with all her heart that she had been able to find out that he wouldn't have. *Get back on track, kiddo; you've got business to tend to,* she told to herself.

Her mouth was dry, butterflies tickled her stomach, and her mind raced full throttle as she anticipated the questions and ran the tape of answers back and forth. Pausing, taking deep calming breath, Crystine opened one of the huge double glass doors and stepped into the lobby of Paramount Studios. She was greeted by a plush maroon carpet, walnut wainscoting that covered the lower half of twelve-foot walls, a soft glowing palatial chandelier hanging from the peak of the vaulted ceiling, casting a warm light on the intimidating space that spoke settled and assured opulence with authority.

Locating the reception desk, she marched up to it, imitating the authority of which the room spoke.

"May I help you?" asked the living mannequin from behind the reception desk.

"Yes, I have an appointment to see Mr. Furlong," replied Crystine.

The receptionist raised her arm, pointed down the hall to her right, and said, "Certainly. The elevators are down the hall, and his office is located on the fourth floor. There is a directory on the wall across from the elevator as you exit. Can't miss it."

Crystine smiled at her. "Thank you," she deadpanned and started down the hallway.

She wondered what the chances were of the receptionist ever becoming an actress. There were probably a hundred thousand breathing mannequins in the LA area. Big breasts were requisite, but she forgot to look, and she chuckled to herself as she approached the elevator doors. The amusement had loosened her up some and calmed down the butterflies. The doors opened, and she exited the elevator. *A little humor can go a long way,* she reminded herself, more relaxed.

Reading the directory on the wall, she headed down the short, wide, carpeted hallway to her right. She opened the glass door at the end of it into another reception area and walked in, her professional heels quieted by the off-white carpet as she approached the desk.

This mannequin seemed at least alert, if not quite alive. "May I help you?" She smiled almost genuinely.

"Yes. My name is Crystine Wheating. I'm here for an interview with Mr. Furlong," she stated in her most matter-of-fact tone.

"Oh, certainly . . . He's expecting you," she said as she pressed a buzzer. "Crystine Wheating for the interview, sir," she chirped toward the intercom.

"Have her come right in," replied a soft, melodious voice.

"This way please," mannequin number two said, moving from behind her desk down a short hallway.

Crystine followed with a relaxed, easy grace. Stopping in front of an oak door bearing an unassuming brass plaque that simply read, JACK FURLONG, the receptionist opened it and gestured Crystine inside.

Mr. Furlong stepped out from behind his polished and orderly mahogany desk, right hand extended. The head of business operations for Paramount Studios, he was not at all what Crystine had expected—not fortyish, not grim-faced, not a shark-like creature at all. She guessed his age to be around sixty-five, and he was bald on the crown of his head, the remaining fringe white like combed wool. A good six feet tall and not noticeably overweight, giving the impression of liveliness, he struck a hazy but pleasant remembrance in Crystine that she couldn't quite place. She felt at ease.

He peered at her over the top of no-frame rectangular spectacles, his alert clear-blue eyes twinkling. "Call me Jack," he said warmly as they shook hands. "And I'll call you Crystine, if that's all right."

"That will be fine," she answered.

"Mr., Mrs., Ms . . . . they're all so formal," he continued with a grin and slight chuckle. "Please, Crystine, have a seat," he said, gesturing at the leather-clad chair in front of his desk. He seated himself behind the desk.

Unassuming, thought Crystine, trying to get a firm read on the man.

"The world is changing faster than I can keep up with," he stated. "So you'll have to forgive me if my interview doesn't quite meet current protocol."

Caught by surprise by the comment, she simply nodded in response. *Hard to read*, she thought again, this time with a touch of anxiety. She sat quietly while Mr. Furlong seemed to study her as well, long enough to put her on the edge of uncomfortable.

"What's your favorite movie?" he asked out of the blue.

Totally surprised and unprepared, she had no time to form a situational answer, no time to pull a Paramount production from her memory. "*Gone with the Wind*," she blurted in honest response.

He eased back in his chair, folded his hands across his slight paunch, and beamed a grin lighting up his grandfatherly face. "When can you start?" he asked.

"What? I'm sorry . . . I mean . . ." she stammered.

Jacks grin grew bigger. "When can you start, here, at Paramount?" he asked.

Recovering slightly she said, "In two weeks, Mr. Furlong . . . I mean, Jack."

He chuckled. "Okay then; two weeks it is. Will that work okay, be enough time for you?"

"Oh yes, sir. That will be plenty. Thank you."

"All right then. Do you have any questions I may be able to answer for you?" he asked.

"I do," she replied. "How could you ask me just one question and decide to offer me the position on that single response?"

Jack smiled at her choice of professional words. "Why'd you hire me?" would have worked, but then, Jack was very down to earth.

"Seemed a little off the wall, I know, but all candidates are qualified regarding education, experience, and background, and all quite equally so. That makes even choosing the ones to interview a difficult decision-making process, one in which I consult, in a very extensive manner, with other high-level staff. These people have done all the reference and background checks, spoken to former employers, and gotten any other available information. The factors separating the candidates at that point are still very minute but are at least discernible."

I'm on a roll now, he thought to himself, trying not to chuckle.

"Now then, during a structured interview, the answers fall within a predictable range of commonality not to be unexpected." He almost laughed out loud on that one. "So," he continued, "being an extremely busy executive I must be efficient in my methods of operation." *She probably thinks she's listening to a textbook by now.*

"My question, then, is designed to reveal part of a person's character, designed so the response cannot be polished or covered over by forethought or practice."

Jack smiled openly and honestly. *Whew! Glad that's over.*

"Oh . . . well, thank you, I think," Crystine replied.

The dam broke, and Jack couldn't hold it in any longer and had to laugh. "You're more than welcome, young lady," he chortled.

Crystine grinned an I-don't-know-what-else-to-do grin.

Jack stood, extending his hand once again. Crystine followed suit. Standing, she took his hand, his grip firm but gentle as they shook.

"See you on the twenty-first, then," he said. "We'll call you the day before, just to make sure you haven't forgotten us."

Not a chance, thought Crystine. This was her dream job. If she thought she could get away with it, she would have kissed the kindly gentleman on the cheek.

"Stop by Karen's desk on your way out. She'll have one paper for you to sign."

"Thank you so very much," Crystine exclaimed. Jack smiled warmly as she left his gentle but commanding presence.

Jack sat down, relieved that he'd found the right person for the job so soon. He couldn't tell Crystine he'd simply taken a liking to her. His gut hadn't led him astray so far, and he trusted that it wouldn't now, protocol or no protocol.

She sat a minute, keys in hand, feeling stunned as she wondered what had really happened. She'd been offered the position and had accepted, yes, but the experience had been so painless and anxiety free—no sweat, as the saying goes. Crystine fired up the Camaro, retracted the ragtop, and headed for home, leaving the radio off and running the interview over in her mind, second-guessing herself.

She wondered if perhaps she had accepted too soon and thought about how she had been so utterly taken by surprise. She considered Jack's speech about interviews and their process. *Oh well, it's done now, nothing ventured, nothing gained,* she thought, reminding herself of the old and worn adage.

And she caught a brief but profound glimpse of the gap that exists between wisdom and knowledge, at the same time realizing she had no idea how to measure its width.

🙢

Now twenty-eight, Crystine was old enough to have shed a lot of naiveté but young enough to handle life's surprises. A recent divorce, maintaining a home by herself, raising two children—Holly entering her teens—and about to embark on a new career. The change was immense but by no means overwhelming.

Karen from Paramount had called her yesterday to remind her that she was to report to Mr. Furlong this morning at eight o'clock.

Filled with enthusiasm for the future, she wheeled her Camaro into the parking lot, pulled the keys from the ignition, checked herself in the mirror, took a deep breath, let it out slowly, and told herself to relax. Leaving the ragtop up, she stepped toward her new career.

Her bronze hair set back in a French bun, single diamond earrings glistening against her olive skin, her soft brown eyes quicker and bolder than usual behind her no-frame glasses, she stepped into the lobby of Paramount Studios and headed straight for the elevators, bypassing the resident mannequin. With her lithe, petite frame, clad in a pure white sleeveless blouse, a light yellow cotton skirt that hit just above the knees, glossy white open-toed shoes laced around the ankles, heels click-clacking on the polished marble hallway floor, she was immediately noticeable but not flamboyant. Professional.

She pushed the button to the fourth floor.

"Good morning, Crystine," piped the receptionist.

Startled that Karen remembered her, she quickly recovered. "Good morning, Karen," she returned, feeling a touch of regret for thinking of her as a mannequin and reminding herself not to judge a book by its cover.

"Mr. Furlong said to go right on in when you arrived," Karen continued, nodding toward the short hallway.

"Thank you."

Crystine walked silently down the hall and knocked somewhere between inquisitive and demanding on Jack Furlong's oak door.

"C'mon in," Jack's voice boomed from the other side of the door. Crystine stepped inside, softly closing the door behind her.

"Crystine!" he exclaimed, standing to greet her. They shook hands warmly. "Please, have a seat," he said, gesturing to the chair in front of his desk as he seated himself. "First of all, welcome aboard," he said.

"Thank you, sir, and I do feel welcome."

"Uh-uh, none of that. Please call me Jack," he said, beaming, happy that she felt welcome. He knew the value of having comfortable but not quite satisfied employees.

"Susan Lolich, our personnel director, will be here in a minute to brief you, have you endorse some standard documents, and introduce you to the person you'll be working with. I think you'll find him more of a mentor than a boss." Jack winked. Crystine's comfort level went up. The term mentor intrigued her as she envisioned an elderly gentleman, similar to Jack in age and demeanor.

On cue the buzzer sounded, Karen's voice audible over the intercom. "Susan is here," she said.

"Great, send her in," Jack replied. He gazed over the rim of his spectacles at Crystine. "If you ever have any problems, or just need to talk about something, my door is always open," he told her with undeniable sincerity.

Turn up the dial on the comfort level.

"Crystine? I'm Susan Lolich," announced the blue-eyed blond product of Southern California.

"Crystine Wheating," she replied, taking the personnel director's proffered hand.

They proceeded to what could only be described as an operating-room type of office space, sterile and devoid of feeling.

Crystine sat through the first-day-on-the-job ordeal of signing this and that piece of paper, listening to the past history and the future hopes of the studio, and being given a snapshot of its current place in the market.

That part over, she was more than ready to meet the person she'd be working with, wondering if he would turn out to be an actual mentor or just another egotistical boss who was defined by his office.

Right on cue again, Susan chirped, "That's that, then. Let's go meet your new boss."

Ms. Lolich tapped lightly on the next oak door further down the hall. "Come in," came an energetic reply through the opening. Susan held the door for her. *The moment of truth,* thought Crystine as she entered the office.

"Step right up," said Susan before closing the door.

He was standing, smiling cordially, and wasn't what she had expected at all. A big man, at least six foot two and a couple of hundred pounds, he was tanned, blond, apparently lean and fit but hard to tell exactly under his suit. His eyes weren't blue but were soft brown, like Crystine's. But it was his age that vanquished her expectations. He was at most ten years her senior, very likely half of that. He for sure wasn't an elderly gentleman. Crystine hoped he was at least a gentleman.

She took his hand and, shaking it, felt gentleness, strength, warmth, and . . . respect.

"Hi. I'm Bill Hopkins, head of Production Budgeting. Make yourself comfortable," he said, indicating the guest chair in front of his desk. "Please, call me Bill," he said. "All right if I call you Crystine?"

"Certainly . . . of course." She liked him so far.

"It probably seems odd to you, not having an interview with me," he opened.

"Yes, actually, it does," she replied.

Bill chuckled. "I thought as much," he said. "But there is an explanation. First, we don't hire a lot of new people. Our last hire was three years ago. Most people stay for their entire career. But don't misunderstand," he quickly added. "You're not the new kid on the block but are an integral part of the team." He paused. "And Jack, well, he's never been wrong with his choice."

"A very unusual interview," she said.

"He won't tell me his secret. Okay, I'll give you as brief and as painless a rundown on our department's operations as I can. Sharon gave you an overview?"

"Yes, and a very thorough one."

Bill smiled. "I know the first day on the job can be quite the information overload. Ready?" Crystine returned the smile and nodded.

"Our department is responsible for estimating the costs of producing a film, and, if the executives decide to actually make the movie, keep track of the production costs, trying to stay within budget."

Crystine knew full well how difficult that could be. She nodded.

"The actual process is, of course, much more complicated, beginning with negotiations for locations, personnel, goods and services, and payments on those goods and services, and ending with final disbursements and the closing of accounts.

"Goods include everything from medieval swords to yet-to-be-discovered spaceships. Services are rendered by actors, actresses, writers, producers, directors, set and costume designers, supervisors, technicians, gods and goddesses, and moguls. Lawyers also." He paused to grin.

"A whole lot of people and a whole lot of coordinated effort go into what is seen up on the screen. Like the tip of an iceberg. Movie locations can be anywhere on the planet."

That was what had interested Crystine. She was ready to travel, to experience more of the world.

"Your first assignments will be local, and your office—which I'll show you in a minute—will be on this floor." Bill paused, waiting for her reaction, hoping she wouldn't be disappointed.

Crystine smiled pleasantly, nodding her assent.

"After you've thoroughly learned the job, normally two years out, then you go on location, restricted to the states. After that, well, you could end up anywhere on the globe, eventually given your choice of where." After not a hint of negative reaction from her, he breathed an internal sigh of relief. "Any questions?" he asked.

"My adjustment period sounds more structured, and involves more time, than I had anticipated. Is that for a specific reason?"

"I'm glad you asked," replied Bill, feeling the depth of her probing intellect. "Initially, of course, it's for the training, so that you will thoroughly understand the mechanics of budgeting and budget control. Next, going on location in the states is designed to get you used to operating away from home, so to speak." He paused to give her a reassuring smile. "After the mechanics of operating away from corporate headquarters are secure, and by secure I mean when you feel comfortable with it, then you'll be ready to function in foreign countries, usually Canada or Mexico to start with. Make sense?" he finished.

"Perfect sense," replied Crystine.

"Welcome aboard!"

Crystine liked him even more. "I feel very welcome and comfortable. Thank you," she said.

"Good!" exclaimed Bill, the comfortable but not quite satisfied employee fully ingrained in his mind. "Before long you'll start to feel like family," he stated matter-of-factly.

Family—that struck her as a pleasant but unusual concept for a corporation to adopt, especially one so large, so visible, and so prosperous as Paramount. But it didn't strike her as being off the mark.

"Come on. I'll show you your office," he said, gliding out from behind his desk.

They proceeded down the hall to the third oak door away from Bill's. The brass plaque attached to it read CRYSTINE WHEATING. Surprised and pleased, she appreciated the efficiency and attention to detail it showed.

Bill opened the door. She halted, drawing in a deep breath. "It's beautiful," she said. A mahogany desk, more than ample in size, riveted her attention. An executive chair covered in leather sat behind it. Two smaller leather-covered chairs sat in front. A cream-colored carpet accentuated the desk, and matching mahogany glass-fronted bookcases stood along the wall. An east-facing window wall framed by light mauve curtains formed the background.

I won't have to fight the afternoon sun, she thought.

"This is very, very nice," she turned and said to Bill, covering her excitement.

"Go ahead; try it on for size," he said, gesturing to the executive chair, his excitement more evident than hers.

Crystine moved like a whisper behind the desk and settled into the chair as easily as a descending mist.

Bill took a seat. "All the internal phone numbers and extensions are in the right-hand drawer," he said, nodding in that direction. "A list of our most common vendors and other companies we do business with are in the left-hand upper drawer, I believe."

Crystine slowly opened it and nodded her head to verify.

"Ann, our secretary, will come in and run you through the use of the intercom, telephone system, requisition forms, and disbursement forms and give a more detailed and specific overview of our corner of the operation." He paused and looked at her for a long moment. "Well, do you like it?" he asked.

"It's more than perfect," she replied.

Smiling as he stood up from the chair he said, "I'll send Ann in right away then. I've also scheduled an eleven o'clock meeting in the conference room where you can meet the rest of the staff. Ann will show you where it is." Pausing a moment he continued, "I'm sure Jack told you that his door is always open. So is mine," he said as he stood up.

"See you at eleven," she said.

He moves very fluidly for such a big man, she thought as she watched him leave her office.

Her office! She'd had an office at ABC that could only be called run-of-the-mill, but this, this was an *office,* plush and spacious and waiting for her personal touches.

She took a deep breath, stepped to the window wall, and gazed over Los Angeles at the mountains to the east.

It is a remarkably clear day, she mused as she moved like a wraith, seating herself into her leather-clad executive chair. *Like a saddle.*

Where in the world did that thought come from? she asked herself. She'd never been atop a horse in her life.

꯭ꕥ

Thirty-three, fit and healthy, a young executive, Bill appeared to have the American dream conquered, but that was not the case. His divorce had hurt enough, but watching the turmoil it had caused the children was the worst part. He didn't miss Carla. True to her nature, she had initiated the proceedings like a Nazi on a blitzkrieg and had taken him for all she could in the process. But he had his kids, and that was what mattered to him. It would have torn him apart to see them singularly raised by their mother. Cautious from the wounding, he stuck to business in his affairs, public and private, as an insulator.

He buzzed Jack.

"Well, what do you think?"

"I think once again you've hit the target."

"Yeah, I'm good, aren't I. She'll work out okay, then?"

"Definitely, but she may be a little overeager," answered Bill.

"All right. She'll be okay, trust me."

"Always do. See ya, Jack."

Bill leaned back in his chair, fingers laced together behind his head, and wondered what kind of person Crystine would turn out to be, her face fixed firmly in his mind.

Chapter Twenty-Two

It was a crisp, cool, invigorating fall morning, and most wondrous of all, the sky was cloudless and a deep azure blue. In the Pacific coastal mountains, the sight was an extreme rarity.

Off in the distance, to the west, fingers of mist curled around the tip of a mountain peak in an early morning caress.

I'd moved out of the brush and setting chokers and was now second-loading for old Hacksaw up on the landing. In between hooking the piggy-back trailers to the truck, having the driver move ahead or back some to balance the load, counting the logs after the load was complete, and a fair amount of BSing with the drivers, I'd busy myself sawing limbs and broken ends off landed logs with my chainsaw.

Intently operating at full throttle, limbing a huge Sitka spruce with six-inch diameter limbs, I was buzzing along, my right leg extended out behind me, my foot on the edge of the road.

We had a gypo trucker, an independent contractor, come up for a load that morning. Hacksaw blew the whistle for him to come back and get loaded. I didn't hear it, didn't hear the truck's two short blasts either. Suddenly, my right foot got twisted and pinned so I couldn't move it. I tossed the still-running saw aside, squatted down on my left leg, and looked back. That damn truck had my foot pinned and was still backing up, slowly, and the second tire was ready to take the place of the first. Then, if the driver didn't hear me holler or otherwise notice my dilemma, the front tire would join the party! I figured neither my foot nor my leg would hold up to such abuse, and so, mustering all the strength I possibly could, I yanked with all my might trying to pull my foot free. Ka-pop! I succeeded!

I also succeeded in splintering my shinbone from ankle to knee, like a popsicle stick would splinter if you twisted and pulled it at the same time.

The force of yanking my foot free, coupled with the bolt of pain that followed, shot me forward, leaving me draped over the spruce log I'd been knocking the limbs off of.

I froze in place, didn't dare to move, couldn't have if I'd wanted to. The pain shot like jagged edges of electricity zapping through me and searing every nerve ending as it traveled up and down and swirled inside and outside my body until time suspended, and the pain became my world. I managed to get turned over with my back against the rough bark of the spruce, both legs extended out on the ground in front of me.

I no longer noticed that it was still a beautiful day.

Looking through bleary eyes, I saw the trailer dangling in the air, held by the tongs of the loader. I couldn't get to it to hold the tongue steady while the truck backed into it to hook up. Hacksaw, not having a lot of patience, tooted his whistle at me. I didn't look at him, didn't move.

The truck driver looked down at me sitting there and noticed something was wrong, by the grimace on my face most likely. He got out of the cab, sauntered over to me, squatted on his haunches, and asked, "You all right?"

"My leg got broke." I ground the words out between gritted teeth and then pointed at my right leg, "This one here."

He leaned a little closer.

"Don't! Don't you touch it!" I gasped.

"C'mon Daniel, you're bullshitting, right? Playing a joke on me, aren't ya?"

"This ain't no joke, Roy. I wish to hell it was. The damn thing's broke for certain," I wheezed.

"I'll go tell Hacksaw. You stay put now," he said hurriedly. I managed a small grin on that one. Wasn't likely to be going anywhere soon.

I liked to wear "corked" boots with eighteen-inch high lace-up tops. Turned out to be a good choice; it helped keep my shattered tibia in place.

The boys loaded me on the crummy and drove me down the mountain to the hospital.

Bam! A shot of morphine in the ass first thing. I didn't protest any as the searing pain subsided.

The doctor couldn't set my leg as it had splintered and not snapped. He put a cast on it just as it was, removing my corked boot first, of course.

So there I was with my right leg in a cast from my crotch to my toes, summer coming on, and me in my mid-twenties.

Hell revisited.

After three months the doctor fitted me with a paddy-bear brace, two steel rods attached to a heavy-duty shoe that ran up each side of my lower right leg. These attached to a padded brace that buckled on my knee.

I walked and walked with this brace on, pounding that bone together to help it knit as good as it could. I'd walk down on the beach to spend time on my private sand dune. My leg needed a lot of knitting, and I was off work for a year.

I kept busy other ways, attending the local college, practicing the guitar, stoking the wood stove, pestering Lynn. Some of my classes at the local community college were very strange. One "professor" said, "You're going to be unhappy anyway, might as well be unhappy with money." Another in an economics class said, "It's our job to increase the wealth of the stockholders." Neither prospect appealed much to me, being unhappy or trying to make other people rich. After my leg healed up, I went back to driving a log truck.

And Lynn and I discovered during that year that we actually *liked* each other and could get along, day after day, just fine, a realization that usually takes years for most couples to discover, if at all. Shortly after I returned to work, Jason was born, a real motor scooter and a sheer joy to watch as he grew. Jenna liked him right off too, and we didn't have to worry about sibling rivalry.

We had recently bought a house in Astoria, a little town full of Finns and loggers and pulp mill workers situated on the south side of the Columbia River where it drains into the Pacific Ocean.

From our back porch, we could look out at that Columbia, the view near breathtaking on a bright sunny day, which numbered about sixty a year. It was still the north Oregon coast.

Lynn and I and the two kids were settled in, had a "good holt," as the saying goes in logger lingo. I had a job I sort of liked, Lynn was happy keeping the home fires burning, and Jenna and Jason were growing, healthy, happy, and being kids. Life was good.

There weren't too many, but a few days I'd have to stay home and tend to the babies. Usually Lynn would have to be not-able-to-get-out-of-bed sick before that would ever happen. But on the rare occasions when it did, I was never so high-strung or exhausted in my life by the end of day, 'Nam excluded of course! It ran me ragged. For me it was a constant response to crisis, a constant vigilance against disaster. Kind of like being in a war. Clean this, prepare that, wipe this, mop up that, mess after mess, without tearing my hair out, and always with sweetness and a smile.

Being a homemaker is no easy task, and not one to be taken lightly or disrespected. Lynn worked every bit as hard as I did, except that I got Saturdays and Sundays off. My respect and appreciation for her deepened, and she always smiled and never once tore her hair out.

A dozen years had gone by since my dad left us high and dry up in Libby. One day he showed up, unannounced and unexpected.

I couldn't hate him in my heart, revile him with my words, or deny him his grandchildren. He was my dad, alive and well, and I was glad to see him.

Lynn made him feel as welcome as if she'd known him all her life. She was genuine and kind, and she treated everyone she met that way, from Oregon state senators to daughters of Country Hall of Fame singers to my rowdy friends and to homeless people. She was sweet and kind and tough. Full of love, wrapped in leather.

We had a good time with Dad over three days, enjoying one another's company, and the kids thoroughly enjoying Grandpa. It turned out to be a real family reunion. I don't even remember what time of year it was.

He never explained why he did what he did, why he'd up and left. I didn't ask for an explanation, figuring that he'd tell me the story if he wanted to. Besides, it was in the past. Some pieces of the past I could put behind me and close the door. Others, I couldn't, no matter how hard I tried.

Dad headed back home to South Dakota, near his childhood roots. I guess we all somehow or in some way, get back there. He did let me know he'd been on a ten-year drunk down in Los Angeles. That in itself would be enough hell for two or three men, at a lifetime each.

Chapter Twenty-Three

An old log-truck driver by the name of Clyde Morehouse lived down the street. A young log-truck driver by the name of Vince Desoto lived a little further down the street. Clyde liked homemade wine, was adept in its making, and always had an ample supply. Vince liked homegrown grass, had a basement full, and always had an ample supply. Between the two of them, they could occupy a lot of my spare time, but I was careful not to let it get out of hand.

One of life's many strange circumstances came about on a fine summer afternoon. Vince, Morehouse, and I were hauling from the same loader operator, a demon by the name of Jack Wilson. There'd been times I'd seen the man in such a frenzy that he'd literally be foaming at the mouth. He had his diesel engine revved to the max from the first turn of the key in the morning till he blew off the last truck at night. He'd toss logs around like matchsticks, on the landing and onto the trucks, timing how long it would take him to finish a load and damn near working his second loader to death. Jack Wilson wasn't easy to get along with. Crown-Zellerbach loved him, though; he was high production.

One particular sunny Friday afternoon I was barreling back for my and Wilson's last load of the week, everyone getting impatient to get the weekend started. Along came Desoto, milking the clock, nursing his last load in to the sorting yard. He flashed his lights at me, so I pulled over into a turnout. He stopped alongside, rolled down his window, and stuck out his definitive Italian face, drooping moustache and all. "Whorehouse is right on my ass, can you slow him down a little?" he asked. Of course, most everybody referred to Morehouse as Whorehouse or Outhouse, but I stuck to Morehouse.

"Maybe," I replied and then asked him, "Why don't you just speed it up some?"

He paused briefly before blurting, "Good idea, Daniel! Hey, you coming over tonight, help me cut up that burl for a clock base?"

"Yeah, probably," I said and then shot, "See ya."

"Hey, Abrams," Vince yelled before I could pull away. "Want a hit?" he asked, sticking a joint out his window at me.

"Not while I'm driving, Vince," I told him for at least the tenth time. "See ya tonight probably," I said as I pulled away, figuring I'd better try to slow old Morehouse down some. Vince wasn't likely to be in much of a hurry and didn't need the hassle of someone on his tail.

As I continued on my way out to the demon loader I spotted a roiling cloud of dust coming at me with barely visible headlights blinking on and off. It was Morehouse driving at a clip that would ordinarily be considered reckless. But it wasn't. The guy had driven these mountain roads for a quarter of a century.

Once he got close enough he flashed his lights in rapid succession, making double sure he got my attention, and then blasted his air horn to boot.

I pulled over into another turnout with my window up, waiting for the dust to settle before I rolled it down.

Morehouse is an expressive person, and a lot of it would show in his face, which was somewhere between Italian, Spanish, and Irish, if I had to guess.

Bald on the top of his head, he never combed the fringe of the dark brown tufts of the remaining hair, which was always on the verge of needing trimming but never seemed too long. And he always had a couple of days growth of beard on his face, always—never more; never less. His dark brown eyes shone with a glint of more than his usual wildness.

He looked at me through my now open window and hollered, "Hey, Abrams!"

"What?" I yelled back, feigning impatience.

"Do you suppose if they made a salve out of pig fat, they'd call it oinkment?"

Laughing like a kid at a carnival, he didn't wait for an answer but gunned his engine and shot away, the dust cloud in place.

I was laughing so hard at the spontaneity and wit of it all that tears sprang up in my eyes. I didn't slow him down any, but he sure did me. It took a few minutes to recover from that journey into surrealism, and Jack Wilson wasn't too happy about me being late.

I paid no attention to him and backed up under the loader as usual. He grabbed the unloading strap and jerked the trailer free of its bed. I pulled ahead and the second loader grabbed the tongue of the trailer, holding it steady as I backed into it. Coupled securely, George cleared out of the way and Wilson let the trailer slam to the ground, rocking the cab of the truck with me in it. I took my sweet time climbing out, slowly walking to the back of the truck and uncoiling the air hoses.

"He's got an appetite for you like a rattlesnake for a rabbit," old George said as I hooked up the air hoses to the trailer.

"That right," I replied and got back in the cab.

Jack was intense and had a fierce reputation. He started slamming logs down on the bunk with more than his usual maniacal intensity. I guess he thought he was going to teach me a lesson. One thing that really gets my hackles up is someone playing boss with me when they ain't, and Wilson was no boss.

Now, no self-respecting logger would ever admit to having a pecker any smaller than that of a horse's. In fact, smaller logs were called just that, pecker poles, and Jack was throwing quite a few of them on my truck. I was inspired to have some fun with such a childish notion.

Jack finished up and tooted his whistle, signaling me to pull ahead. I cleared, got out of the cab, threw the chains over my load, and finished by cinching it down with the binders, taking care of my business.

Jack was foaming at the mouth, throwing logs around the landing. From a safe distance I hollered and waved my arms at him until I got his attention. He stopped.

"What!" he barked, glaring at me with a killing look. I moved very slowly up to the loader; that way I wouldn't have to yell at him. It got real quiet when old George shut off his saw so he could listen in.

Jack was about twenty-five years my senior and had been a logger all his life.

"Say, Jack," I started.

"Whadda ya want?" he barked again.

"Well I . . . I was wondering."

"Ya, what!"

"Does your pecker reach your asshole?"

He faltered for a split second and then said, "Goddam right it does, and then some. What the hell's it to ya?" he blurted, puffing up his chest a little.

"Well, that means you can go fuck yourself."

He looked like he'd been punched in the gut. His eyes bulged out as his face changed hues from pink to red to crimson and finally to purple. Beads of sweat broke out on his forehead. He wheezed for breath.

I grinned at him real big, turned around, casually strolled back to the cab, climbed in, and started to pull away. Looking in the side mirror I saw Mr. Wilson staring after me—if looks could kill—so I thrust my left arm out the open window and offered him the international high sign.

Glancing out the window I saw old George doubled over, like he'd been punched in the gut, only this was from laughter, probably the best he'd had in years.

I guess Jack didn't have a coronary over the matter, I was afraid for a short while he might. His face hadn't changed from purple the last time I saw him in my side mirror. Anyway, he was back at work the following Monday. I didn't haul from him for a while. Guess he dropped a hint to the truck boss that he didn't want to see me, which didn't hurt my feelings any.

But the day finally came around. I got to camp before daylight had broken. Checking the dispatch list, I saw that I was scheduled to haul from Wilson. *Could be more than a routine day,* I thought as I headed out to Biddle Creek.

Jack was in his usual frenzy by the time I arrived. He saw my truck, idled down, set his tongs, and whistled me back. I backed under the tongs of the loader. Wilson grabbed the unloading strap and lifted the trailer off the truck. I let out the clutch and started to pull ahead. Somehow, before I was clear, the trailer broke loose from the grip of the tongs and came crashing down on the back of the truck.

Imagine a teeter-totter. Imagine a person on one end of it, seated on the ground. Imagine another person jumping from the top of a two-story house on to the other end. Imagine the sudden thrust of force driving the seated person up into the air.

That was me.

The weight of the trailer slammed the back end of the truck to the ground. The cab flew up, reaching the peak of its explosive arc at about forty-five degrees from the horizontal. The problem was, when the truck stopped, I didn't, the upward thrust trying to keep me going. I gripped the steering wheel white-knuckle tight with both hands. Ain't no horse could have bucked as violently as that truck. It felt like my arms would rip loose from their shoulder sockets!

The upward thrust, its abrupt stop, and the resultant downward force caused my back to arch severely backward. The truck slammed down to the ground and I followed, still gripping the steering wheel. I hit the seat at the precise angle and with enough force to cause a jarring pain in the lumbar area of my spine. I heard something crack.

Stunned, nauseous, momentarily paralyzed by the pain, I sat still. My mind was foggy, almost nonfunctional; my instincts told me this was a big one. I vaguely heard Wilson leaning on his horn, his innate impatience prevalent.

"You okay, Abrams?"

"Huh?" I looked over at the face of grizzled old George framed in the window.

"You okay?" he asked again.

"Oh . . . yeah . . . fine, just a little shook up is all. What the hell happened, George?"

"The unloading strap slipped out of the tongs," he flatly stated and disappeared.

I turned painfully around to look out the small back window. Sure enough, Wilson had another grip on the unloading strap. I nodded at George, and he signaled Wilson, who then lifted the trailer without incident. George stabilized the suspended trailer, I eased back, and we made the hookup. I climbed, very slowly and very carefully, out of the cab, barely able to walk. As I uncoiled the air hoses, I looked up at Jack the Demon. He wouldn't look me in the eye, but I would bet he was feeling damn smug about then. The bastard.

I managed to finish out the day and then sporadically made it to work over the next few weeks. With a lot of coaxing from Lynn, after she'd seen me driven to my knees several times by the bolts of pain, I went to see the doc. My instincts proved true. I had a couple of cracked vertebrae in my lower back. On top of what was previously there, that put an end to my logging career. No more driving, no more logging, over—dead and done. Only this time it wasn't just me. I had Lynn, Jenna, and Jason. We had just begun paying on the mortgage of the house we were going to make our home, where we were going to live and love, raise our kids, and grow old.

So much for plans.

Twenty-eight years old, unable to work, back trouble for the rest of my life.

So much for hopes.

Next step? No idea.

Chapter Twenty-four

"Are you nervous?" asked Nikki, helping her with final preparations. "No," replied Crystine, "Are you?"

"Of course not. This is the third time I will have been your bridesmaid, remember?"

"Third time's a charm, they say," Crystine replied, the nervousness in her voice more than the flippancy could cover.

Deciding to jump in the stream, Nikki said, "To be totally honest, girlfriend, I am a little nervous."

"About what? You look gorgeous."

"No, no . . . about you. Do you think he's the one . . . that this is the one?"

Crystine stopped what she was doing. Carefully placing the hair brush on the dresser, she turned to her friend. "Nikki dear, I'm entering this relationship with my eyes wide open, and so is Bill. We've both been around the block, and we're mature enough to know that a relationship can't be sustained on sex alone. In fact, we haven't slept together yet, believe it or not."

Nikki raised a brow in disbelief.

"Honest. We've talked extensively about what we want and need from our marriage. We've discussed our goals as partners and individuals. We've come up with plans for our kids. Yes indeed, I think this will definitely last. And if it doesn't, well, I won't have lost much, if anything at all."

"Except maybe part of your heart," replied Nikki softly.

"What? I'm sorry; what did you say?"

"You won't have lost anything, except maybe some of the gentle places in your heart," Nikki said, afraid that her friend was locking up her feelings.

Crystine looked up at her. "It's time," she stated.

"Is he fun? Spontaneous? Exciting?" Nikki asked, almost in desperation.

Crystine didn't want to answer. She didn't want to even think about the question.

He's no Tyrone Power, she playfully thought to herself, a warm memory of her mother bringing comfort. *Or Daniel Abrams,* she thought. Caught totally by surprise, she had no idea where the thought had come from, or why. She only knew she could never forget him, ever.

"Nikki, I've known Bill for a year. He's mature, deliberate, and very cool under fire, everything I want in a man . . . in a partner . . . now."

⚜

Light from the low-angled sun filtered through stained-glass saints bathed the interior of the Catholic church in soft light. Burned into the structure by countless thousands of masses, the aroma of incense teased the air. The organist struck up "Here Comes the Bride." Crystine took a deep breath, exited the waiting room, and entered the rest of her life. The colors of the saints painted fleeting rainbows on her pale yellow chiffon gown as she walked in step with the music toward the beautifully adorned altar and her patiently waiting husband-to-be.

Absolutely radiant, thought Bill as he watched her approach through adoring eyes. He was not a religious man. When Crystine asked him if he had a church preference he had teased her with the reply "white stucco," and so she arranged the ceremony and he arranged the honeymoon. The kids would stay with Bill's parents in Thousand Oaks.

✿

The weather was crisp and clear and brilliant, the sun a ball of molten bronze in a pale blue sky, an unusual touch for this time of year as they rode north on the Pacific Coast highway, Bill comfortably in control of his BMW sedan.

Crystine stared out the window at Malibu passing by. She had never been to San Francisco and had no idea what to expect over the long weekend, but she did know that whatever it was, Bill would have it meticulously planned. She knew he loved her, but not with all his heart. Parts of it he kept protected, as she did hers, from the possibility of further wounding. But, with a dash of guarded optimism, she thought this marriage could last, if they worked at it.

Noting her pensiveness, Bill asked, "Happy?"

She turned dreamily to look at him. "Oh, yes, of course. I was just thinking about us, our future, our kids. About how our lives have changed . . . for the better, I'm sure."

"Everything is in place," he responded.

"You mean for the weekend?"

"Well, yes, but what I meant was legal papers, property-ownership transfers, company stock transfers, insurance papers—all the documents that needed to have your name on them; you'll just have to sign them when we get back to LA."

"Oh, Bill, you're so thoughtful and so caring, and I love you for it," she said, her smile one of genuine affection.

"Lyin' Eyes" finished playing off the Eagles tape Bill had plugged in. "Desperado" followed. Crystine listened closely to the mournful lyrics, the desperation in them. Inexplicably, the song triggered memories of Daniel, causing her to sit up a little straighter in her seat, able to pay more attention to the words. She could picture him on horseback in a snowstorm. She wondered what might be going on inside of him by now. *Maybe someday I'll get to Montana,* she thought, blushing inwardly for having such imaginings on this, her wedding day.

The Golden Gate Bridge reflected the rays of the setting sun, subduing all else into background.

"It's absolutely gorgeous!" exclaimed Crystine.

"This is just the start. This city is one of the most fascinating places on earth," he said, looking forward to showing it to her. Bill loved San Francisco, wishing someday to move here, but home was where the work was, and work in LA treated him, and now Crystine, extremely well.

"I like Frisco already," Crystine quipped, breaking in on his thoughts.

"Let's get to our suite, unload our stuff, and have some dinner, okay? We've got a full schedule ahead of us, and we'll need to keep our strength up." He winked at her. The meaning wasn't lost on Crystine, and she flashed him a mischievous smile.

The valet and bellhop appeared the instant the silver BMW pulled to a stop in front of the Queen Anne hotel, an historic Victorian offering views of the Golden Gate Bridge and the bay and within easy walking distance of Fisherman's Wharf.

She stood breathless at the suite's threshold. "It's beautiful . . . gorgeous." Before she could blink, Bill lifted her up in his arms. She giggled. "What are you doing, sir?" she quipped.

"Carrying you across the threshold, where yonder I shall be ravished by your love," he replied.

Crystine giggled again and then kissed him lightly on the cheek. She hadn't seen this playful side of Bill before.

Carrying her to the middle of the main room, he gently set her down on the leather sofa, and taking a seat beside her, he enfolded her in his arms.

"It's absolutely gorgeous," she exclaimed once more.

"Might as well get used to it," he said. "You'll be staying in places like this when you go on location."

"Really?" she replied with a tinge of disbelief covered by surprise.

"The studio takes good care of us, and you're ready to go much sooner than most—congratulations!" Bill said.

"Thank you, Bill. I thought my apprenticeship would last another year. I had no idea . . ."

"Let's go have dinner, shall we?" he said with a wink.

"Whatever is your pleasure," she replied with another mischievous smile. They stood up off the couch. Her body pressing up against his made it hard to refrain, but he managed to keep it to one light kiss. "Dinner it is, then," he replied. She put out her lower lip in a mock pout, and Bill chuckled. They hurriedly unpacked, took the elevator to the lobby, and strolled arm in arm into the luxurious hotel restaurant.

They had dined together often over the past year—part pleasure, mostly business. Tonight's dinner was purely for pleasure, and Bill had pulled out all the stops.

"Yes, monsieur?" asked the host.

"Reservations for Mr. and Mrs. Hopkins," he replied, beaming at Crystine. She returned the same intensity of light.

"Oui, monsieur. Right this way, please." Flitting out from behind the podium, the garçon led them into the candlelit dining room. A single crystal chandelier hung from the high ceiling in the center of the room, reflecting the soft lighting. Unobtrusive mood music wafted smoothly through the air, its source indeterminable.

Their host, dressed in a black silken jacket with matching slacks, a white shirt with ruffled sleeves and front, a black bow tie, and a red cummerbund wrapped around his waist, gestured with perfect grace at an elegant dark mahogany table lit with a single candle in the middle. "Here monsieur, madame," he said with a slight yet precise bow.

It was perfectly situated, looking out at the famous bridge and the now-darkened bay that it spanned. The night was absent of its usual fog. The lighting on the bridge transformed it into an object of art, its function completely absorbed by its beauty.

Ships and boats anchored in the bay and in their slips directly below them, added a twinkling dance of lights, giving the scene a perception of Christmas.

Bill slipped around behind his bride, pulled the chair out for her, and then gently pushed it against the backs of her knees, seating her comfortably.

While he moved to his side of the table, Crystine looked pensively at the substantial diamond on the third finger of her left hand, reflecting on it as the candlelight reflected off it. Dazzling, and certainly the largest and most expensive wedding ring she'd ever owned, she hoped it would be the last. Looking across the table at her husband looking at her, they smiled in unison, offering her some assurance.

Bill ordered a glass of Dom Perignon and the famous Full Sail Fisherman's Wharf Platter, heavy on the oysters.

Crystine smiled. "Do those really work?" she asked demurely.

"What?"

"Oysters."

"I don't know for sure, but it certainly won't hurt to try," he answered with a broad grin.

"Well, if they're good for you, they're good for me!" she retorted playfully, ordering the Petite Fisherman's Wharf Platter along with a small filet mignon to go with her customary glass of merlot.

The dinner was a banquet of perfection, delicious, quiet, unhurried, and romantic. With the hunger of their palates sated to the balance point of just right, their hunger for each other moved from a low rumble to a full growl.

❧

Crystine again drank in the stunning appropriations of the penthouse suite. Not adorned with an air of temporary frivolity, no heart-shaped water bed with a red satin cover, no mirror on the headboard or ceiling; it was not a Valentine card brought to life. It spoke of timelessness and permanence.

The bed was a huge four-poster of deep, rich mahogany, cloistered in its own room. The headboard was shelved and had its own music system with a discretionary selection. A dozen red roses lay on the cream-colored chenille bedspread, its fringes embroidered with heavy mauve thread. A dresser and a nightstand, also of deep rich mahogany, stood by both sides of the bed. On each nightstand a tranquil lamp rested, adorned by a stained-glass shade from Tiffany's. A mahogany cabinet concealed a state-of-the-art television and stereo set.

The carpet, a rich dark maroon, was offset by cream-colored drapes. Currently closed, they covered a sliding window wall that opened onto a balcony overlooking the bay. The main room was earthen-toned with a splash of orchids here and a splash of lilacs there, their vases not garish, but tastefully subdued. A crystal chandelier hung from the center of the room. Two candles in silver sconces were placed on the four-seat mahogany table, a silver bucket of ice containing a liter of Dom Perignon between them. A Moroccan leather sofa faced the window wall, a low table in front and end tables at each side, all of highly polished mahogany.

On the opposite wall, two maroon wing-back chairs, upholstered in velour, faced the wood-burning fireplace.

An ornately carved mantle of white marble settled the fireplace into the wall.

A hot tub, waiting to soothe and embrace, raised thin inviting mist in an anteroom off the main bath.

The suite was welcoming, warm, and cozy within its spaciousness.

Crystine's tension began to seep away. A monumental day in her life now completed, the night awaited exploration.

"Let's have some champagne while we relax in the hot tub," she whispered as she and Bill snuggled on the sofa, gazing down at the velvety blackness filled with the twinkling lights of the ships.

Bill nodded. "Why don't you go on in. I'll follow with the champagne after I call room service."

"Room service?"

"I'll have them start a fire. I'll open the window, and it'll be cool enough in here to enjoy it by the time we get out of the hot tub. Help us cuddle."

"Perfect," Crystine replied, kissing him on the cheek and then moving languidly toward the hot tub anteroom. She undressed and eased into the welcoming water. Leaning back and closing her eyes, she let the rest of the day's tension drain out of her. She opened them just as Bill was slipping into the water, holding a glass of chilled champagne out to her in the dim light.

He shifted his glass from his left to his right hand, and they hooked elbows.

"To us," he said.

"You and me, and all of our days."

Gazing lovingly into each other's eyes, they sipped champagne in perfect synchronization, beginning the night's ballet.

"I love you," Bill said, leaning forward to kiss her softly on the mouth. She responded immediately and totally. She rose. Bill toweled her off and then lifted her as he stood up. She rested her head on his right shoulder. As they entered the candlelit bedroom, Crystine noticed that a dozen roses had been placed in a crystal vase on her nightstand.

Bill laid her down on the bed. The slightly open window let in a soft harbor breeze. Their bodies entwined in synchronization, the soft glow of the candlelight caressing them as they danced the ballet to its climax.

Crystine hadn't gotten a good look at Bill's body in the sensual light, but she knew it, and he knew hers. Their hunger totally abated, their desire resting in satisfied languor, they let the moment sink into them.

"I think they work," she quipped.

"What works?" asked Bill.

"The oysters!"

They shared the laugh, and then Crystine rolled over to lie on her back with Bill on his at her left side. Rising up on his right elbow, he leaned over to kiss her lightly on the mouth. Opening her eyes, she noticed the button-hole scar on his left shoulder, like a polio vaccine only much larger, the tanned skin surrounding it accentuating the pale crater.

"What happened here?" Crystine asked, gently placing the tip of her forefinger on the scarred tissue. Bill rolled over onto his back, staring pensively at the ceiling for a few seconds. Taking a deep breath, he exhaled very slowly, as a reluctant heaviness descended on him.

"It happened while I was in the army," he answered.

"You never told me you were in the army! Want to tell me about it?" she gently pressed.

"Vietnam."

"My God, Bill, I had no idea. You never—"

He held up his left hand, stopping her. "I wasn't that proud of it, but I guess it's something you should know about," he said.

"Sure you're all right with it?" she asked.

"Yeah, fine," he said at the end of a slowly exhaled breath. "I'd just finished up at UCLA—there went my draft deferral. So instead of waiting around for them to call me, I got it over with and enlisted. They sent me to officers' training, I was made a second lieutenant and shipped to 'Nam. Another ninety-day wonder, as we were called by the troops over there."

"Why?" she interjected.

"That's about how long it took to complete our training, not a lot of time first off; plus we had no experience. And for the men who'd been over there, in combat, for nearly a year . . . well, you can understand . . ." he looked questioningly at her. She nodded an affirmative.

"I was assigned to the 101st Airborne Rifle Infantry Division."

"Wasn't that extremely dangerous?"

"Yes and no. My men were well-seasoned veterans, and looking back on it, they covered for me beyond the call of duty, as the saying goes. So I actually survived more than ninety days in the jungle—which was considered another wonder." He paused long enough to let out a chuckle, the kind that says thank you.

Crystine listened intently.

"The first day I arrived I was all afire, ready to lead my men. I introduced myself to the sergeant—he'd been there about a year by then—to let him know right off that I was in command. He didn't have a problem with that, but it didn't take me long to understand he was the leader of that platoon, at least until he decided to turn it over to me."

"Wasn't that insubordination?' she asked.

"I'm talking from hindsight and reflection here. I didn't know what was going on at the time, and my sergeant knew that I didn't know. They let me believe I was in command." He paused with the same intoned chuckle of amusement and affection. "All the while they were keeping me alive," he continued. "Are you bored yet?" he suddenly asked her.

"No, not at all. Please, keep going."

"Eventually I took over command. We were sent on a recon—that's reconnaissance—mission."

"I'm with you," she encouraged him.

"We were south of the town of Hue near the north coast, just scouting around, alert, but not really expecting anything. We came to a clearing; the day was hot and steamy." He glanced at her and smiled, remembering the evening of a few moments ago. The innuendo not lost on her, she smiled and snuggled closer.

"Both my sergeant and I scanned the area, a normal operation. He gave me a single nod, which meant proceed with caution. I agreed, and we moved out. He was kind of a strange sort, soft-spoken, unassuming, at times almost shy. Even in the compound he'd be off by himself, or he could be in a crowd and be off by himself."

He shot her a quick, intense glance.

"But his instincts were uncanny . . . unerring," he continued. "We could all be talking or laughing, you know, relaxing. All he'd have to do is hiss sh-h-h, put his finger to his lips, and you could hear a butterfly flap its wings.

"We'd talk some, not a lot. He did tell me he'd spent some time in California nearly a lifetime ago, which I thought was a strange thing to say for a man maybe twenty years old. But like I said, he was sort of strange. I never had any doubt that he'd cover my back, though.

"Anyway—sorry I got side tracked—Sarge gave me a single nod and we moved out into the clearing, the platoon strung out behind us along the trail, quiet, cautious, but not on edge. I was on the point, and Sarge was right behind me. All of a sudden he bellowed, 'Hit the dirt!' and then grabbed my shirt sleeve, yanking me down and sideways. A fifty-caliber machine-gun slug tore through my shoulder." He put a finger on the bullet wound. "Where my heart had been a split second earlier."

"I . . . I'm sorry, Bill. I had no idea," Crystine said.

"Oh, it's no big deal now. That ended my combat days, though, and now, here I am . . . with you." He smiled at her. "Bored yet?" he asked again.

"There's more?" she returned. "Please, go on."

"Sarge tore his shirt and bandaged my wound as best he could, and then he and Lopez dragged me to cover in the brush, and all the while bullets whizzed over our heads like a storm of angry wasps.

"He set my head on his helmet, took his eyes off me just long enough to make sure the men were doing what they needed to do—returning fire, radioing for a chopper and a medic—and then he said, 'You're gonna be all right, Wild Bill.'

"It's funny. I relaxed then, which probably kept me from going into total shock."

"Wild Bill?" Crystine asked.

"Oh, they gave me that nickname because I'd shown I was calm, cool, and collected under fire. I wasn't given command; I'd earned it."

Bill paused and drew a breath. "Just a little more," he said.

"I'm fascinated," she replied. "I didn't know you were such a good storyteller."

"Not hard to relate just the facts, ma'am," he retorted. They giggled a little, but not enough to make her interest wane.

"So he said, 'You're gonna be all right, Wild Bill,' and I relaxed. Funny, I felt assured, calm, like being warmed from the inside out."

Crystine stiffened as surprise jolted her.

"You all right?" he asked.

"Fine. I just got a strong visual of you lying there . . . shot, and . . ."

"Hey, it's okay," he reassured her, gently taking her hand.

"Any more?" she asked.

"Some; want me to go on?"

"Yes," she replied, pulling her robe up around her.

"Lying there, waiting for the medics, I asked him how he knew. 'There wasn't any music,' was all he said."

"What did that mean? Do you know?"

"Yeah, I do; I think, anyway. It's kind of a side story, want me to . . ."

"Honey, we have all night," Crystine interjected.

"Every now and then Sarge would borrow someone's guitar and play the same chord progression over and over. He'd sing, 'My sweet lord . . . he's so fine . . . gonna make him mine . . . I really want to see you.' Only tune I ever heard him play. He'd put the guitar down, shake his head a little, and say to no one in particular, 'Funny how they fit so close. I don't think George meant it.' It was as if he was trying to solve a puzzle or some kind of riddle."

"George . . . who did he mean by George?" Crystine asked.

"George Harrison. Supposedly he infringed on a copyrighted song. See, what Sarge was doing was comparing the songs 'My Sweet Lord' with 'He's So Fine.' Strange guy, like I said."

Another jolt nearly stiffened her.

"One day I asked him if he knew any other music. He said, 'Sure, Wild Bill.' Then he put his finger up to his lips, quieting the men. Looking at me he said, 'That music.'

'What music?' I asked. 'All I hear are birds chirping, insects buzzing, and the wind moving around in the brush.' Sarge smiled. 'That music,' he said. He was always off somewhere, even in a group, listening to his own music."

"The marching to the beat of a different drum type," Crystine said.

"I suppose that could be. Doesn't matter; the man saved my life."

"Did he have a name besides Sarge?" Crystine asked, her breath a whisper and close to catching in her throat.

"We all called him Sarge because that's what he wanted. He always said, 'Don't get too close to anybody . . . you're likely to lose them if you do.' Strange. Anyway . . . let me think . . . Davey . . .

Donny . . . no, it was Daniel, yeah, that's it, never Danny, always Daniel."

Her heart beating like a timpani drum, she asked, "Did he have a last name that you remember?"

"Let's see . . . Adamson? . . . Abrahamson? Something like that . . . maybe, I'm not exactly sure. Said he was from Montana, though, and that he was going back to see an old friend. Don't know if he made it. I never heard from him again."

From across distance immeasurable and time without passage Crystine knew she had heard from him. Her emotions skyrocketed from confused to delighted to astonished and then settled into warmed from the inside out.

"Oh, Bill, hold me, kiss me, make love to me," she murmured.

"Those oysters must work really well for you," he said, gathering her in his arms, a smile lighting his face.

Crystine knew that it wasn't that. Her longing came from a plane not physical, a need much deeper, a need to feel the closeness of he with whom her soul was entwined while his presence lingered near.

"What is this?" asked Bill, gently wiping the trickle from her eye.

"I'm happy, Bill," she said. "I'm so very happy." She smiled, a tear releasing from her eye, caressing her cheek as it slid to kiss the satin pillow. The fire in the main room crackling.

Chapter Twenty-five

Entering the realm of the gods several times as a young man in Montana and a soldier in Vietnam had left me forever impressed, and maybe somewhat weird. Looking at the world from a purely physical viewpoint as something to be manipulated, controlled, and reshaped made no sense to me, and I told myself I would never be in a technical profession, nor would I ever live in a city or work in an office. After my log-truck accident, I finished a technical training course and went to work for a branch of municipal engineering as a draftsman in the downtown section of Oregon's largest city.

Never say never, as the saying goes.

A film called *The Draughtsman's Contract* came out not long after I began my career as one. "How could a movie about a draftsman possibly hold any interest?" I asked Jim, a veteran of twenty years at his desk, whose only interest in life was how much time he had to put in before he could retire.

He surprised me. "Me and the wife went to see it over the weekend. This young man was contracted by a wealthy landowner's wife in 1694 England to make twelve drawings of the lands and house for her husband, since that was all he cared about. He finally agreed when she threw into the deal that he could sleep with her after each drawing was completed, making it part of the contract. Get it?"

"Yeah, I think so. Sex is the main theme of the story with a little intrigue thrown in. Still boring."

"I should be so lucky," he said and then got off his stool and headed for the door. Time for lunch.

First a movie about a logging family when that was going on in my life, and now a movie about a draftsman when that was going on in my life.

$$\text{\textsc{*}}$$

A year passed, and I was standing next to Lynn in the hospital room. Groaning, almost screaming, her sweaty face contorting in sync with the bolts of pain shooting through her, she gripped my hand hard enough to make it hurt. Then it would subside and she'd look at me and smile.

I couldn't share her pain and would never know what it was like. She was in labor. All the comfort I could offer her was to remind her to breathe.

When Jenna and Jason were born, I wasn't allowed in the room with Lynn. Though the process itself hadn't changed much since then, allowing such visitors wasn't in vogue at the time.

Lynn and I hadn't decided that we weren't having any more children, but we took extra care not to press the issue, and her pregnancy was a surprise to us.

And so for the first time I was allowed in the labor room, by her side the whole night. My appreciation for women increased exponentially after witnessing that ordeal, and my love for Lynn deepened by an equal proportion.

Daniel Junior finally decided to enter the human race, and Lynn delivered all ten pounds two ounces of him. The nurses did what they do to brand-new people, and then, to my utter surprise and near shock, thrust the little guy into my arms! I froze, afraid to breathe, and was so tense my biceps started cramping. But what a miraculous, sacred, and holy moment it was, and I was awestruck, being the first person in the world to hold him. Babies being born a common, everyday occurrence? Not our baby; not anybody's baby. The gods had revealed another part of their realm to me. I turned the little guy over to Lynn. She took him and held him to her breast, smiling through her exhaustion, the sweetest smile I ever did see. He cooed, that little sound only babies can make, the one that gives the world pause and a reason to continue on. Jenna was fourteen and Jason had just turned eleven, and now we had a teenager, a preteenager, and a new baby in the house.

When we first married, we read some silly books and manuals and heard and sometimes listened to advice on how to raise children. We raised each of them in the same environment, with the same boundaries and rules, the same discipline applied, and the same values taught. We did let them follow their own bent, not trying to mold them into our or anyone else's image. It seemed the most natural, the most beneficial, and the most rewarding for each, and in the end, the determiner of character. And each of the three turned out different as night from day or as east from west. What fun!

Eventually, through the natural progression of life, Jason entered his early teens and was starting to feel his oats and sowing a few wild ones with his buddy, Toby Tyler. Toby's mother and Lynn were good friends. Somehow, Toby's mother had gotten Toby to agree to take kung fu lessons, and she and Lynn talked about Jason joining in. Lynn and I discussed the possibility, and it took about ninety seconds to agree that it would be a good thing.

Goal setting, focus, building self-esteem, physical conditioning, discipline, all that keep-'em-out-of-trouble kind of stuff, seemed like a great idea, and Jason agreed to try it.

I took the boys to the academy to check it out, where I met Sifu Dupree (Sifu being the Chinese form of Sensei, both meaning teacher) and watched part of the class. They got a free lesson, and Jason said okay, he wanted to do it. I liked the place, and they had a summer special going on, so I paid for him in full.

But, as frequently happens, when desire fades away, discipline doesn't kick in, and the boys ended up quitting.

Rather than going through the rigmarole of juggling money and books, I asked Sifu if I could finish out Jason's remaining month and a half to see if I'd like it and to find out if my back would hold up to the rigors of training. I ended up training three nights a week for four years and only made it halfway to a black belt.

About six months into my training Sifu said, "Get your sparring gear on, Daniel." I strapped the foam pads on my feet and hands, put in my mouthpiece, and saluted to him and he to me. This was the first time I had sparred with him, so I thought, *Let's see what he has.* I hit him square on the jaw with a left hook, snapping his head to the side. He slowly turned back to face me. Tall, lean and lanky, with sandy hair and blue eyes, he gave me his Clint Eastwood look. He seemed almost too thin, but that was deceptive; he was simply wiry and sinewy, and he could hit like a sledge hammer.

He popped me with a back fist—I didn't even see it move—and then another between the eyes. I stepped back, circling to my left and trying to avoid him. Bam! He threw a roundhouse kick to my left side, stopping me in my tracks. I didn't—I couldn't—touch him the rest of the session. I'd ram him, thinking to move him away. His body would seem to turn to iron, and I couldn't budge him. I'd try kicks. He'd be in range, in front of me, and then not. Gone, like smoke, or wind. A punch? Forget it. He knew what was coming before I threw it.

He said, "Stop," and I was more than glad to. Soaked with sweat, huffing and puffing, my legs like rubber, I weakly saluted out.

He looked fresh as a daisy, the same as when we'd begun, an eternity ago it seemed. Ten minutes, tops. He'd used me for a punching bag, a light workout. Some of his strikes stung but never caused pain. That was due to his control. He wasn't vindictive; he was simply teaching me a lesson, one he taught to all his students— a little humility.

After the match Sifu told me I suffered from PMS. I wasn't sure how to take that comment. Did he mean I fought like a girl?

"What?" I returned.

"PMS," he said, expressionless. "Primitive-Mechanical-Slow; that's how you fight." He flashed a grin as my ego reeled. I had learned an object lesson that day, with me as the object.

Funny thing, though. Whenever we sparred after that, he could use me as a punching bag at will. It didn't make any difference how long or hard I trained and practiced. But I kept up my training, taking lessons, grunting and groaning my way along, and making excruciatingly slow progress.

Debbie Heely stood a shade over five feet tall, weighed around 110 pounds, had a brown belt in the art, and reminded me of Crystine.

"Am I hitting too hard?" she asked after snapping my head sideways with a roundhouse right.

"No, not at all, don't even worry about it," I said, trying to keep my male ego intact.

"Any hope of me getting better?" I asked Sifu after he'd watched Debbie kick my butt . . . again.

"Mushin and zanshin," was all he said.

"Okay . . . is that related to PMS?"

He turned and hollered, "Put your gear away," to the class. We did and then lined up in front of him.

"Mushin and zanshin. Some of you may have heard these words; most of you haven't. I'll explain their meaning as best I can.

"Mushin is the mind of no mind, instinctual automatic motion and response without thinking. The essence of zanshin is having the foreknowledge of absolute and total dominance. Athletes recognize it once in a while and call it the zone.

"Is there a set of steps to getting there? No, and it is the same with mushin. Some get there soon, others take longer, and some never get there. But when you do, you will know, because mushin and zanshin are not merely words to be defined; they are a state of being that cannot be known until experienced. Salute out!"

He covered his right fist with his left hand and bowed slightly. We did the same, and class was over.

So there was hope for me beyond PMS.

We had a drill called the monkey line. The whole class attacked one defender. The rules were that the attackers came at you in a line, one by one, and threw a noncontact right roundhouse punch when they got in range. The defender then countered with any strike or kick they chose, placing them in spots vital enough to knock the attacker out of the action and then engage the next in line, all the while moving to keep the attacker between him and the others in the line. The motion of the line resembled the tail of a monkey as it whipped about; thus the name monkey line. Another rule was if an attacker thought your defense was weak, he or she could get up off the floor and come at you again.

After sifu's explanation and a hundred or so monkey lines, I finally understood its purpose to be twofold. The obvious goal was getting used to defending against multiple attackers, and the other was to let the grueling hours of training and the buckets of poured out sweat bestow a reward; the ability to move and act with purpose without forethought. The mind of no mind. And eventually I experienced mushin and understood its meaning.

❧

Up against a deadline at work, the day had been like sharks at a feeding frenzy with nothing to eat. I was in a foul mood when I entered the training hall. I went straight to the changing room, not looking at or speaking to anyone, and lined up for class. One of the brown belts warmed us up. I went through the motions. There, but not really *there*.

Sifu Dupree barked, "Monkey line." Inwardly groaning, I tried to hide somewhere in the middle of about twenty of us as we lined up.

"Abrams, first out." I stepped to the front of the line and then turned to face it, trying to focus and get into the moment.

"Full speed," Sifu hollered.

They swarmed me before I could blink. I was in the moment and into survival mode without thinking about it. After what seemed like forever, Sifu hollered, "Stop." My chest heaved, my pulse pounded in my ears, my red T-shirt and black pantaloons were drenched in sweat, and I was drained of energy. I retreated to a safe place against a wall and looked over the room. *Wow, looks like I did all right,* I thought, rather pleased at all the bodies scattered around on the concrete floor. I glanced over at Sifu. Debbie had come from somewhere and was standing next to him. He remained stone-faced. I turned and surveyed the floor again. What? One guy had gotten up and was coming at me, dragging a foot behind him, suggesting I'd injured his leg, but not bad enough to keep him down. Anger flared from my belly to my chest in less than a heartbeat.

Kicks were not my forte, and I limited them to the waist on down, but in the heat of anger I thought, *I'm going to kick this dude in the head.* Not sure how, I took off toward him with small running steps. When I gauged the proper range, I leaped straight up in the air and continued up and up and up until my feet were level with his head. It seemed that I had all the time in the world while I hung in the air. Without doubt or strain, I snapped out a perfect right-front kick, stopping it an inch from his nose. Feeling lighter than the air I was suspended in, I floated down to the floor, landing in a perfect tiger stance. The guy stood frozen in place with his mouth hanging open.

I'm five feet ten inches tall. My feet were at least five feet off the ground, I could easily have dunked a basketball. In fact, the top of my head would have been a little above the rim.

Exactly what had happened? I wasn't sure. I did know that I had performed a physical feat beyond anything I had ever done or dreamed I could do, but what amazed me the most was that my *intention* had been focused like a laser beam, and that *intention* had manifested immediately.

Could intention, the setting of the will, be that powerful? Possibly. Some time-worn sayings flew through my mind.

"Where there's a will, there's a way."
"Be careful what you wish for; you might get it."
"Hope springs eternal."
"Faith can move mountains."
"Love will find a way."

I walked over to Sifu and Debbie standing at the edge of the training hall. "Ever play sports in school Daniel?" he asked.

"Just playground stuff," I replied. He looked me over for a brief moment and smiled; he knew. Zanshin. I looked at Debbie. Maybe it was the supercharged moment, but when she looked back and smiled, I saw Crystine. I had to come to grips with the fact that my love for her had never died, but it was a spark I dare not fan into a flame I could not quench. And I believed, perhaps foolishly after so long a time, that the love Crystine and I had once shared would never die and would find a way back to itself. Right then and there, I set my intention on seeing her again someday.

Chapter Twenty-Six

A movie was made called *The Seven Year Itch*, with Marilyn Monroe. Rosanne Cash sang "The Seven Year Ache" twenty-five years later. What the effect that particular time frame has on marriages I'm not sure—anything from boredom to fear of barring one's soul to being unable to reach a place of trust where rest is found, or an undefined restlessness.

After seven years of what was, Crystine thought, a stable and steady relationship validated by marriage, not entirely devoid of passion and one they'd worked at, Bill told her, "I'm unhappy, and you're the reason why."

She hadn't the slightest inkling of an idea he felt like he did. But then Bill never was one to reveal his feelings. Always cool under fire, he had dropped a megaton bomb on Crystine.

Her mouth dropped open. Her eyes widened in disbelief. She stared dumbfounded out the kitchen window of *their* house, at *their* pool. But right now, those things were of no significance. She remained silent, remembering how she had once gazed out Nikki's kitchen window at her pool, thinking she'd never have one, but she did have Daniel then, and he was all she wanted. But that seemed a long lonely lifetime ago. Suddenly, she wished Nikki were there.

They hadn't talked to each other in six months, busyness getting in the way.

Carefully placing her after-dinner glass of merlot on the table, she focused her eyes on the man sitting across from her. "What?" she asked.

"I said, I'm unhappy and you're the reason why," he repeated.

The Arctic zone spread across her heart.

"Bill . . . wha-a-a-a . . . What are you saying?" His lightning bolt of devastation, disguised as words, hadn't fully hit the mark.

"Crystine, our marriage isn't working; it just isn't. There's no more to it than that."

"But . . . we've worked at it, Bill . . . tried . . . give and take . . . partnering. What's gone wrong? Where did we . . . I, fail?"

"I don't know. I've tried to pinpoint a reason. Tried to find a specific problem we could solve and correct. No luck. I'm stymied for an explanation, other than I'm simply unhappy."

"Do you want a divorce then?" Crystine asked, her innate boldness kicking in and jolting her out of the shock.

"No-o-o . . . not necessarily, maybe a trial separation . . . space of our own for a while. Time to think . . . give us a chance to maybe work this out."

Crystine quickly assessed the situation, concluding that Bill's stunning revelation was unfair and absolutely off the mark. Burning sand replaced the polar ice in her heart, and she became flushed with anger. "I'll be gone in two days, at the most. Holly and Davey will come with me," she snapped.

"Crystine . . ." Bill held up his hand pleadingly, trying to make it easier on her.

"Don't! If this is the way you want it, this is the way it will be. No sense putting it off!" Pushing her chair back, she stood up and stormed out of the kitchen, her bravado sufficient to mask the hurt twisting inside of her. Slamming the door behind her, she threw herself on the bed, a river of tears cascading down her cheeks.

And she longed to return to that oasis between the polar ice and the burning sand, where Daniel's love once filled her heart but now was only desolate ground.

With Holly a junior in high school, Davey two years behind her, and Crystine in her mid-thirties, transitioning to a new house was not at all difficult. Crystine made sure they stayed in the same school, knowing that established friends were important at that, or any other, age.

"Nikki?"

"Crystine? Wow! Hi, girlfriend! It's been so long. I'm always meaning to call, but you know how busy we can get, and how quickly time slips away," she said.

"Sometimes it does; sometimes it doesn't."

"Is something wrong?" asked Nikki, picking up on the tone of her long-time friend's voice.

"Bill and I split."

"Oh-h-h," Nikki groaned. "What happened?"

"I'm not sure, but right out of the blue he told me he was unhappy and that I was the reason why, so I left."

"Where are you now, dear? What's going on?"

"We've been split for a month. I'm in my own place. Holly and Davey are in the same school; I made sure of that."

"Why didn't you call me sooner?" asked Nikki, her voice anxious.

"I know you, Nikki. You'd have come running over, knocking yourself out trying to help or rescue me. By the way, did you get your master's yet?"

"Yes, I did. Three months ago, in fact."

"Big raise?"

"Not big, but a raise, I have more flexibility in decision making, though. Plus a whole lot more upward mobility—God I hate that phrase; it sounds so . . . mechanical."

Crystine couldn't help herself; she had to chuckle—down-to-earth Nikki, helpful Nikki, always-there Nikki, and her best friend since forever.

Nikki had been raised on the well-to-do side of town, at the high end of the upper-middle class. She had for a brief time and years ago, as was in vogue, tuned in, turned on, and dropped out. More mature now, she understood that she couldn't change the world—not even one person, with the exception of herself, maybe. She realized that the best she could do was perhaps ease a little suffering here and there and had devoted her career to that end. The work didn't pay a lot, her salary half of Crystine's, despite the advanced degree in social work. But Nikki didn't care much about money or the things it could buy.

Still bubbly, still energetic, and still single, she had never married, had never truly been in love. She'd seen the heartaches that came from both and made it a point to avoid them. She didn't need those burdens; she helped carry too many other people's. And she was somewhat of a realist, with a dash of cynicism, who thought happiness was an illusion not to be pursued. So she did what she could to alleviate some suffering here and there, not realizing that the satisfaction she got from work was her happiness in disguise.

"I'm going to ask you a huge favor," Crystine said.

"Sure, anything," replied Nikki.

"No, I mean really huge, as in enormous . . . gigantic."

"Okay, lay it on me."

"I need to see you, tonight, if you can."

"I don't have any plans. I can make it tonight," Nikki assured her.

"Great. I think it's better to talk face to face, and I can tell you then what I have in mind. About seven?"

"Seven it is! I'll be there."

"Uh . . . Nikki, my address?"

"Oh, yeah, right." They laughed.

"49502 Placid Lane, can you find it okay?"

"Just fine, honey. I'm LA bred and born too, remember?"

"Sure, see ya."

"Bye, sweetie. See ya in a while."

Nikki, always there. Crystine hung up the phone, a silent prayer of thankfulness briefly gracing the desolate ground in her heart.

Crystine made a high-end income and could easily afford to be on her own. The only price she had to pay for her independence was absence from her home, her family, and from those she loved. She had purchased the house with the idea of having a live-in nanny. Holly and Davey only needed a watchful presence in the background, an ally of Crystine's, someone she could implicitly trust. She hadn't really thought about Nikki, but to her own amazement the idea just felt right.

Nikki pulled up in her two-year-old gloss-black Chevy Camaro. Looking at the house on Placid Lane, she thought it perfectly fit Crystine. Bold, straightforward, and at the same time welcoming. It was Southern California optimized, Spanish style, with stucco siding and a red tile roof. The roof ran at an upward angle from the front until it was intercepted by a bank of clerestory windows. From there, the roof angled down toward the back of the small hacienda. Along the east-facing front, now shadowed, ran a full-length porch, its roof beginning under the main one and protruding at a slightly sharper angle. The porch was entirely open, the roof supported by four-inch-square posts of a dark wood. The exterior windows were framed by the same rich material. A wide curving walkway, its color matching the roof, wound through the luscious green lawn. A green space about fifty yards wide lay on the south side of the creamy yellow house.

Nikki strode soundlessly up the slightly inclined walkway, sprang up the four steps to the porch landing, and pushed the buzzer. Chimes sang within, their music wafting through the open windows that ran along the sides of the oversized oak entry door.

"Hi, Nikki!" exclaimed the black-haired beauty standing in the open doorway.

"Holly! Hi, honey! How are you, kid?"

"I'm fine for a no-direction, lost-and-lonely, dazed-and-confused teenager," she quipped.

"Give me a hug, kiddo!"

Nikki was like a second mom to Holly and Davey. She didn't think of them as her own, but she did think of them as her niece and nephew.

"Hello, Aunt Nikki!" a voice called from somewhere down a dark hallway.

"Hi, Davey! How are you, dear?"

"Busy . . . way too busy to talk right now," he fired back from some unknown room down the hall.

"I see how you are!" laughed Nikki.

"Davey! Quit being so rude," Crystine piped in from the kitchen, off to the left. "Come on in, Nikki!" she hollered, and Nikki seated herself on the sofa.

Holly turned and winked at her as she started down the hallway. "Homework," she called over her shoulder, disappearing in the general direction of the lurking Davey.

Crystine clattered through the swinging door that separated the kitchen from the dining-living room carrying a tray of iced tea, cheese, crackers, and smoked oysters.

"Hi, girlfriend, don't bother to get up. I've got everything under control," she said teasingly.

"It's so extremely good to see you," Nikki said as Crystine put the refreshments on the coffee table and then seated herself on the leather sofa.

She looked over at Nikki. "Wow, time sure flies, huh?" she said.

"How are you doing?" asked Nikki. Due to the nature of her work, she liked to get right to the heart of the matter.

"Oh . . . not bad . . . Okay, I guess." Due to the nature of *her* work, Crystine liked to feel and probe, analyze and negotiate.

"Really, how are you holding up?" Nikki asked again.

"We're not to the divorce stage yet. He thought we should try a separation, give it some time. See how that goes."

"How about you? What do you want? How do you feel about it all?"

"After I got over the initial shock and anger and was able to sit down and think about, I came to the conclusion that . . . I don't know!" She smiled at Nikki, but the laugh they shared was muted.

"Come on now; what do you want? What are you planning to do?"

"You're not practicing your social work skills on me, are you?" asked Crystine.

"Sorry. No. I'm just concerned; you know that."

"I know. I know you are, Nikki. I'll give it some time. I'm trying not to think too far in the future, of course. Maybe Bill is going through a midlife crisis or something."

"That could very well be," mused Nikki. "Do you love him?" she asked.

"What kind of question is that?" Crystine responded, her defenses beginning to show. "Of course I love him."

"But can you live without him?"

"If I have to . . . Yes, I suppose so. I wouldn't want another man, though. I wouldn't want to take that risk again."

"That risk?"

"You know, marriage gone dull or stale or bad, the shock, the fights, the tension, the turmoil, the divorce, the . . ."

"Broken heart?" injected Nikki.

"The aching heart. I don't think it can be broken more than once."

"Yours was broken, wasn't it, Crystine?"

"Yes."

"Daniel?"

"Yes."

Nikki moved over and put her arms around her. Crystine couldn't be tough any longer, the sobs washing through her like waves breaking on a beach. "It's all right, honey . . . go ahead and cry," said Nikki, her own heart near to breaking.

"I'm sorry," Crystine murmured, looking at Nikki through bleary eyes.

"It's okay. Feels kind of good, doesn't it?"

"I can't remember the last time I bawled like that."

"You should do it more often. It's a great relief, and that's not just textbook psychology; it really works," Nikki said, the light of compassion glowing brighter than usual in her eyes. Crystine gave a barely perceptible nod with a smile to match.

"Now, what was that *huge* favor you wanted to ask of me?"

Crystine hesitated, gathering herself. "I want you to move in with me . . . us," she replied, composure being the street her bold and straightforward manner traveled on.

"Why?" asked Nikki. She wasn't looking for a reason to weigh her decision; it was already made. She was simply curious.

"Well . . . let's see . . . to make a long story short, Bill and I are split, I've put a down payment on this house, I've been promoted to a production accountant, which means I'll be traveling and staying on location for months at a time, Holly has a year and a half of school left, Davey, three, and I'd like you to be here to help keep an eye on them and the house." She drew a deep breath, closely watching Nikki's unchanged expression.

"Okay."

"Huh, what?"

"I said okay. I'll do it. I'll move in."

"Just like that?" asked Crystine.

"Just like that. I've only got my apartment, my stuff will fit nicely here, and it's not any further to work. Sure, I'll be glad to."

"Nikki you're truly amazing."

"I know," she replied, laughing. Alleviating a little suffering here and there was what she did, and she was good at it. She would never have accepted pay for helping out, and Crystine wouldn't dream of charging her rent. The setup was perfect, the transition imperceptible. Aunt Nikki, pseudo-mom.

Chapter Twenty-Seven

Crystine worked exclusively on set locations, in the states and abroad, and the more time she was away, the less poignant was the hurt. Globe-hopping, working long hours, keeping busy, she tried to convince herself that she was happy, but at moments of pause, the core truth revealed itself: she was running, trying to hide from the feeling that she'd failed in life.

She returned home from England where she'd been working on Paramount's latest project.

Whenever she could she got autographs from the stars, not for herself—her opinion of them had steadily declined, and she assessed that their average IQ hovered around room temperature—but for Holly and Davey. Nikki could care less. She was under no illusion, understanding that the business of Hollywood was to create illusions, which she and Crystine laughed about many times.

"The business of providing vicarious living," Crystine quipped over her glass of merlot.

"Better living through celluloid," added Nikki, sipping on her beer.

And they think I'm an airhead, thought Holly, seated on the other side of the room. "Cellulite, how can anyone live better with more cellulite?" she asked, purposely mixing the word, and they all broke apart with laughter.

Davey closed the door of his room down the hall, surrendering to ladies night. His makeup was much like his mother's, a practical application of intellectual curiosity.

Holly's makeup was more like her father's, free-spirited, freewheeling, somewhat restless, oriented to the moment.

Crystine heard the phone ringing down the hall. She set her glass on the coffee table. "Mom, it's for you. It's Bill," hollered matter-of-fact Davey. Holly ceased her laughter, and Nikki shot Crystine a concerned look and touched her reassuringly on the shoulder as she stood to answer the phone.

"How did Bill know you were here?" asked Holly.

"I don't know, hon. We do work for the same company, so he probably knows where I am all the time or can easily find out. No big deal."

Crystine moved into the darkened hallway, her eyes adjusting to the dim light. Her mind and mood, only seconds before loose and relaxed, were snapped to instant attention and defensive alert. Focused beyond professional, her intellect and senses were those of a warrior. She steeled herself.

"What do you want?" she asked crisply and straight to the point. Crystine at her best; Bill had expected it.

"I think you should start dating," he replied with the same straightforwardness. Crystine had not expected that.

"What do you mean, start? What makes you think I haven't been seeing other men? Besides, my private life is no business of yours right now."

"Not my business, no, but it is a concern of mine."

"You're serious? Have you filed for a divorce or something?"

"No, it just doesn't seem right for you . . . us . . . to be bottled up like we are. We need to get out, explore a little, test the waters to find out how we really feel."

She felt as if she'd been stung by a wasp and after a long pause replied, "Okay . . . sure Bill. Let me know when and if you have your mind made up about . . . *us*!"

She slammed the phone down on the hook, angered and upset that this was one more step toward a permanent parting.

Dating? What would be the point? Fun? Maybe. A fling? Maybe. A relationship? *No, that's the last thing I need,* Crystine thought as she traversed the length of the hallway, *and if I do decide to "test the waters" it will be on my terms, and my terms alone.*

In her mid-thirties, she was beginning to doubt her attractiveness. It was not only her age; it was also the fact of two divorces with a third pending. Although the first two were predominantly her doing, the relationships had still failed. Bill had instigated the third, and it hurt. Some of the blame for not being able to sustain a relationship must lie with her, she surmised. But she really didn't care anymore. Relationships were out.

Well, I'll go ahead and date, she thought to herself. *And then some,* she added as an afterthought.

She rejoined Holly and Nikki in the front room, but the festive mood of only moments before eluded recapturing.

❧

New York City, the site of countless movies, plays, productions, extravaganzas, extravagance, and the home of millions of everyday, real, essential lives. Crystine couldn't see the Manhattan skyline. The building she was in was part of it. Standing up, she pushed her chair back and gazed out the window of the twentieth-floor office. Winter was drawing near. The sky, the streets, all she could see was gray and dreary, a reflection of the Big Apple. Well-seasoned in her job, she found that the interval between thrills stretched a little longer each time, and the transition to winter in New York was a season of dreariness, a time of loneliness.

Her intercom broke the reverie.

"Yes, Carla," she said as she pressed the receive button.

"Your two o'clock interview is here," replied her long-time receptionist-friend and first-line filter.

"Thank you, Carla. I'll be right out," she said. Crystine appreciated Carla and everyone else who worked in her department.

They returned her appreciation with long-term loyalty. She held firm to the doctrine of having comfortable but not quite satisfied employees, always allowing room for suggestion or improvement.

Not as pampered as those showcased on film, she and her staff were nestled snugly in the lap of luxury just the same.

For her third and final interview of the day, she put on her best professional demeanor.

The young man sat stiffly in one of the two chairs in the reception area. Tall, dark, and vacuously handsome, he appeared to be in his mid-twenties and was of Italian descent.

Crystine came out of her office, gliding lightly toward him with her right hand extended. He stood to greet her, towering over her.

"Rocco?" she asked.

"Yes."

"I'm Crystine Hopkins. Nice to meet you."

She was, according to self-proclaimed sex experts and women's magazines, at her sexual peak, that point of most insistent desires that every woman on the face of the planet reaches sometime in their mid-thirties, according to the *experts*.

The word stud galloped across her mind as he grasped her hand, gentle and firm, no sweat on the palm.

"Please, come into my office." She smiled and turned, and he followed. Leaving the door open, Crystine stood behind her desk and waited for him to take a chair before seating herself.

"Let's see, a graduate of Syracuse, you worked for Seaboard Construction," she paused and looked over the rims of her glasses at the impeccably groomed young man.

"Yes, for two years as their construction accountant," he stated.

She found him desirable and wondered if he would find her desirable, minus any leverage she could apply as his boss. The idea intrigued her. At least ten years his senior, she decided to challenge the norm. A simple dating game. A what-if. A fantasy. An image booster. Admitted to or not, she needed a refilling of her self-esteem. After two divorces and with a third pending, she had to find out if she could still attract a man.

"And the company went out of business?"

"Yes, they had to declare bankruptcy."

"Because?"

"Too much owed in taxes. I wasn't involved in that part of the business."

"Well, we're in need of a person with your qualifications and experience. When could you start?"

"Right away . . . tomorrow!"

Crystine smiled. "How about Monday? Tomorrow is Saturday."

Yes, she would date, and then some.

Exposing her heart to further wounding was out of the question; turning on the charm was not.

"I won't be in further need of your services," she said to Rocco.

"You're letting me go?" he asked, leaning slightly forward in his chair.

"In a sense, I suppose so. The movie isn't quite a wrap, but all the construction is complete, and all the scenes have been shot. You will have two more weeks on the payroll."

"The next movie?"

"I'm not sure where or when it will be, but I have all of your current information if I need to get ahold of you."

"What about . . . us?"

"As I said, I have no further need of your services."

He blinked twice, swallowed hard, stood up, and strode quickly out of her office.

Over the course of a year she had validated his vanity, and he had validated her need to know. But it hadn't taken long for Rocco's suave handsomeness to reduce to vacuousness, and, like any toy, he was discarded.

Game over, doubts removed, discoveries made, and she understood that no sensual indulgence, no sophisticated thrill, no material acquisition could replace the sweetness of pure love remembered.

She turned in her chair to gaze at the blue sky above Manhattan. A single tear found its way down her cheek to rest in the corner of her mouth. Her winter had been long and dreary and lonely, even with Rocco handy.

꽃

The Big Apple to the Big Amoeba, she thought as the 747 dropped down into LAX from NYC. Another ride on a jet plane, another landing in a labyrinthine airport, another surge into another megalopolis. Funny how days and months, seasons and years, locations and cities blend together after enough repetition, but still, be it ever so gargantuan, uncaring, and dangerous, there's no place like home. Crystine chuckled at her musings, the touchdown giving her a slight jolt.

"Crystine, over here!"

She looked to see Nikki waving her arms over her head. "Over here!" she hollered again.

"How do you stay so young looking?" Crystine asked as they buzzed through LA in Nikki's two-year-old Impala.

"I wasn't aware that I looked young," she replied.

"Sure you do; amazingly so. You should really compare yourself in a mirror against some pictures taken say . . . ten, twelve years ago. Amazing."

"I'll take it as a compliment," Nikki said. She paused to consider what Crystine had told her. Maybe it was the heartaches she hadn't suffered. Maybe it was the high-profile, high-stress job she didn't have. Maybe it was not striving for anything more in life than to be content and lend a helping hand here and there.

A silver Corvette zoomed by on the left, horn blaring; the driver leaning sideways to give Nikki the finger. "Life in the fast lane surely make you lose your mind." She laughed and glanced over at Crystine. No comment.

"Go on in and see the kids. I'll get the luggage," said Nikki.

"Oh no, I won't hear of it. Holly and Davey can get it later. Come on."

So much change in one short year, thought Crystine as she hugged first Holly and then Davey, who was more of a man now than the boy she remembered.

"I hope you're hungry, Mom, 'cause Sunday dinner is waiting," chirped Holly.

"I'll get your luggage," offered Davey. *More of a man.*

"Thanks, hon, and then we'll sit down to eat. I'm starving!"

Nikki was in the kitchen, setting the table.

Fried chicken, mashed potatoes and gravy, corn on the cob with butter, and apple pie a la mode. It was more special than any gourmet fare, and Crystine savored every bite. *Home and hearth, family and friends, nothing better,* she mused, but a vague sense that it was passing her by intruded on the happy thought.

She took her first bite of apple pie. The phone rang. Unexplained, a twinge of anxiety fluttered in her stomach. She put down her fork, having to concentrate on working up enough saliva to swallow the mouthful of pie.

"I'll get it," Holly exclaimed, pushing her chair back from the table. "Probably one of my suitors ready to beg me for a date," she laughed as she bounced down the hallway. Returning, she stopped and braced both hands against the hallway door frame.

"Mom, it's for you. Bill," she deadpanned, covering her own anxiety.

Nikki gave her an inquisitive look. Crystine shrugged her shoulders, returning an I-don't-know look.

Easing back from the table, she walked down the hall to the phone and placed it against her ear. She was angry. Her dinner, and more important, her time with family had been interrupted.

"What do you want? It had better be important."

Bill picked up on her mood. "Sorry to bother you. I didn't realize what time it was. Were you in the middle of dinner?"

"As a matter of fact we were, so could you please make this brief?" she said, her coolness more than implied.

"I need to talk to you," he replied.

"You are, Bill," she pointed out, resisting the urge to add "you idiot" at the end of her statement. The New York City doldrums lingered.

"I know, but I mean face to face."

"Why?"

"It's about us, Crystine. We need to get on with our lives . . . one way or another, so I've had divorce papers drawn up. You need to come over, look them over, and decide if you want to sign." She understood the reason for her sudden anxiety.

"All right, Bill, when?" she asked, thinking there was no sense putting it off.

"Tonight?"

"No, that's too short notice. I just got home, and I'd like to spend some time with my family. Tomorrow evening at the soonest, around seven."

"Okay, around seven," he agreed.

"I'll call if I can't make it," she replied, moving into the Arctic zone that was now a permanent place in her heart, and the ground between there and the burning sand was not only desolate but numb. She kept it that way as insulation from hurt. She slammed the receiver down.

She could hear laughter coming down the hall from the dining room, the double-you-over, make-your-belly-ache kind that comes around once in a blue moon. She was determined not to let Bill's intrusion spoil the festive mood. True joy should always be given full welcome and full sway.

Nikki looked up as she entered the dining room. "Wha . . ." Crystine put her forefinger on her lips, asking for silence. Nikki nodded in understanding. Holly and Davey didn't notice through the tears of laughter running down their faces.

"Hello, Bill," Crystine said coldly as she stepped past him into her former home.

"How are you?" he asked in that casual, cordial, not-meaning-it frame, neither expecting nor wanting an answer. Not giving one, Crystine glanced at the stack of papers that lay on the dining room table. Turning back to face Bill, she tossed her head in their direction. "Those the papers?" she asked. Not waiting for an answer, she marched directly to the table, pulled up a chair, and seated herself. Removing a pair of glasses from her purse, she put them on and picked up the sheaf of legal documents.

Bill seated himself across from her.

She hadn't set foot in the place for over a year. Orderly, tidy, spotless, it reflected Bill perfectly. He was not one to do anything sloppily or without a good amount of deliberation, including having divorce papers drawn up. Crystine wondered if she should have her attorney present. She laughed inside to herself, thinking, *I'm not being interrogated here,* but she remained uneasy just the same.

"Crystine," he began, "I've missed you, and I'm willing . . . I want . . . to try to work things out." She remained silent. "And I think we can," he continued. "But I've decided that we need to settle our situation. So . . . either come back with me or sign the papers. If you want, you can contest, of course, and string this out, but we both need to get on with our lives one way or another."

She mulled over the idea of turning on the sarcasm and lacing it with acid. *Didn't all the pretty young women fall for you like you thought they would? Didn't turn out to be quite the stud you thought you were, huh? Feeling old, Bill? Looking for a companion now? Well that's just what you'll get, a partner and nothing else.*

"Okay," Crystine replied.

"Okay?" He was taken aback. "Okay what?" he pressed, not anticipating such a quick or succinct response. Pulling a pen from the depths of her leather purse, she tapped the sheaf of divorce papers with it. "Okay, I'll come back home. So I won't be needing this," she held up the pen for Bill to take a good look at and then dropped it back in her purse. *"Let us be partners and marry our fortunes together."* She thought, changing the lyrics of a song she'd heard a long time ago.

She knew that Bill's divorce papers would be ironclad in his favor, no loopholes. Take it or leave it, as is. *Besides, if you've experienced one Rocco, you've experienced them all,* she thought to herself.

Holly was on her way to college, Davey not far behind. She'd be on location eleven months out of the year, and two incomes were always better than one.

Arctic ice, burning sand, and desolation in between; why fight it?

❧

"Have you decided where you're going to school?" Crystine asked Holly over coffee in the kitchen.

"Yes, UCLA."

"That's a good school," Crystine smiled. "It will give you a good foundation for the professions within the business world. Good choice."

"Mom, I'm going to major in art."

Crystine stopped her cup half way to her mouth. "Art? Like a broker through a gallery or some type of dealer traveling to exotic places around the globe procuring unusual objects for your shop or gallery? That could turn out to be fun."

"No, Mom, I'm studying art because I love it and am going to be an artist."

"Well, then you can keep an eye on the market and give them what they want."

"I can't work that way. I have to be inspired, passionate about what I create, enthralled and entrenched in the moment in order to do my best work."

"Are you going to teach?"

"No, Mother, I'm going to paint."

"Not very practical, Holly, and quite risky. Do you want to end up one of those starving-artist types?"

"I don't want to, but that's not to say I won't."

"I have seen some of your paintings. You did win some contests in high school. I think you're a good artist, Holly, and you certainly didn't get it from me. But I also think you'll grow out of that school-girl notion once you get to UCLA. Some people change their majors three or four times before they graduate. Did you get accepted?"

"Yes, got the letter today."

"That's wonderful, hon. I have faith in you that you'll make good decisions down the road."

"Thanks, Mom" was all she could say. No sense in trying to explain much right now; her mom wasn't listening anyway.

Holly just couldn't grasp the importance of living life in a practical, contemporary fashion with a good-paying job, a house in the suburbs, a flashy new car, and an exotic vacation once a year, all standards in her family. What she sought was inspiration, and what welled up inside of her she expressed in paintings. That was how she lived and what she lived for, and she had faith in herself.

She graduated holding a degree in art and holding a work of art, her newborn baby girl. She had no husband—none required; times had changed. She lived with an art professor and was working toward her master's degree.

"Oh my, what a darling, may I hold her?" Crystine asked Holly, who handed the baby over to her grandmother. "A grandma at forty-one. Well, I guess that's about right. Twenty years here, twenty years there, give or take. "How are you, baby?" The baby cooed. Crystine looked at Holly. "What prompted you to name her Crystal?" she asked.

"I remembered the story Grandma Julie told of how she had decided to name you Katherine but fell in love with Crystal, like the vase that held a dozen roses. So, she combined them into Crystalline . . . Crystine."

"That was sweet of you, honey," she said and looked down at the baby. "My beautiful Crystal," she said, and the baby smiled, her eyes big and brown and sparkling with delight. Crystine looked up at Holly. "It's like she knows who I am," she said, and in the desolate ground between the polar ice and the burning sand in her heart, an oasis took root and began to blossom.

Chapter Twenty-Eight

Like a mutated Greek goddess revisited, Portlandia squats on a raised dais, a huge copper-clad idol, plunked down in front of the Portland Building. The window of my sixth-floor workspace was located directly behind her butt.

Our department had started a huge public works project, and about the same time computers came on the scene. We attained three work stations for computer drafting, and the three senior drafters out of the ten of us began using them. The problem was that we needed immediate production, so I volunteered to work swing shift and at the same time learn computer drafting.

I had to laugh as I remembered my vows to never live in a city, never be confined to an office, and never engage in a technical occupation. Now here I was, doing all three, gazing out my window at Portlandia's butt in the dark.

Life can be sublimely funny at times.

It was nearing midnight. I saved my work, shut off the machine, stood up, stretched, went over to the window next to mine, and stared out at the blackness of the uneasy night. The street was devoid of traffic. The street lamps cast a halo of copper-tinged light onto the black hole of the pavement, like huge bright copper pennies lining each side of the empty street. Even from this height I could see the raindrops explode, dance, and then splash as they hammered into the halos cast by the lamplight. The scene spoke loneliness, sentient and powerful. The night, the scene, and the overpowering feeling of loneliness gripped me and would not let go.

It was as if the tines of Portlandia's trident somehow pierced my mind, making me realize how acute the pain was that had pierced my soul. And then, as if to counterbalance the grip of loneliness, sweet memories, long buried, resurrected themselves, flooding my heart and soul, and again, the strength of the moment encompassed my being.

"Crystine, where are you?" I whispered into the black and uncaring night.

Then the counterbalance once again. *What's wrong with me?* I thought. I'm only forty-two, I'm contentedly married, love Lynn, Jenna and Jason are in high school, and Daniel Junior is three years old. I told myself I was being a fool. But Crystine remained in a secret place within my heart, and to deny the strength of that fact would be true foolishness.

Over the next decade, starting from that intense and revealing night, a pattern of very odd but very similar events emerged. Some would call them coincidence, or happenstance, or a quirk of fate and pay no more attention to them than that. But there is a word for what may appear to be a chance event but has meaning on a personal level: synchronicity, a glimpse of the tapestry being woven that reflects, or affects, one's life.

Movies were following me around.

I could chalk off *Sometimes a Great Notion* and *The Draughtsman's Contract* to coincidence, but it didn't stop there.

I found out years after seeing it that the big dance scene in the movie *Grease* had been filmed in the gymnasium of Huntington High School. Crystine probably graduated from there, as I would have if we hadn't returned to Montana.

The love scene between Sarah Connor and Kyle Reese in *The Terminator* was filmed at the Tiki Motel in Huntington.

Goonies, Short Circuit, and *Free Willy* were filmed in and around Astoria, Oregon. They shot the movie *Kindergarten Cop* in Astoria and in the grade school my daughter attended.

Always, a movie of fire fighting in the woods, was filmed mainly in Libby, Montana, where I went to high school and fought forest fires the summer afterward. The theme of the movie is about love so powerful that it carries across the boundaries of time and place, of life and of death. The strength of the love portrayed in the film reminded me of what Crystine and I once had, and my thoughts turned strongly toward her, the poignant memories of what was, the hope of what could be, the loss of what should have been, overwhelming me. That our love was as powerful as that depicted in the movie, I had no doubt. If and how it would ever connect again, I had no clue. But if it could be borne in the imagination, it could become a reality, couldn't it?

The River Wild used Kootenai Falls, named "The Gauntlet" in the film, for the dangerous part of the river trip. Kootenai Falls is located just outside of Libby. I hung out at the falls a lot in my high school years, drinking beer and doing what teenagers do.

Dante's Peak used Wallace, Idaho, as its setting. My sister reminded me we had lived there when I was three.

Many major motion pictures, some worthy of Academy Awards, filmed in or near places I'd lived, little podunk towns like Wallace, Libby, and Astoria. Portland was easier to understand as a location, being a full-blown city. But I had to wonder about Los Angeles. How was it that out of the thousands of high schools and motels in that megatropolis, Huntington was chosen to be in the films *Grease* and *The Terminator?*

Body of Evidence was filmed next door from where I worked in downtown Portland.

Mr. Holland's Opus was filmed at the high school two blocks from my house in Portland. All my kids went there.

Part of *The Hunted* was filmed at Portland's wastewater treatment plant while I was temporarily assigned there.

So . . . what, if anything, did it all mean? I asked myself. It seemed obvious that it went way beyond circumstances. It was too strange for me to ignore yet too puzzling for me to decipher.

Movies following me around, some practically landing on my doorstep. What were the odds? *What would the odds be,* I asked myself, *if I had lived in LA, of movies following me around?* Practically nil.

People generally follow movies; my case was just the opposite. But as hard as I looked for some tiny thread of synchronistic meaning, it eluded my sight.

Chapter Twenty-Nine

"What do you know? You're just the bean counter."
The man's superior demeanor made Crystine's temper flare.

"Do you really think we should get into kid games here, Bob? Maybe start calling each other names? *(you arrogant ass)*. The fact is, we're not on schedule. And why? We could start pointing fingers and throwing accusations around like the production designer didn't give it enough thought, the actors don't like cold weather, too many script revisions, or . . . the production manager is too lackadaisical." Bob shifted uneasily in his chair. "But that childishness wouldn't solve the problem, would it?"

"I think it's obvious that we need to step it up; devote more hours, hire local technicians and extras, do whatever it takes keep on schedule; sounds simple enough," interjected Ira, the director.

A generous amount of enthusiastic agreement flew around the conference room. Bob leaned back in his chair, arms folded across his chest, his grin so smug Crystine wanted to vomit.

"That's the point I'm trying to make. Along with the production schedule we have a thing called a budget, and to throw more hours or hire more people or gather on Sunday and pray it doesn't snow will have an associated cost, and any increase in cost has to be approved by the main studio." She paused to look around. She had their attention. "So, first off, we simply need to focus and pay more attention. If that doesn't work, I'll need a detailed request for extra goods and services so I can estimate the costs and then forward it to the studio, Bob." He unfolded his arms and nodded.

"Good suggestions, Crystine. All right, we'll try the first one, and . . . focus, focus, focus, kids," said Ira.

Crystine returned to her office. Convincing the freewheeling types of the necessity of staying within budget was often exhausting. She turned in her chair and gazed out the window at the panoramic view of Vancouver, British Columbia. Beyond breathtakingly beautiful, the place somehow refreshed her spirit, in turn refreshing her outlook on life.

The sun seemed stalled in its descent into the Pacific, visible to the west. The mountains, to the north and east, glowed a rosy hue, the low angle of the sun's rays turning their snowcapped peaks into strawberry cones. Drawing a deep breath, drinking in what her eyes beheld, she began to relax, letting the natural beauty of the scene melt into her.

She remembered Daniel telling her of the raw purity of the land he'd grown up in, how much he had loved it, how he could draw energy from it, how that energy allowed him to enter the realm of the gods from the top of a mountain peak or in the depths of a pristine lake or on the back of a pony flying on hooves that barely touched the ground. She got a glimpse of what he meant as she looked out the window and let the peace of the scene refresh her once again.

Returning her gaze to the screen of her desktop, she reviewed the information she had typed in: Crystine Mercado, Huntington High School. She clicked okay and then went to her personal site and typed in Crystine Hopkins and the other information she was willing to reveal. Double-checking, she clicked okay, making herself available on the Internet site.

Chapter Thirty

I was back on day shift, and after spending the day working on a computer, I'd hurry home, grunt a greeting, eat, and then spend the evening on the computer in my upstairs office. What obsessed me were the people finder sites.

I searched California for Crystine Mercado. I got a few names in a few towns, but no street addresses or phone numbers or the e-mail address. I searched the other western states, my chances decreasing with each blank return. I expanded my search eastward, getting a few of the same names but never any solid contact information. My fervor burned out, and with shoulders slumped and head down, I gave up.

The despair went deeper than the hope had climbed, and I sank into the darkest possible shade of lethargy, moving like a zombie through the motions of existence, for it could not be qualified as living. I numbed myself, afraid to expose my heart to further torturous treatment by whatever malignant force ruled the universe. Perhaps it's a neutral cosmic energy and I had it coming, or it could be a deliberate intention, but, when at a loss for explanation, we dub it fate. The acquiescence is to say that the circumstances and events of our lives are written down before they occur, and there is no escape. Maybe, but if so, who is the author? And is the author benevolent or malevolent?

My life became fraught with duty, and drudgery was my singular response. I was back in the status of a human *doing,* rather than a human *being.*

One evening it occurred to me that I had never checked out Oregon on the people finder sites. I tossed the remote on the table, shot out of the La-Z-Boy, and bolted up the stairs two at a time! Plopping into my chair, I clicked the desktop on. I bopped into the site I'd been using, and up came the little multiple choice box; I clicked on Oregon and typed in Crystine Mercado. My mouth dropped open. There she was! I thought my heart would stop. I paused to catch my breath before I reread the information. Yes! It read Crystine Mercado and a name, address, and phone number in Willamina, Oregon. It wasn't more than forty miles from Portland. I had taken Jason and some of his buddies to play a pee-wee football game in Willamina a few years back. Oh man, Crystine! Right there, practically in my own neighborhood! Maybe a benevolent presence ruled the universe after all and a miracle had occurred in my behalf.

I stared, transfixed, at the screen, heart trembling, mouth gone dry, perhaps in a mild state of shock. The clock in the lower right-hand corner of the screen read 7:32, non-atomic time, but close enough not to be considered too late in the evening.

I took a blank sheet of copy paper out of the printer bin and copied her phone number down in large letters to avoid misreading it. I double-checked it for any errors and then laid it on the desktop under the light of the lamp. Holding my breath, I tried to punch the sequence of numbers on my wireless phone. I couldn't. I tried again. I couldn't. My hand trembled and wouldn't hold steady.

Gently returning the receiver to its cradle, I stood. My knees were weak, rubbery. I sat back down, staring at the screen, still not believing what I was reading. It just could not be. Exiting the search site, I logged off and shut down the machine. My mouth was as dry as Egyptian sand, and my heart raced, my mind alternating between spinning and racing all that night and into the following day.

If Crystine was in Willamina and I did get ahold of her, what would I say? How would I react, what would I do if I saw her? How would our meeting affect our lives and the lives of those around us? What if she didn't remember me? What if she rejected me? What the hell was I thinking?

Come on; get a grip.

I couldn't, no way. The desire, the intensity, the obsession was too overpowering to allow doubt, to allow the weakness of . . . what if? I had to find out. I had to find *her*. I had to know if she was still alive in this world, and if she was, how she was.

That night after dinner I quickly excused myself and retreated upstairs to plop down in front of the computer. I called up Crystine Mercado through the site once again. Grabbing the paper with her phone number on it, I double-checked it against the one on the screen. Check. I drew a double lung full of the breeze coming through the open window. Exhaling slowly, I picked up the wireless phone and punched in the sequence of numbers.

What would I say? "Hi, this is Daniel. Remember me? How ya doing?" Or something equally as silly. I really had no idea. Three hollow rings. I drew in another breath. Another ring.

A nasally, computerized voice said, "We're sorry . . . the number you are trying to reach has been disconnected. If you feel this message is in error . . ." I shut it off and dialed again. Four hollow rings. "We're sorry . . ."

My mind, my body, my very soul went numb.

So close.

No golden ring for me.

I guess happiness was a word not meant to be part of my vocabulary, not part of my life experience. I was convinced of it now. But even at that, my obsession would not allow me to give up on this one thin thread of hope. I would travel to Willamina on Saturday.

My sister Lauren and her husband Dale came over for dinner on Friday night. We saw each other about four times a year even though they lived right across the Columbia River in Vancouver, Washington. Jason had been at the coast and brought back fresh clams, crab, and salmon that he and his buddies had dug, caught, and fished out of the Pacific, and Lynn had prepared a feast fit for a king. We sat around the table after dinner, idly chitchatting, drinking coffee, eating mincemeat pie, and enjoying one another's company.

The discussion turned to politics, which I don't care much about. It's a game nobody wins, except perhaps a few very wealthy families, no matter where it's played.

"Remember the Cold War?" I asked Dale.

"Sure. We're the good guys, the Russians are the bad guys, and at any minute an all-out nuclear war could happen."

"Yeah, I remember we had drills to train us to duck under our desks in case Russia shot first," Lauren added.

"It caused a lot of anxiety in us kids; I know that," I said.

"And in our parents," Dale said.

"Well, since then we've had the War on Crime, which became the War on Drugs, which has filled the jails and prisons to overflow. Ever seen a dog chase its tail?" I asked. Lauren and Dale nodded. "That's the surreal wars we've been fighting. But I suppose some get rich off of wars, don't you think, Dale?"

"Come on—that's a given. Now we have the War on Terrorism, which will ultimately result in the further eroding and elimination of freedoms and promote the establishment of a police state."

"Right here in America?" I said with unmasked sarcasm.

"Yes, Daniel, right here in America. And isn't it sad?" added Lynn.

"I hope Iran doesn't turn into another Vietnam," said Lauren.

"Not specifically, but I imagine a lot of folks will profit from it, and it will go on for years and years like Vietnam. Just a guess," I quipped.

So we decided at the dinner table that honest disclosure by the government is seriously questionable and that objective reporting is a thing of the past. I believe it's called manipulation. The world didn't change any though. Wag on.

Daniel burst through the swinging door connecting the kitchen and dining room, ending our political nonsense. "Mom, can I have some more ice cream? Aunt Lauren, did I tell you I made the Royal Blues?"

"No, you didn't. What, or who, are the Royal Blues?"

"A school singing group. We'll travel all over the state, sometimes out of state. Fun . . . don't you think?"

"Way to go, kid," Dale exclaimed.

Daniel was fourteen, in high school, and six feet tall, 190 solid pounds, and he could care less about sports. His loves were art, music, entertainment, and animation, and he for sure didn't get his singing voice from me.

"Sure, Daniel, help yourself," Lynn replied. He pulled the biggest bowl he could find out of the cupboard and filled it with Rocky Road and spun back into the living room.

Lauren looked across the table at me.

"Did you know Jan Schultz and Todd Erickson got married right out of high school and are still together?" she asked, right out of the blue.

"Oh, yeah," I replied with a small amount of interest. "They still up there in Montana?"

"Uh-huh."

She was a girlfriend of mine in high school, but Todd had won her heart, and she dumped me. It hurt for about a week, near as I can remember. It felt like a hundred years and a couple of lifetimes ago now.

"How do you know that?" I asked.

"On the Internet, I stumbled across this site called Classmates. It's very cool. Every public school in every state is listed. All you have to do is go in and register your name and the years you attended in the registry of the school. Easy. Then, if there is someone you want to find out about, you can look up their last name under the years they attended school, and . . . bingo, there you are. Maiden names are changed to married names at each person's own site. E-mail right there, everything, like I said, easy. And . . . great for catching up on gossip." She winked. "You really should check it out and register yourself. It's lots of fun," she said.

I was way ahead of her.

We said our good-byes, Lynn retreated into the living room, and I headed upstairs. Afraid to get my hopes up, I typed "Classmates" into the search engine box and clicked on the first choice offered, and it popped onto the screen. My hands shook slightly as I fumbled my way to the list of states, clicking on California. Maneuvering the cursor to the letter H, I clicked on it. Scan down. Stop! Huntington. Click. Huntington High School. Click. So close again. I typed in the year Crystine would have graduated, *if* she'd gone there and *if* she'd graduated, and hit enter. The list of names appeared in alphabetical order. Scan down to the *M*s. Stop! Mercado, Crystine.

Afraid to breathe, as if I could upset some delicate balance at this moment, and more afraid to hope, I carefully placed the cursor on her name and firmly pressed down with my right index finger. A little hope flared as it immediately zapped me to her site. It *was* her! A hundred thousand sparks erupted throughout my being in the atomic split of a second, an eye-popping, mouth-dropping, heart-stopping, stunned suspension of time.

It seemed impossible for fate to play such a twisted trick, but there it was: Crystine Hopkins. I had married a Hopkins. She had married a Hopkins. Mere coincidence? I didn't know, but it seemed to be more synchronous than circumstantial.

Chapter Thirty-One

The environmentalists had succeeded in destroying logging as the backbone of the Oregon economy. Using the spotted owl as the fulcrum, they put over four hundred people out of work in Clatsop County. Save the owl's homes, dislodge the families from theirs.

Besides home to the logging families, Seaside had been a resort town from Memorial Day to Labor Day, offering relief to the heat-drenched people in the Willamette Valley. After having its foundational economy torn away, the city fathers turned it into a full-time resort.

A convention center sprang up, hosting the annual state Republican gathering. Old beach-front hotels were razed. Newer, fancier, bigger, and of course, taller ones were built in their place. Broadway, the main street that culminated in a turnaround at the beach, was redesigned to accommodate more foot traffic and to offer more shelter from the inevitable rains.

The town could easily have died. It not only didn't, but it thrived, and thrill seekers cruised in and out year around. Young people in cutoff jeans, open-toed sandals, and sleeveless shirts—or no shirts at all—weren't seen anymore. The party had adopted the ruse of sophistication, trading beer for champagne.

"We'd better go so we can get settled before dinner," said Bill.

"Yeah . . . I guess we'd better," quipped Crystine dryly. She had found the replica of Lewis and Clark's winter fort just south of Astoria less than inspiring, and the day was beginning to wear on her.

Bill wheeled the Navigator through the heart of Seaside, going west on Broadway. "This looks like a quaint little burg," he remarked as they reached the turnaround at the beach. Instead of going around the circle, he pulled off to the right into the parking lot of the Shining Inn, the fanciest, biggest, and tallest of the new hotels. Elegant by Oregon standards, it was adequate for world travelers.

After checking in at the lobby they rode the elevator to their top-floor suite. Dropping off their few travel items, freshening up and putting on a change of clothes, they rode the elevator in the opposite direction, returning to the lobby.

The hotel restaurant was situated with its wall of windows looking out over the ocean. The sun hung about an hour away from its plunge into the Pacific. Crystine stopped to gaze out the windows as the hovering golden orb began its nightly painting of the misty sky, its finished work to be the day's crowning glory. Smitten with a romantic impulse, she lightly grasped Bill's hand as they were about to enter the restaurant. "Let's hold off on dinner for a while. I'm not especially hungry. We could stroll down the promenade and watch the sunset. It looks like it will be glorious," she said.

"If that's what you want, I can wait," said Bill, taken by surprise.

They stopped at the monument centered in the middle of the turnaround. Crystine read the attached plaque.

"It says that this is the spot where Lewis and Clark spent a week boiling much-needed salt out of the sea water. This tub is an exact replica of the salt cairn, as it was called."

"Look out over the ocean," Bill said to her.

She looked. An ocean, one of many she had seen; in fact, all seven of the seven seas.

"Okay, I'll bite," Crystine replied. "It's an ocean as far as I can tell. Nothing special . . . is there?"

"No surfers, no piers, no freighters, just ocean."

She looked again, this time stricken by the scene. "Let's walk," she said, nearly breathless. She took Bill's hand in hers, and they strolled southward down the promenade.

Tillamook Head, a prominent mountain robed with lush evergreens, jutted out into the ocean just south of them, ending the view down the beach. Crystine pointed out the fire-colored cloud resting on its peak.

"A very unusual color," Bill commented. "Even more unusual because it's the only cloud in sight," he continued.

Crystine quickly scanned the sky and couldn't find another. "Yes, very unusual," she agreed. Suddenly stopping halfway between the turnaround and the mountain, she whispered, "Let's stop and watch the sunset from here." Turning his face toward the setting sun, the setting sun turning his face into the likeness of a bronze statue, Bill agreed without saying a word.

The sky of the northern coast rises straight up out of the ocean, like a vertical pane of glass. Upon this window the clouds, the mist, and the fog join together to form the canvas upon which the sun paints an unmatched scene nearly every evening. Sometimes its colors take on a pastel hue. Other times its lines and colors are bold and sharply defined, like an oil painting. At all times the colors are without name and beyond description, impossible to match and put in a can.

And the sky seems near, almost as if a person could reach out and touch it, smearing some of its colors on their fingertips, and then run the tips of their fingers across a matte or canvas surface, producing a sun-blessed masterpiece.

That night's display, a mixture of watercolor and oil paint, light pastels and dark clarity, fuzzy edges and sharp definition, was mesmerizing, and it took Crystine's breath away. Transfixed, her eye fell on a small sand dune, crowned by a few clumps of beach grass, lying halfway between the prom and the ocean's edge.

"Bill, I want to go sit on that small dune," she said, pointing at it, "just to watch the sunset. It's so incredibly beautiful as it shifts and changes, and . . . shimmers."

They settled on the same small dune that long ago had held a young man wearing cutoff jeans, open-toed sandals, and a sleeveless shirt; a young man who had pondered everything but had arrived at nothing . . . except that the heart of the matter is that it is the heart that matters.

The small cloud, now tinged by the sinking sun to the color of orange sherbet, lifted off of Tillamook Head and remained suspended over its peak. Across the vast water, hovering just above the horizon, clouds were rendered in shades from lavender to purple, their western edges lit on fire. The sun's rays slipped past the clouds, bathing the coastal mountains to the east in a pastel hue of pink roses. Above Tillamook Head, as if a fire burned within its body of vapor mist, the hovering cloud transformed from orange to pink to rose.

The sky clouds became deep purple, their western edges blood red, the background of sky splayed with the colors of fire. A fog bank hung at the seamless juncture of sea and sky. Kissed by the sun, its color shimmered between purple and orange. Returning the kiss, the fog rendered the sun into a golden-red ball, kind to the naked eye. The world was engulfed in a pastel rainbow, and Crystine was held in its thrall.

"Bill, kiss me please," she whispered with an urgency she didn't truly understand. He kissed her, long and deep and wet and dripping with passion.

As it neared dark they rose slowly, took one last lingering look at the lavender horizon, and headed back to the hotel, walking north, hand in hand, on the promenade. Deferring their passion, they decided to savor dinner as a precursor to it. The waitress seated them by the window wall where they could view both the scenery and the scene. The promenade below was rapidly becoming crowded with thrill seekers.

After taking their order for Seaside's famous razor clams, the waitress brought them a liter of white wine and poured them both a chilled glass, Crystine foregoing her customary merlot.

"Well . . . what do you think? Need we look any further?" asked Bill as they clinked glasses in a toast to the future. He gazed longingly into her soft brown eyes as the last of the sun's rays coaxed her burnished bronze hair into a dance of rose and copper highlights. Looking forward to the night ahead, a twinge of welcome anticipation surged through him. A long time gone, the strength of it surprised and thrilled him.

"It is a beautiful place . . . amazingly lovely . . . But I wouldn't care to live in a resort town. Yet . . . there is something about it that seems so oddly familiar . . ." she trailed off.

"Déjà vu?"

"M-m-m . . . maybe. No, I don't think so. I've never been here, at least not in this life, that I can recall. Have you?"

"No, this is my first trip to Oregon," Bill replied.

Crystine rose with the sun. Leaving a note for her still sleeping husband, she took the elevator to the hotel lobby. Stepping out into the cool morning air, she was thankful that she had purchased a designer sweat suit last night, its fleecy warmth shielding her from the morning chill. Traversing the half circle of the turnaround, she continued south on the promenade. Looking up at Tillamook Head, she wondered if the small cloud that resided on its peak was the same one as last night's.

The sky was clear, gray yielding to pale blue, as the sun ascended on another day. The scene was nowhere near as spectacular as last night's display, but the promise of another was offered.

Stopping halfway between the turnaround and Tillamook Head, Crystine stared pensively at the small sand dune they had sat on the night before. It compelled her, like a mystery that needed solving. She had to return to it and try to understand the pleasant suddenness of her romantic inclinations begun there the previous evening.

Seating herself comfortably, pulling her knees to her breasts against the remaining chill, she gazed up at the mountain. The cloud was now the color of liquid gold, the sun's early morning rays having penetrated the crystalline structure of its mist. The ocean was deep blue, tinged with gun-metal gray, befitting the north Oregon coast.

The sun burnished the beach to a molten bronze, matching Crystine's hair, and then radiated her face with a golden glow. Basking in the chill-chasing warmth, she drank in nature's display of changing hue and shifting shadow as a symphony of wind and wave and gull played gently on her ears. Closing her eyes, she breathed deeply of air filtered over thousands of miles of ocean.

Peace settled over her, and from within, in that secret place in her heart, a long ago familiar warmth stirred and spread outward, warming her from the inside out. She sighed. She knew.

Opening her eyes, she was not surprised to see the resident cloud rise and drift away from the top of Tillamook Head, like the cloud that had been lifted from her mind. She uncurled herself and headed north on the prom to the Shining Inn. Stopping at the house phone in the lobby, she opened the Clatsop County phone book to A, certain in the hope of what she would find. But her hope was dashed, disappointment settling in its place.

No Abrams, not a single one in the county. Not in Seaside, not in Astoria, not anywhere. Yet she was sure of what she had felt on the beach, and it could only come from one source, Daniel. But how, and why, after so long a time? Perhaps the mystery was beyond solving.

Chapter Thirty-Two

Wheeling the Navigator out of the Shining Inn's parking lot, Bill turned left, heading east down Broadway. The lush green carpet of the coastal range, brilliantly lit by the early morning sun, matched the color of the SUV. Reaching the intersection of Highway 101, he turned south onto it. Being a weekday, the traffic was light, and he looked forward to a leisurely cruise south down the coast.

Occupied with his own thoughts, he didn't notice Crystine's silence. But her silence was like the surface of the Pacific. Underneath, currents ran deep and swift as she tried to fathom the thoughts of Daniel that came so sudden and so strong, wondering if feeling his presence was only delusion. Her emotions shifted between wonder and disappointment, like a ship tossed on the sea, vacillating between assurance of what had occurred and denial that it hadn't.

She glanced over at Bill, grateful that he didn't notice her inner turmoil. Relaxing somewhat, she decided to let things work themselves out, or better still, let them go. She had a bright future, and the past was the past. But her feelings refused to line up with her mental assertions.

Sighing, she peered out the window at Tillamook Head. The cloud had returned.

❧

The warm spring weather held for several days as they traveled down the coast from Cannon Beach to Newport to Coos Bay, the sky clear of clouds or hanging mist. The coast itself, from the beach inland, remained free from the intrusion of fog.

The three-day trip was leisurely, and Bill enjoyed every minute of it. Crystine remained in neutral, pondering the occurrence at the Seaside beach, trying to get her feelings to line up with what her mind told her. By the time they reached Coos Bay, the intensity inside her subsided and she could focus on the present.

The beauty of the landscape—clean, open, and refreshing—had not eluded her along the way, and she deeply appreciated it. The nightly sunsets, beyond matching by any artist, crowned the closing of each day, their beauty different but always taking her breath away.

The artistry reminded her of Holly, still fluttering about UCLA as a part-time instructor. She hadn't talked with her in over a year. Every now and then she had a twinge of doubt about whether adopting her granddaughter Crystal had been the right thing to do. Materially, yes; as to the important parts of life, only time would tell.

Nikki was watching Crystal at their house in Thousand Oaks. Crystine reminded herself to call her this evening. Good old Nikki, now the director of Human Services for Los Angeles County, was always uplifting and often insightful and could answer puzzling questions about life with an ease that Crystine recognized as a gift.

"Have you decided anything at all?" Crystine asked as they pulled into Coos Bay for the night.

"Just that I'm not only ready but am *positively* going to retire," Bill replied. "But I still want to travel a little further south, to the California border. Maybe some quaint little town along the way will reach out and grab us," he continued.

"Grab us? That's an unusual thing for you to say."

"Well . . . retirement is about relaxing and *feeling,* especially feeling good. Let the taxes and the markets and the numbers be damned. We can afford to live about anywhere we want. With your income and my pension, we'll have more than enough," Bill said.

"Oh, I know. I just thought you'd have everything thoroughly researched. You know, market values, tax values, and the tax base of property in every little town we visit along the way."

"I do," he answered, laughing, "but I'm trying real hard not to let those considerations influence our decision. So I hope something reaches out and . . . *grabs* us," he said, laughing once again.

"Your decision, Bill, remember?"

"Sure I do, but I'm going to want to know what you think," he grinned.

"I like Oregon," Crystine said. "Seaside the best so far, even though it is a resort town. I don't completely understand why, just a feeling . . ."

Bill turned his eyes away from the sleepy main street of Coos Bay to look at her. "We don't have to settle on anything during this trip. We can always come back and give it another try." He paused. "I like Oregon too. Just haven't found the right town yet. Or, I should say, the right town hasn't *grabbed* me yet."

"Grabbed you," she exclaimed, chuckling, enjoying Bill's relaxed approach.

With the sunset dimming to deep lavender and Bill in the shower, Crystine picked up the phone and dialed her own number. Nikki answered.

"Hi, Nikki. Any news on the other side of boring?"

"Nope. Things are smooth as a newborn baby's butt. How's the trip going? Anything clicking?" she asked.

"Not in terms of finding property."

"Well, it'll happen soon enough. Retiring is a big life decision, uprooting . . . just as big, and then the reality. So, not to hurry; not to worry."

"I know I couldn't handle being retired. Not right now, anyway. Is Crystal doing okay?"

"Just being a teenager. We've talked some. She goes back and forth between being sad at the thought of leaving and looking forward to a new adventure. I think deep down she hopes to stay. You know, having all her friends here and her place established with them, that kind of stuff; you remember those days."

"Sure, some with precise vividness."

"But I pointed out that changes happen, once in a while severe and unwanted, so she might as well start learning how to deal with them. Eventually all your current friends will be gone, and that will happen no matter where you go to high school—you and I excepted, of course." Crystine smiled; good old Nikki. "And I told her to look at the opportunity to make new ones. She's at Sarah's right now, probably talking about . . . ummm, boys, what do you think?"

"I would find that rather shocking!"

A thousand miles apart, they shared the laughter.

"So, what clicked that brought up such vivid memories?" asked Nikki.

"In Seaside, I was sitting on a small dune on the beach, with Bill, mind you, when out of nowhere I felt or sensed, but absolutely did not imagine, Daniel's presence so strong that it physically affected me, and the emotional affect still lingers. And Nikki, I'm not exaggerating, not in the least. So what do you think?"

"He was there, at that precise spot at some point in the past, how long ago doesn't matter. My guess is that he experienced something profound then and there."

"Like what?"

"I don't know. An epiphany, a revelation, an angel dropped down to visit, or . . . he fell in love," replied Nikki.

"Don't say that."

"Or was still deeply in love."

"You don't think I'm crazy, then?" asked Crystine.

"Not in this instance, but I am worried about you."

"Why? You just said not to hurry, not to worry."

"This is different. This is a matter of the heart. What will you do, girlfriend, if Daniel should suddenly pop into your life?"

"I've fantasized about it but never seriously thought about it . . ."

"I'll tell Crystal you called."

"Bye, Nikki, and thanks . . . for everything."

Nearly exhausted after their third trip in four months to Oregon, Crystine let out a sigh of relief as they landed at LAX. Bill's search was over and it felt good to be home, but the feeling didn't last long. The traffic to Thousand Oaks was heavy and suffocating, and after the openness and cleanness of Oregon, LA closed in on her in a hurry.

"This sucks. I'm so glad to be getting out," Bill said as horns blared in the stinking smog-laden air.

"I'm happy for you . . . us, too. I don't think I'll miss this much . . . Crystal might, she might miss the whirl of LA excitement, and that concerns me a little. But after I tell her of our new home and what the town has to offer, I think she'll be okay with it."

Crystal, in her early teens, was naturally interested in being popular and having fun. That she would be popular was a given. Her Hispanic blood prevalent, she was a beauty, the flower of her youth in full bloom, with her black, long, wavy hair, deep, soft brown eyes, perpetually tanned skin, and early physical development, she would definitely stand out in a small town. Or in a large town.

Bill and Crystine had purchased one of the oldest, finest, and most expensive houses in Cedar Harbor, a four-bedroom, three-bath, two-story Cape Cod built by a former lumber baron and situated on two acres of beachfront property on a bluff overlooking the ocean.

Crystal's questioning was relentless.

"What's there to do in Cedar Harbor?"

"How big is it?"

"Is the high school close?"

"How many schools are there?"

"What do the kids wear?"

"What do they do?"

"How big is the house?"

"It looks over the ocean?"

"How big is two acres?"

"Eighty-seven thousand, one hundred twenty square feet, to be exact," Crystine replied.

"Let's see, that'd be about three hundred feet squared. Not bad." Crystal had also inherited a knack for numbers. "Big enough for a horse?" she asked.

"Maybe . . . we'll see. We can talk about it tomorrow, okay, honey? I'm really tired right now and in need of a hot bath and a good night's sleep."

"Sure, Mom," she replied. Skipping into the kitchen she hollered, "Aunt Nikki, guess what! We're moving to Oregon!" But of course Aunt Nikki already knew that.

Crystine stepped out of the soothing waters of her bath into the warm, steamy room. Relaxed and comforted, she wrapped a towel around her still damp hair, donned her terry-cloth robe, slipped her manicured toes into her fuzzy slippers, and strode languorously across the bedroom, through the door, down the hall, to her home office, refreshed enough to check her e-mail.

Flicking on the light switch, she crossed the room and sat in the leather executive chair behind her oak desk. Turning on the desktop, she waited for the screen to come to life.

Entering her e-mail site, she began scrolling through the messages. Pretty sparse for being gone a week but confirming her decision to disengage from the electronic world while gone. No apparent emergencies or work-related brush fires to be put out; she breathed a sigh of relief on that one. But the usual unsolicited stuff was garishly prevalent, enticing advertisements, spam, other garbage, and virus-infested crap. People will be people.

She scrolled down the list, deleting as she went. The very last message brought her to a pause. Titled "For a Long Time," it had been sent by "dunkeyhead at excite.com". She paused, holding her finger above the left click button of the mouse, ready to press it down, tempted to see what the message might say, but decided instead that "dunkeyhead at excite" referred to some sneaky porn message and clicked delete.

Chapter Thirty-Three

A week had gone by since I sent my e-mail to Crystine. I had gotten no response. I'd expected something, if only a "get lost, bozo!" Maybe she wasn't the same Crystine that I'd known. It could be possible; in fact, when I listened to my head and not my heart, I thought that it was likely the case.

It was Saturday, the crispy kind of day that holds promise of excitement and adventure. Checking all its vital fluids, I climbed into the cab of my Chevy van. It was old and getting rusty but was as dependable as a faithful hound. Double-checking the map, making sure of my route to Willamina, I backed down and out the driveway, telling myself I had to be the world's biggest fool for heading there in the hope of finding Crystine. But I went. I cleared the on ramp, shifted the old rig into fourth, and cruised south on Interstate 5, knowing that this was my last chance.

No one lived in the abandoned house I had come in search of except the ghost of hopelessness taunting me with the blackness of despair. Unless I had an e-mail message waiting for me when I got home, that was that, done, finished. No more reason to obsess; my hope had been broken and thrown in my face.

It was still early in the day, and I decided to go to the beach, being halfway there already. Maybe go on a good drunk—at least it would kill the pain . . . for a while.

It had been a dozen years since I'd been to the coast, almost twice that many since I'd lived there. I turned right on Highway 101 and headed north to Seaside. I knew the place had changed into a year-round resort, but I was amazed at how much; it was no longer a sleepy little place during any time of year. Broadway was a cauldron of specialty shops, selling everything from salt water taffy to midnight promises. For the first time I laid eyes on the Shining Inn dominating the western end of Broadway. I wasn't in a cordial mood and decided that it wouldn't be a good idea to spend the night there. If I did drink, I'd end up making fun of the façade of snobbery and probably get my face punched. Instead I visited the old motel my brother and I had run many summers ago. It was still there, and in decent shape, so I booked a room. Maybe some good memories would help override the twisting in my gut.

After checking in, I strolled west down the street to its dead end at the promenade, about halfway between Tillamook Head and Broadway. The beach hadn't changed much. Of course, sand shifts now and then, but that's to be expected. The little sand dune where I spent many hours pondering what, I couldn't remember, was in the same spot. It had changed some, but I recognized it without any trouble. The overcast sky was omnipresent, coloring the world a dull gray, the Pacific a darker shade of the same color. That suited me just fine; the world could have been shrouded in black for all I cared. Off to the south Tillamook Head had a singular heavy cloud covering its peak. I wondered if the same cloud had been there all these years. I'd never seen the Head without one. No, that couldn't be possible, but it was fun to think about and say, "Why not?"

Vaulting over the concrete railing, I walked slowly to the dune and sat gazing out at the giant cesspool called an ocean. The breeze coming off of it felt as though it could temper the heat of anger and the edge of bitterness that boiled inside me. It is so damn dark when hope is lost.

Closing my eyes I breathed deep of the ocean air. It had a mild calming effect on me, and I continued taking the air down into my lungs, for how long I don't know; more than a minute, less than an hour. I opened my eyes to the world, dull and gray, but felt better, not so thrust through with rage. And there was something else, like a whisper stirring a feeling, vague and yet familiar. I couldn't put my finger on it, but I knew it, and it felt good and right, an aura from long ago or yesterday, a warming presence. Perhaps an angel came to minister grace to my despairing soul. Whatever the source, it was a welcome release from rage. I turned my head left and glanced up in time to see a flash of brilliant light within the cloud on Tillamook Head. Lightning? I couldn't remember ever seeing it on the coast. But regardless, I waited to hear the thunder. It never boomed, only silence. Maybe it was an angel, and the light a flash of its wings. *Could be*, I thought. But I'd probably never know this side of what we call death.

Strains of music, distant and haunting, came drifting through my mind, louder and clearer until my breath caught in my throat at the recognition of the strong sax riff with a guitar back: "Harlem Nocturne." Maybe it was nostalgia night and the band in the hotel at the turnaround was playing it. I hadn't heard it or thought of it for years, since my early teens, in fact, when Crystine and I had danced slow to its mesmerizing melody and melded our hearts together. I was flooded with the memories it stirred, and I recognized the earlier vague feeling. But how could it be? It was as if Crystine were very near, I knew how her presence felt. No, not possible.

Why not?

Was it an extension of mercy? Or a tantalizing tease by something malignant? Or was it her presence? Logic and intellect said no to all of those impressions, of course, so I went deep inside myself, sorting my feelings and trusting my instincts to filter the possibilities. No angel; no demon; it was her. I was absolutely certain of that, and somehow, someway, our paths had crossed. I accepted it. She was alive, somewhere; I knew that, and right now, that was all I needed to know.

Hope restored.

I looked again at Tillamook Head, my mouth dropping open as I watched the cloud lift off its peak. And then I remembered what it was I had pondered many lifetimes, and yet like yesterday, ago. It is indeed true that the heart of the matter is that it is the heart that matters, and right now, mine was soaring with hope and awe and joy.

Enough daylight remained so I could make it back to Portland before dark fell. The clerk at the old motel was kind enough not to charge me for the room and credited my Visa.

At home I checked my e-mail. No return message from Crystine, yet my hope remained while my obsession ended. I settled down after my trip to Seaside, wondering if I had gone through a period of madness, certainly one of foolishness. How many first loves ever reunite or spend a lifetime together? Maybe not a single one in all of history.

And something else: I looked at Lynn through new eyes, realizing just how deeply I loved and appreciated her. It had been thirty years now that we had been married, and she had never given me reason to mistrust her, nor had she ever insisted on having all the finer things in life or always getting her own way, though her arguments could be quite persuasive.

I had to concede to the fact that my intention to find Crystine wasn't powerful enough, or maybe it was a false idea in the first place. Didn't matter; I was content to go on with life and appreciate what I had, and that was miracle enough.

Chapter Thirty-four

The Hopkins house, clad in cedar silvered by the coastal weather, sat like a sentinel atop the bluff. Facing the Pacific, an enclosed sun porch opened onto a redwood deck that ran the frontal width of the house. A round tan-colored marble table surrounded by three wicker chairs was on the north end. A deep comfortable chaise lounge with a small table at the side was on the southern end. Potted ferns were placed at the corners of the deck. A waist-high railing of redwood slats surrounded the sides and front of the deck, except for the center front, where a four-foot opening led to three long flights of stairs with a landing after the first and second flights and the third one ending at the beach. The stairway treads were old-growth Douglas fir, as were the railings, anchored to withstand the gale-force winds of winter. No expense had been spared and no quality of materials had been compromised when the house was built.

The beach at Cedar Harbor, though not isolated, was unfrequented and quiet. No big bonfires, big parties, or bevies of bikini-clad babes. It was early June, and a beautiful quiet day graced the Oregon shore. Not a hint of breeze blew off the ocean or from the wooded inland. Under the deep blue of the sky, the sand took on the color of eggshells.

Mid-morning, the temperature hovering around seventy degrees, Crystal descended the second of the three flights of stairs. Without a breeze to blow her hair back, she had it tied up in a loose-hanging ponytail. Jet black, the wavy mane hung down between her shoulder blades. Her lime-green halter top, matching the color of the tie in her hair, pronounced the deep olive tone of her bare arms and midriff. Loose-fitting cream-colored shorts, mid-thigh level, and slip-on leather sandals completed her attire. Her beauty was only marginally surpassed by that of the surrounding day.

She would begin her college career in the coming fall but was as yet undecided whether to attend UCLA or Oregon. Crystine wanted her to go to UCLA. Acceptance there would not be an issue—money would talk, and very persuasively. But Los Angeles was not Crystal's home, and its promise of glitter held no attraction for her. The University of Oregon had accepted her on her own merit, and no other persuasion would be necessary.

Crystal had become attached to Oregon and its people. She liked the country and three years ago had gotten a little quarterhorse mare, a sorrel with a white blaze face, and being too far from her was not something she wanted.

Stepping off the last stair into the cool soft sand, she glanced quickly south and then shifted her gaze north as she headed for a small sand dune situated halfway between the water and the back of the beach. The shore extended in a nearly perfect straight line in both directions, with jutted land stopping the eyes on either side about a mile to the south and maybe twice that far to the north. She noticed a small speck to the north as she approached the dune; probably a beachcomber. They came around once in a while but were otherwise quite scarce in the area. Crystal settled herself on the sand dune.

As time had passed she had come to think of her grandmother as her mother, not in word, but in truth. Her sister-mother Holly, being a full-fledged professor at UCLA now, was . . . well . . . extremely artsy and busy. She got in touch with Crystal on her birthdays and at Christmas, just in the form of cards, but they were original and hand-painted.

Crystal and her mother had spent many pleasant hours on the same dune, engaged in talk about life's ups and downs, its triumphs and tragedies, and its possibilities. Mostly about its possibilities. To Crystine, possibilities and opportunities were part of the train that ran on the same track, so she pushed her daughter to attend UCLA. "And," she said, "with Holly a professor on campus, you and she could begin a closer relationship, maybe a healthy one." But Crystal wasn't convinced, not about possibilities or opportunities or relationships, and these were the things she needed to sort through.

A bit free-spirited like Holly, her sister-mother, she thought education should have some other value besides getting a job that allowed you to claw your way up a corporate ladder. *Now there's an unusual opportunity,* she chuckled to herself. So today was a day for contemplation, and Crystal was torn between what her head told her and what was in her heart. It's hard to make life-affecting decisions at seventeen. But she had to start, and its factors were not to be weighed with a defective scale, as her mother would say, and her mother could be quite persuasive.

Gazing out at the ocean as she had thousands of times before, she whispered her hope that whatever the decision, it would be the one best for her. She moved her head slowly left, panning south down the beach, and then straight ahead to the seamless juncture of sea and sky. Panning north, she noticed that the solitary speck had grown larger, forming into the shape of a man.

Up at the house, Crystine stepped through the double French doors leading from the sun porch to the deck. Carrying a steaming cup of morning coffee, she sat on one of the deck chairs and set her cup down on the table. She drew in a deep breath of the balmy ocean air, allowing the relaxation of its timelessness settle into her. She knew that Crystal was struggling with a major life decision, and she hoped and prayed that it would be the best one for her.

"Hi," the speck from the north said. It had grown into a full-sized young man with dark brown hair, nondescript in style, parted on the left side and combed over, sort of. He stood around six feet tall, lean and sinewy, and Crystal guessed he weighed about two hundred pounds. His blue eyes bordered on gray. She was surprised, not at his less-than-stunning appearance, but that he appeared with stunning silence, like a whisper of vapor.

But she wasn't the least bit startled.

"Hello," she said. "What are you doing on my beach?"

"Your beach? It must have cost a fortune! How much did you pay for it?"

"Well, it's not really *my* beach, but it is in front of our house, and no one hardly ever uses it, so I think of it as mine."

"Okay," replied the young man.

"Okay what?"

"It's yours. You can have it. But, I pray thee, oh Queen, that I may join you in the realm of *your* beach. Perhaps you will grant that I may sit with you on your throne for a brief but no doubt most thrilling time of my life."

Crystal liked him.

"Boon granted. But mind you, you are here at my discretion, so behave, lest the knight become the knave."

They shared a laugh saturated with delight as the young man seated himself not too close to Queen Crystal.

Crystine smiled as she took a sip of her cooled-down coffee. She was used to boys, and now young men, approaching her daughter, getting next to her. She sighed at the bittersweet memories of her own youth. But, all in all, life had been good to her. She had found a measure of contentment, and she had gotten almost everything she had ever wanted. But still she felt a void deep inside herself, a vague incompleteness. Knowing the reason for it, she could reluctantly accept it, and hope, above all, that Crystal would not have to live with the same emptiness.

"Aren't you a little old to be wearing a Donald Duck shirt?" asked Crystal, amused by the macho image her new knight lacked.

"I like Donald Duck and Mickey Mouse, and Walt Disney is my hero," the young man retorted.

"You don't really look like a geek," said the queen to Sir Speck.

"Besides, m'lady, this is not Donald Duck. This happens to be the mascot of the University of Oregon Fighting Ducks. Rumors of that magical kingdom, the very model of Camelot, have no doubt reached even to this far realm."

"*Animal House.*"

"Wha-a-at?"

"The U of O, where they filmed *Animal House*; you know, the movie," said the queen.

"Sure, I know. It's one of my dad's all-time favorites. One of mine too, as a matter of fact."

"My mom works on them."

"She's a veterinarian?"

"No-o-o . . . the movies; she works on the movies."

"She's an actress?"

"No . . . she works in the financial area. It costs money to make a movie, you know."

"I suppose."

"Do you go there?" asked Crystal.

"No, I've never been to Camelot, but I do go to see a movie now and then," replied Sir Speck.

"No . . . I mean to the U of O, to Oregon!"

"Oh, yeah . . . quack, quack . . . a Fighting Duck all the way," he said, sticking out his chest to accentuate the logo. "I'll be a senior this coming year."

"Well, I still think it looks like Donald Duck," exclaimed the queen.

He laughed with a delight unremembered.

Reaching down with his right hand, he scooped a golf-ball-sized rock from out of the sand and, with a flick of his arm and a snap of his wrist, sent it rocketing with a resounding smack into the face of a small wave two-thirds the length of a football field away. Being low tide, the beach stretched for fifty yards before reaching the water's edge.

Crystal turned and for the first time really *looked* at him, deciding immediately that the word geek did not apply.

"Do you play sports there?" she asked.

"No, I've never tried surfing," he replied.

"No . . . not *there*," Crystal said, pointing at the surf, her exasperation undisguised. "*There* . . . at the U of O!"

"No, I don't care about sports."

"Oh . . . what's your major?"

"Art and design, with an emphasis on computer graphics and animation."

"You didn't answer my question."

"Art and design, with an emphasis on com . . ."

"No, no, not that one. What are you doing on *my* beach?"

"Bumming."

"That's obvious. What else?"

"Exploring."

"Exploring, for what?"

He turned to give Queen Crystal a straightforward and penetrating gaze. "New cartoon characters," he answered.

She was taken aback. Most young men would have fallen at her feet by this time.

"That's a nice color on you," he said, his gaze dropping to her halter top.

Crystal had inherited her mother's endowments and had gotten used to the ogling.

"It's lime green," she replied.

"What's lime green?"

"My halter top."

"I was referring to your shorts. More tan-colored, I think."

Delighted by the surprise, Crystal burst into laughter, Sir Speck joining her. She liked him even more.

"Do you live around here?" she asked.

"Well, no . . . my dad does . . . in a small trailer house about twenty miles north of here. I'm visiting him for a while before I go back to Eugene, to the U of O. He comes here once in a while, told me how it just feels good to be in this area . . . the good vibes thing, so I drove down to take a look.

"He must be an old hippy."

"Yeah, something like that." He laughed. "And so some whimsical muse inspired me to stop and explore this beach. Haven't found any new cartoon characters, though."

Strangely, an internal sigh of relief escaped her. Crystal didn't want him to view her as a cartoon character.

"What about your mom? Does she live around here too? Somewhere else?" she asked.

He stared out at the ocean with a faraway look much older than his age should have allowed. Crystal let the moment be as he slowly turned to look at her.

"Uh . . . no . . . she died from cancer right after I got out of high school," he replied.

"I'm so sorry," Crystal said. She could not resist putting her hand out and touching the young man's arm, offering comfort if she could. "Your dad's a widower then?" she asked.

"Huh . . . oh, yeah, I guess that's the word for it. He's pretty much a recluse now. Doesn't want any more hurt."

"That's sad. I'm so sorry," Crystal said with a depth of sincerity she didn't know she had, but it was comfortable, and she suddenly felt more grown up.

Not wanting the conversation to drift further toward sad, the man-speck asked, "And what, pray tell, doth the queen do, alone and unattended, in her realm?"

"I'm contemplating," she replied.

"Uh-oh, that could be serious. So I shall attend m'lady, if thou wilt dub me with knighthood," he said.

"I will. And I dub thee Sir . . . Donald!" exclaimed the queen.

They shared another sparkling laugh permeated with delight.

"Contemplating what?" Sir Donald asked.

"School. I start college this fall."

"Are you going to Oregon State or to Oregon?" he inquired of the queen.

"I haven't decided. My mom wants me to go to UCLA."

"What does your heart say?" asked Sir Donald.

"What's that got to do with anything?"

"Well, my dad always says that after careful consideration, after assessing all the facts, after weighing all the pros and cons, and after analyzing different scenarios and outcomes, most decisions should be made with a clearly informed and rational mind." He paused. "But the really important ones should be made with the heart."

"Is your dad strange?"

"Sort of, but who isn't? So . . . what's in your heart?"

"I don't want to go to Los Angeles," she blurted with surprising, comfortable, and more grown-up honesty.

"Oregon it is then!" Sir Donald robustly exclaimed.

"Wait a minute! I didn't say I was going to Oregon. There are still Oregon State and other schools to consider," she protested.

"How else will I be able to attend m'lady, unless you come to Camelot?"

"Do you like Camelot?" she retorted, playfully serious.

"I do, and like my dad says, all an education does is get your foot in some door that hopefully won't be slammed too soon in the future. Where the education comes from doesn't matter much in the long run."

"He is strange," said the queen. "Camelot it is then," she proclaimed as she stood up from her throne. Offering him her hand she said, "Rise, Sir Donald." He gently took it, and she felt his touch all the way to her shoulder and beyond, to her heart.

"Will you be . . . exploring here again?" she asked, grateful her thumping heart wasn't revealed by a stammering tongue.

"I will. But not for a cartoon character," he answered, gazing deeply into her eyes.

"Tomorrow? Maybe?"

"As m'lady wishes," Sir Donald replied, bowing slightly at the waist. His hand remained in hers as their eyes locked in a look that flirted with longing. She smiled, its brightness almost dimming the sun.

"Tomorrow then, Sir Donald," Crystal chirped as she headed for the stairway leading up to her house.

He watched her walk. Tan was an excellent color on her.

Crystal stopped on the second stair landing to turn and look north. A single dark speck receded on the otherwise empty beach. She wasn't certain what had just happened down there, but she had no doubt of the affect.

Her eyes had just cleared the floor of the redwood deck when her mother asked, "Who's your new friend?"

Bouncing up the remaining four stairs Crystal replied, "Oh, someone I just met. He's a duck . . . I mean . . . he goes to the University of Oregon. He'll be a senior this year."

"Does he live around here?"

"Sort of. He's visiting his dad for a week or so. His dad lives in a trailer house about twenty miles north of here."

"A trailer? Hm-m-m, what does his dad do for a living?"

"I didn't think to ask. It doesn't matter to me anyway. He did say his dad is a widower, though."

Crystine paused for a moment in her interrogation and then asked, "Does he have a name?"

"Who?"

"Your friend . . . the duck."

Crystal laughed. "Yes. I dubbed him Sir Donald. I asked him what he was doing on *my* beach, so he started playing this game, calling me a queen, and it went from there. It was fun, and easy, and . . . sort of strange."

"Strange? How so?"

"Well, he made me feel warm . . . from the inside out."

Crystine managed to hold on to her coffee cup without spilling its contents or causing the table to shake as she set it down. Standing, she focused her gaze northward on the receding speck.

"You never told me your friend's name," she said to Crystal without turning to face her.

"You know, I never asked. He doesn't know mine either, come to think of it. Like I said, sort of strange. But he told me he'd be on the beach tomorrow. Wanna meet him?"

She turned toward her daughter. "Yes, Crystal, I'd very much like to meet your Sir Donald," she said.

"Mom, there's something else you should know." Crystal drew a deep breath and then said, "I've decided to attend the University of Oregon."

After a long look, Crystine said, "For some reason, I'm not surprised."

"I hope you're not disappointed," Crystal continued.

"No, honey, I'm not. Only if you were unhappy would I be disappointed, and that wouldn't be with you, but with your circumstances," her mother replied absently, her mind wandering to that place in a corner of her heart where peace could be found.

Chapter Thirty-five

The weather mirrored yesterday's. Crystal and her mother sat at the deck table, Crystine drinking coffee and Crystal enjoying a cup of tea and rhythmically alternating her gaze between the blue of the ocean and the eggshell white of the sand to the south and then to the north. A small speck appeared, and to her surprise, her heart soared with a strength of anticipation she was unable to temper with reason or denial.

The speck grew.

"Is that Sir Donald?" asked Crystine.

"I think it is. I'd better go take up my throne, just in case," replied Crystal, laughing, her mother joining in, her own anticipation growing.

"Bye, Mom," Crystal said as she began her royal descent to the beach. "Will you be here for a while? I'll bring Sir Donald up to meet you if it's okay," she quipped as her head disappeared below the level of the deck.

"Okey-dokey," her mother called after her, surprised at the youthful slang that flowed so easily from her mouth. She smiled and took a sip of her still hot coffee.

Settling herself on the same small sand dune, Crystal turned her head to the north. The speck had disappeared. Her heart caught in her throat, and again the strength of the emotion took her by surprise. Refocusing, she scanned down by the ocean and then back again to the eastern edge of the sandy beach.

Still no speck.

"And how is m'lady this glorious morning?"

Twisting around to her right, Sir Donald filled her view.

"How'd you do that?" she asked.

"I used my voice."

Standing as if to verify the young man's presence, she said, "No, I mean, how'd you sneak up on me like that?"

"It was easy, I just moved from dune to dune along the back of the beach. And I didn't really sneak up on you. I just approached very quietly . . . in case you were contemplating. Were you?"

"Were I what?"

"Contemplating."

"No," she said.

"Did you change your mind then?"

"Sir Donald, you weary me with your questions, so I shall be seated, and you may seat yourself next to me," she said, patting a spot on her left, nearer to her than yesterday's.

Suppressing an amused smile, he bowed slightly, his eyes not leaving hers, and then seated himself on the designated spot.

"About what?" she asked.

"Going to the U of O."

"No."

"Glad to hear it," he stated.

Crystal returned a wan smile, thinking that his response would be more exuberant, but maybe he was putting on a cool front. She thought they were on the same wavelength, but only time would reveal yea or nay.

Time accelerated as they bantered back and forth, sometimes for fun, sometimes with purpose. Deep in the moment, talking of many things—moms, dads, backgrounds, histories, school, hopes, and dreams—time revealed its yea, and they were on the same wavelength, but lost track of time.

"Oh my . . . I promised my mom I'd bring you up to meet her!" Crystal blurted out of nowhere.

"Are you sure the queen mother wants to meet me? I mean, I feel more like a stray dog than a worthy knight."

"Don't be silly. You're Sir Donald! Come on," she said as she stood and, taking hold of his right hand, helped him to stand with her. The connection went deeper than momentary. Crystal didn't release his hand as she half tugged him toward the stairs.

"Whoa, m'lady. I go willingly to yon castle keep!" With a shy smile she let go of his hand.

The queen and her knight bounced up the stairs side by side until they stood on the lustrous surface of the redwood deck.

Crystine reclined in the chaise lounge, its tan color accentuated by the glowing redwood. Her burnished bronze hair, now with a few strands that matched the silvered cedar on the house, hung loose to her shoulders. Her brown eyes were still quick and intelligent but also carried their allotment of life's weariness and were now more wise than inquisitive.

She looked up at the young couple as they landed on the surface of the deck. The sun on their faces was overshadowed by the brightness shining through them. She remembered the same brightness in herself, once upon a time.

"Good morning," she welcomed them. "There's coffee and coffeecake on the table if you'd like some."

"We'll be right back, Mom. I want to show Sir Donald my horse."

"Take your time; the coffee will still be hot."

Crystal grabbed his hand and led him through the sun porch, the living room, and the kitchen, across the back porch, and into the backyard. A sharp whinny came from a shed at the back of the acre.

"I didn't know you had a horse," he said.

"That's because I didn't tell you," she said as they crossed the grounds to the shed. Crystal slid out the bolt and swung the door open. The blaze-faced mare tossed her head up and down and whinnied a greeting.

"Hey, girl," Crystal said, laying her hand on its neck and gently stroking the sorrel to calmness. "She's one of the big reasons I didn't want to go to UCLA. I'd never see my baby."

"What's her name?"

"Pogo."

The mare walked over to him and gently placed her muzzle on his chest. "Wow, she must really like you. That's the first time I've ever seen her do that to a stranger," said Crystal. He stroked the blaze on her face a few times.

"So, I did find a cartoon character." he said.

"Uh-huh. We'd better join Mom. She really wants to meet you."

Sir Donald closed the door of the shed and slid the bolt into place. They retraced their steps through the house and onto the deck.

"Man, I'd bet three or four of my dad's trailers would fit inside this house," he remarked as they left the sun porch and stepped on the deck.

"The coffee and cake are on the table. I'll join you if you don't mind."

"Oh, Mom! Of course I . . . we don't mind," replied Crystal glancing at her grinning knight.

Crystine watched the young man move with an easy fluidity. He pulled the chair out for her daughter, seating her as if they were in a fine restaurant. He gave her the slightest of bows, his grin not foolish but sweet and oddly knowing, like that of the Mona Lisa's on a masculine face.

Crystine rose from the chaise. Still plenty of litheness in her body, she was at the table in a few steps. To her surprise, the young man pulled her chair out and, with great confidence and ease, seated her as he had Crystal.

"Thank you, that was very thoughtful of you," she said. "I'm a knight in training," he quipped, his voice soft yet carrying easily over the sound of the surf.

"Help yourselves to the coffee and cake," she said. Then looking at Crystal she added, "You haven't introduced me to your new friend."

"Oh, I'm sorry. Mom, this is Sir Donald. Sir Donald, this is Mom."

Crystine directed an amused look at the young man. "Sir Donald?" she asked.

"Yes. I was dubbed thus to attend to Queen . . . Queen . . . Saints preserve us. I do not know my queen's name!" he exclaimed with a gasp. Crystine laughed. The moment relaxed and shifted into easy.

"I am Queen Crystal."

"Queen Crystal!" blurted the knight.

The words resounded in Crystine's ears, reverberating like a musical refrain wafted on the winds of a distant dream, its tremulations reaching to her soul. She didn't know why. A single voice, a few simple words—it didn't make sense, perhaps didn't need to.

"And yours?" Crystal asked her attendant knight.

"Cream and sugar," he replied.

"Cream and sugar? That's a really weird name, weirder than Sir Donald."

"No . . . I meant for my coffee. I thought you were asking what I wanted in my coffee."

Shared laughter was the loom upon which a thread was woven into the lives of Crystine, Crystal, and . . . "Daniel; my name is Daniel," he said.

Hope triumphing over disbelief, belief pushing astonishment past fear, wonder overwhelming the shadow of doubt, her heart pounding like a tympani drum, Crystine managed to set her cup down on the table.

"Pleased to meet you, Sir Daniel," Crystal said, offering him her right hand. Their fingers touched. Crystine thought she saw electricity arc, but that could only be imagination, couldn't it? Their hands lingered beyond an introductory shake.

"Pleased to meet you Queen Crystal . . . uh . . ."

"Hopkins," she interjected.

"Pleased to meet you Crystal Hopkins," he said. "That was my mom's maiden name, before she married Dad and it became Abrams," he continued.

Crystine's heart galloped, thundering against her ribs. Her eyes swam, or maybe it was the entire world she had known until now that was swirling out of focus. She couldn't tell. She focused out on the ocean and then up to the sky, making sure *the* world hadn't altered the same as *her* world.

"Very pleased to meet you Daniel . . . Abrams?"

"Daniel Abrams Junior, to be precise. But I like Sir Donald better," he laughed. Crystal joined him. Crystine couldn't; her mind was racing in sync with her runaway heart, *His dad lives in a trailer house about twenty miles north of here.*

"Junior!" exclaimed a delighted Crystal. "Why weren't you called Danny?"

"Just wasn't. Dad never was."

"Is your dad still alive then?" asked Crystine, hoping the question sounded casual.

"Mom! I told you yesterday," her daughter reminded her. But she needed to hear it from the young man's own mouth.

"Yes, he lives about twenty miles north in a little trailer house. It's all he wants. My mom died three years ago, and he says he doesn't need his heart broken anymore, so he isolates. The quintessential hermit slash beachcomber I guess."

"Heartbroken? Anymore?" asked Crystine.

"Three times, he says. When mom died, of course. The other one is what Montana has become. He grew up there."

Crystine almost slipped and said, "I know."

"And how is that?" she asked.

"He just says it isn't the Wild West anymore. Freedom is restricted there as much as anywhere, maybe even more so."

"That's unfortunate. And the third?"

"He never says. Would you like to meet him?" Daniel suddenly asked her. "He's retired, writes poetry, and listens to music, really really old music. One tune he listens to a lot. I don't think it was ever a megahit, just an instrumental with a strong sax riff and a guitar back. I'm making him sound a little eccentric, but he's not, really."

"Let me guess the name of the tune," Crystine interjected. "Harlem Nocturne."

"That's amazing!" he said, eyes wide, mouth dropped open.

"I've been around a while too," she said, for the first time seeing the resemblance in the young man's face to the one she had adored a lifetime ago. "Yes, Daniel, I would very much like to meet your dad," she said.

He looked at Crystal and grinned. She returned him a puzzled look, and he turned back to Crystine.

"How about today?" he asked.

"My, that's awful sudden. I don't think it would be doable," replied Crystine.

Daniel gazed out toward the ocean, pushed back his chair, stood, and pointed to the beach. "That's him down there," he said.

Chapter Thirty-Six

Crystine stood up and looked in the direction Daniel was pointing. A solitary figure strolled along the beach, near the ocean's edge, moving with an easy fluidity as a breeze ruffled his shoulder-length gray hair. His loose-fitting denim jeans were faded by wear and time, as was his ocean-blue shirt. He wore open-toed leather sandals allowing the sand to tickle his feet as he walked toward the dune only moments before occupied by the queen and her attendant knight. Reaching it, he sat unmoving, gazing out over the Pacific, the sun high but at his back.

"I'll take you down to meet him if you'd like," offered Daniel.

"I'll come too," Crystal piped in.

"If you don't mind, I think I'll go down alone and introduce myself."

"Uh . . . no, of course we don't mind," said Crystal, Daniel adding his agreement with a nod and a smile.

Not knowing what to expect, Crystine placed her hand on the stair railing, steadying herself should her knees go any weaker. She swallowed the lump in her throat as she stepped onto the sand, her heart racing out of control with anxious anticipation of the moment ahead, when her past, her present, and her future would converge into a single point. She took another step. The man rose off the dune and walked toward the ocean, stopping at its edge. She had no way of knowing if he was aware of her as he stood fifty yards distant, gazing out to sea.

She took another step. Feeling weightless, she glided across the hard-packed sand left behind by the receding tide. True to her nature, she took the direct approach and stopped at the water's edge a few feet to his left. His profile was not as she remembered.

"Daniel?" she queried, her voice quavering despite her resolve. Time froze, and it seemed to take an eternity for him to turn toward the sound of her voice, as the far gaze of his eyes flickered into the present.

"Yes," he responded, as much a question as an affirmation. Their eyes met, and in one shared beat of their hearts, they knew.

"How is m'lady today?" he asked.

"Daniel's been talking to you," she said, her voice just above a whisper.

He nodded. "Wanna dance?" he asked, holding out his hand.

"Oh, Daniel! It's been longer than . . . forever!"

They crushed themselves together and held tight, dispelling the wondering, the longing, the searching and the years, their hearts melding into one, and in a single moment of time, the pain of the past disappeared, the joy of the present rang out, and the hope of the future soared on wings.

"I don't hear any music," she said.

"Just listen for a moment."

The surf, the gulls, the newborn ocean breeze rustling through the swaying clusters of dry beach grass combined to play the soothing rhythms of nature's orchestra. They swayed back and forth, holding each other in a never-ending moment, dancing in the realm of the gods.

Crystal looked down at her mom and Daniel's dad sitting side by side on yesterday's magical sand dune.

"How strange," she quipped.

"I've been called worse," replied Daniel from his chair at the coffee table.

"No, no, stand up and take a look."

He stood and moved to Crystal's side.

"Look at them. They've hit it off like they were old friends."

"How strange," Daniel commented.

"That's what I just said."

"How weird."

"How lovely," she mused.

"You are," he said. Their embrace took flight on the wings of promise and joined together with hope.

Daniel turned to Crystine. "I've been driving down to roam this beach for a while now. It just felt good, and I liked being here." He got lost in her soft brown eyes. "Now I know why."

"I saw you here once in a while, if I had known it was you . . ."

No more words required, the look between them said it all . . . boundless and endless love, capped by a miracle. "I have found you. I never thought it would happen," he said.

"Welcome home," she said, gently squeezing his hand.

"I also came here to try to solve another lifelong mystery of my own," he said.

"And what is that?" she asked.

"The ocean."

"The ocean is the ocean—often mysterious and often the inspiration of poems or great works of art. The sunsets over it are gorgeous."

"I think it's a cesspool."

"You're very romantic."

"Always." Youth revisited and its wonder held them in thrall.

"I told Daniel about this place." He glanced up at the castle keep, "I think he may have found something too, a life long treasure perhaps."

Crystine looked up at the deck. "Do you think a marriage is in our future?" she asked.

"Yes."

"How soon?"

"Well, we're not getting any younger, so I hope not more than a year."

"Why so long?"

"That's when Daniel will finish up at Oregon, and then he's going to grad school at UCLA. Every serious grad student should be married, don't you think?"

"I love you," she said, and the words were like a dam that broke, releasing the reservoir of love she had held in her heart for so many years. It gushed, and not only did I feel her profound love but the release it gave her, flooding us with a warmth and joy so long absent but still remembered.

"That feels so-o-o right," she said.

"You know that we belong to each other. We always have and always will," I said. She nodded and then in a quiet voice she told me she was married. I told her I wasn't.

"I know," she said. "I met Daniel . . . Junior . . . yesterday, and he told me about his mom. He also told me how your heart had been broken three times. At what Montana has become, when your wife died, and the third you'd never say."

"He usually doesn't open up to people like that. Could it be there is something special about you? And you know the third, when our souls were wrenched asunder."

"Yes, Daniel, mine too. I just never realized how much. He said you write poetry?"

"I dabble around. I've got one here; wanna read it? It's kind of long—got time?"

"I have all the time in the world. I'm where I want to be, where I'm meant to be."

I pulled a piece of paper out of my shirt pocket, unfolded it, and handed it to her. She began to read . . .

The Night Rains

In rhythmic patterns, the night rains fall
to misty days and gray
while all along the fortress wall
the hounds are held at bay.
Foundations laid on pain and grief
is built the cold stone tower.
In solitude was sweet relief,
yet loneliness devours
a heart that knew the joy of love
and its killing power to
embrace the lightning or crush the budded flower.
Away! Keep distant, mischievous light.
False rays of hope launched in the night
shall not pierce the armored walls.

While one by one the hurting falls
into those jaws known so well,
they've broken loose
the hounds of hell.
Spring forth! Unsheathed, soul's blade of steel
whose fired edge defiance wields
against those beasts from vapor mist
who devour one's heart with loneliness.

But wait! What stirs upon the stair?
A universe in radiant smile
calls silently, come stay a while,
as soft and gentle melting feeling
through mortared walls comes slowly stealing
the unknown touch
that brings
love's healing.

A single teardrop, turned into a glittering diamond by the sun, trickled down Crystine's cheek. "You wrote this?"

"Yes, over two decades ago, on a lonely, rainy night. The loneliness was palpable, sentient, and so powerful I had no choice but to write it down. It was a mystery then; I understand it now. It showed me what was going on inside me, how I isolated and insulated myself against pain, but the memories always returned to haunt me. And only one person could bring the healing touch, and that is you, Crystine," I whispered to her.

"And you bring mine," she said. "Why didn't you answer my last letter?"

"It was a Dear John."

"Not that one, and I'm sorry, but my *last* one."

"I never received it until about a year ago."

"A year ago! That's too incredible!" she exclaimed.

"It's a long story."

"We have the rest of the day . . . and the rest of our lives," she smiled.

"My daughter, Jenna, decided to move to the Flathead Valley from Portland."

"You lived in Portland?"

"Up until I retired, about three years ago."

"My God, Daniel, we were in Portland three times in five months the year before you retired!"

"I remember I was in a frenzy during that time, trying to find you. Do you suppose I somehow felt you near?"

"I believe it's possible and probably is what happened."

"Why didn't you answer my e-mail? I sent you one," I asked.

"I don't remember anything from a Daniel or Abrams, or anything that would remotely clue me in to your name."

"It was, at the time, 'dunkeyhead at excite dot com'."

"Oh, no! I remember that weird name. I thought it was a sneaky porn message and deleted it. How did you choose such an oddball e-mail address for yourself?"

"My little nephew. He called me donkeyhead probably because I teased him first and called him turtlehead, you know, the Teenage Mutant Ninja—"

"Turtles," she interjected.

"Yeah, only my nephew pronounced it dunkeyhead. I thought that was pretty unique, so I used it."

We laughed, and our delight continued.

"The letter?" said Crystine, back on track. She was, after all, a professional and beautiful and delightful, and oh so right.

"Anyway, Jenna moved to the Flathead for a summer and while there visited my cousin Denny and his wife Marion at the farm on Lower Valley Road. They're the third generation to live in that house and run the farm.

"And so after dinner, Marion told Jenna to wait while she retrieved something for her out of the storage room. She returned with a small box containing old newspaper clippings, photographs of the family, report cards, old drawings we'd done as kids—things that somehow or other Aunt Louise had gotten ahold of and saved."

"And my letter?" she asked.

"Yes, your letter. I'd left the farm for town by the time it got there. Aunt Louise had a stroke that year, and we didn't go out to her house for Thanksgiving dinner. I think she planned on giving it to me then, but she probably would have forgotten all about it anyway."

A tear rolled from Crystine's eye down her cheek. I gently wiped it away.

"And there was something else," I said.

"What?" she whispered.

"A newspaper article about my grandma and grandpa celebrating their fiftieth wedding anniversary out at the farmhouse. There was a big gathering, and I remember it well. My granddad's brother had come up to attend. What I didn't know, until I read the article, was that he was from, of all places, Huntington, California. This was seven years before we met."

"What was your granddad's name?"

"Thomas McDermitt."

"And his brother's, the one from California?"

"Galen . . . Galen McDermitt."

"What did Galen do?"

"He was a schoolteacher."

Crystine's breath caught in her throat.

"Your presence was there before you were, Daniel," she breathed.

"What do you mean?"

"My all-time favorite teacher, who taught fifth grade, was an elderly gentleman named Galen McDermitt."

My turn for the breath to catch in my throat.

"And he, being of the same heritage and blood and closely related to you, contained your presence, in a sense. Don't you see?"

"Yes, I do. Quite amazing."

"And I still remember the last words he spoke to me, which at the time seemed quite odd."

"What did he have to say?" I asked.

"He said, 'You're a very special young lady, Crystine, and I'll bet there's a special someone out there just waiting for you.'"

"And that was me."

"Yes. Daniel, do you think we're trying to cheat fate?"

"No. I think fate tried to cheat us, and lost."

"It did," she said.

I placed my finger gently under her chin, tilted her face up toward mine, and kissed her. She kissed me back.

"What are we going to do?" she asked.

"About what?"

"About us, silly."

"Well . . . we're not full of juice anymore, so no sense in running off to a motel." She laughed, the sound of it like music to me.

"But, I am retired and do have a lot of time . . ."

"So is Bill," she said.

"Who's Bill?"

"My husband."

"Oh. Bill who?"

"Hopkins."

"Wild Bill?"

"The very same one. I never noticed the scar from the bullet wound until our wedding night and so he told me the story of how you saved his life over in 'Nam. I didn't tell him I knew you, but it certainly gave me the tingles.

"And it figures, doesn't it?" I said.

"It does. So what are we going to do?"

"Sneak off into the night?"

"No."

"Contemplate the ocean together?"

"Okey-dokey," she said and giggled.

To hear her voice, to feel her presence, to breathe of her breath, to drink of her soul, was bliss beyond description.

"I figured it out!" I exclaimed, startling her.

"What?" she asked.

"Love is the fulfillment of dreams and the end of wishes."

"That's what the ocean means to you?"

"That's what you mean to me, Crystine." She threw her arms around my neck and kissed me. I hoped the kids weren't looking. They weren't.

Chapter Thirty-Seven

I t would make no sense to go off in a mad rush at this point in our lives, disrupting the lives of so many around us.

Crystal and Daniel got married right on schedule and live in LA with their two boys. I'm not sure how they came up with the boys' names: Canaan and Connor. I have my suspicions, though. Without consciously realizing it, Canaan, I think, represents a settled searching, like when the Israelites reached the Promised Land. And Connor represents hope for the future, as in Sarah and John from *The Terminator* movie. Makes sense to me anyway.

I met Wild Bill again. I don't why he got to spend so much of his life with Crystine and I didn't. Maybe he was able to give her something I could not. Materially, this was true. Maybe by now she was just the old lady to him and it didn't matter. He seemed somewhat detached from life anyhow.

He understood the situation and didn't mind if I came around. Maybe it was his way of thanking me for saving his life. He was gone to San Francisco most of the time on business. He didn't like Oregon as much as he thought he would, I guess.

Crystine and I would never go into the house alone if no one was there, and only as far as the sun porch if it was raining. Part of being adult, I guess.

She globe-hops here and there on movie locations for six to eight months a year and is always home on Christmas. I think we figured out one thing, though. While she was working on movies and movies were following me around, it was our love trying to get a message through, trying to get us connected, or trying to get me to look in that direction. Sounds crazy but possible, considering all of the mysterious threads that ran so close together throughout our lives, lived separate yet together. Like parallel lines.

It was the Fourth of July. I'm not all that patriotic, but I do like barbecues, and Crystal and Junior were doing a bang-up job of fixing one up on the deck. We were waiting for dinner, sitting on Queen Crystal's sand dune, gazing out at the ocean.

"What do you think?" Crystine asked.

"It's salty," I replied.

"Is that a step up from cesspool?"

"I suppose so, but why would it be salty? All the rivers running into it are fresh water, and so is the rain."

"Tears?"

"You're crying?" I said.

"No . . . well, some tears of joy lately." She smiled up at me, and I squeezed her against me a little tighter. "But what if it's God's tears?" she asked.

"God cries?"

"He could. Maybe his heart breaks too."

"I suppose it could, considering the world nowadays . . . being so backasswards and all."

"You're still a cowboy, aren't you?"

"Yeah, but there's no place for us anymore, not even in Montana."

"I know. Daniel told me. Heartbreak number two."

"When did I tell you that?"

"Not you, silly; Daniel Junior."

Nothing better than sharing a laugh wrapped in delight.

"We'd better call him Junior or I'll keep getting confused," I said.

"Okay. What about Crystal?"

"We'll call her Junior too."

"Then I'll be confused and so will they."

"So . . . one Junior?"

"One Junior," she said.

"All right, but what about him?"

"Him who?"

"God. Not supposed to call him that anymore or some lily-livered, no-convictions, sonofa . . ."

"Easy, cowboy," she said touching my arm.

"Okay," I said. "So is God a he? A she? An it? A thing? A neutral force to be manipulated?"

"May the force be with you," she said, grinning.

"Something like that. Is God . . . God in you? Is God . . . God in me? Wait! I've got it! We'll cover them all!"

"How?"

"We'll call God . . . Shmee! That works for me, how about you?"

"Me?"

"No . . . Shmee!"

"Okey-Dokey."

"I love you, Crystine."

"And I love you, Daniel."

We couldn't help ourselves; we kissed.

"They've gotta be crazy," Crystal said, looking down from the castle keep.

"Maybe . . . probably . . . but it sure looks like fun," Junior said as he gathered her in his arms and kissed her. She kissed him back.

"I have a new poem. Wanna read it?" I said to Crystine.

"Of course."

I pulled the folded piece of paper from my shirt pocket and handed it to her. "It's not long. Got time?"

"I have all the time in the world. I'm where I want to be, where I'm meant to be. The fulfilling of dreams and the end of wishes, remember?" She smiled with such brightness it would match any schoolgirl's. Her light had been rekindled, my broken heart healed.

She opened the paper and began to read.

What I Have Learned

Once had me a wife, coupla young 'uns at home. They were my life, since I lost 'em been alone. Found sweatin' for the gettin' and strainin' for the gainin' to be a lot like chasin' the wind. Thar ain't no replacin' kin. So I reckon there's only two things I own, my words and my deeds; by these I am known. And there's only one thing I work hard at keepin, that is my word; to do less I'd be cheatin'. This life I've been given appears low, that may be. Still, to do the forgivin', that's left up to me. Ya see, it ain't how life treats me that amounts to concern; it's how I treat life that counts, I have learned.

Crystine slowly folded the paper and turned her radiant face up toward mine.

"Life's really pretty simple when broken down to basics, isn't it?" she said.

"It is, and it's also more complicated than writing a check."

"Can I keep it?"

"The poem? I'd be honored, m'lady."

We passed a moment of silence wrapped in peace.

"What are you thinking?" she asked.

"I'm thinking that the heart of the matter is that it is the heart that matters."

"That is true, isn't it?"

She couldn't help herself; she kissed me. I kissed her back.

"Daniel. There is a gap between wisdom and knowledge, isn't there," she stated more than asked.

"I believe there is," I answered.

"I think I've been shown the bridge." And she was warmed from the inside out with a warmth that would never diminish.

As for me, I still don't know. I don't know if I believe in God or destiny or even in Shmee. I'm not so harsh toward fate, although if fate is the ruler, I think it cheated Crystine and me . . . almost. I don't believe in miracles, particularly, but I believe in the *possibility*, like I used to believe in the possibility of Santa Claus.

"Daniel," Crystine said. "Do you realize we never had any children together, but we have the same grandchildren."

"Strange, isn't it?" I replied.

"No, not so strange, I don't think, because our love is so powerful it grew to be bigger than us and continues on. It tried to move mountains for us, it seems."

"I read somewhere that love is strong as death. Could be true, don't you think?"

She nodded.

An instrumental tune wafted down from the castle keep. It had a strong sax riff with a guitar back.

I looked at her.

"Yes, I *wanna* dance," she said.

Junior and Crystal waved at us from the deck.

We stood up, lightly holding each other and swaying back and forth. Crystine gave me her melt-my-heart-with-one-look smile.

"Thank you, Daniel."

"For what?"

"For being you." Her lovely soft brown eyes glowed with a light beyond ethereal.

"You, m'lady, are the queen of my heart."

"And you, my gallant knight, my noble sir, are the crown that I wear."

"Gammah! Gammah!"

Crystine looked down at Connor tugging at her pant leg. "Is dinner ready, honey?" she asked.

"Uh-huh," he said, letting go of her pant leg. "And Gammah."

"Yes, dear."

"You make me feel all warm inside," he said, taking her hand, his grin so wide it did stretch almost ear to ear.

And as we walked down the beach toward the house, Connor between us, Shmee painted us the most unutterably magnificent, gloriously beautiful sunset I have ever seen before or since in my entire life.

And isn't it nice
when love strikes twice
upon a time.